WAVES OF A
TEMPEST

WAVES OF A
TEMPEST

Book Two of the
Fires of an Empire Saga

JESSICA BARBERI

Waves of a Tempest / Jessica Barberi

ISBN: 979-8-227-23647-0

Dedication

I am dedicating this book to my daughter, Louisa. When I started writing this, I did not anticipate how big Roshin's story would grow. I enjoyed crafting a character that I feel is compelling and heroic but in a distinctly feminine way. May you come to see your own strength and draw inspiration from heroes like Roshin and Ashlyn in your life. You don't have to wield a sword to make a big impact.

L. Br

L. Mor

TAUGHMON

L. Enda

DROCHIT

L. Batle

SCOUT RUN RIVER

L. GORM

SOUTH TRADE ROAD

THE LIGHT

MILITARY ENCAMPMENT

LOCH DA CRUN

ARDVAR

DEERVAR

THE CAPITAL CITIES

VARGAH

THE FRESH SEA

ANCALAH

IV

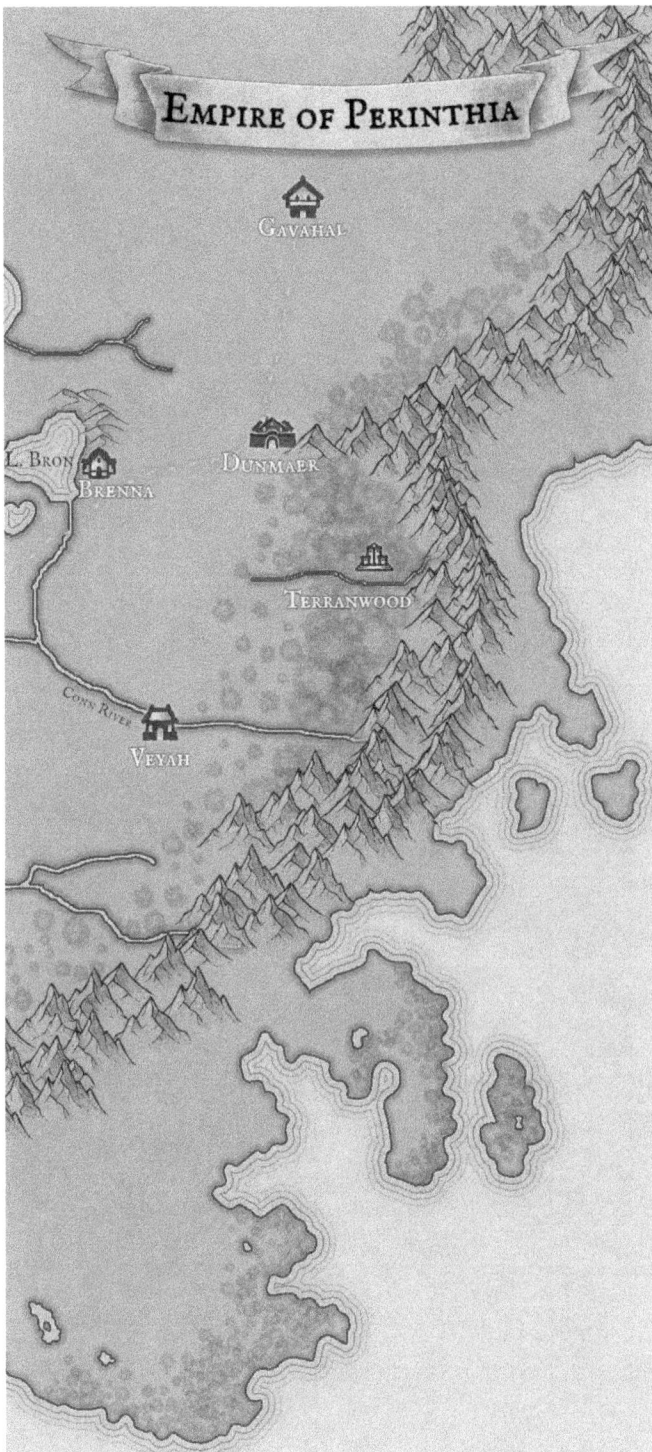

EMPIRE OF PERINTHIA

GAVAHAL

L. BRON
BRENNA
DUNMAER

TERRANWOOD

CONN RIVER
VEYAH

Section 1
A Tale of Bondage

1

Beginnings

It was a gentle touch on the shoulder that drew Roshin from her dreams. The room she occupied was still dim, lit only by candlelight. She blinked open her eyes to see her fellow servant Ashlyn standing beside her.

"The waves are coming faster. It should not be long now," Ashlyn spoke in a whisper. Roshin nodded in understanding and rose to her feet. She took a minute to tuck a loose lock of auburn hair back into her snood and then adjusted her veil so that it draped evenly over her head. Her last effort was to smooth her skirts.

"I am ready." Roshin whispered to her companion. The pair walked out the door of the small cottage and proceeded down the dirt lane which was bathed in moonlight.

"I remember it said that the babes prefer to come on the full moon, seems true this time at least!" Ashlyn was looking up at the shining moon beaming, an excited skip in her step. "How many babes have you seen born?"

"I would guess some more than twenty at this point," Roshin replied with a smile back to her companion. "How is our mother doing this night?"

"It has been a long labor for her, but when I left, she was still in good spirits. Servant Granya was readying some broth for her," Ashlyn explained.

Roshin nodded. "The first babes often take a bit more time to come, but joy is found in patience and grace. I am gladdened to hear her spirits are still high."

The women quickly shuffled down the lane until they reached the door they were seeking. Without knocking Roshin slowly opened it and slipped in without a word. Ashlyn slipped in behind her. The room they walked into was dark with a dirt floor and clay walls. A fire in the hearth and a few candles placed about provided the only light in the space.

An older woman was seated before a wooden table, ladling a liquid out of a pot into a wooden bowl. Like Roshin her head was covered with a linen snood and veil. She had a simple tan overdress with an apron tied at her waist.

The woman raised her wrinkled face and smiled at their presence. "Just in time! Our sweet mum has said she has started to feel a need to push." Her quiet voice showed excitement, and the two girls turned and smiled at each other.

A low-pitched moan pulled their attention over to a woman in the opposite corner of the room, leaning against the back of a chair. The woman's bulging belly hung below her, and her hips swayed back and forth in the fire light. Her long brown hair was tied back, and eyes were closed as if deeply focused on something. Shortly her moaning transitioned into a low and rhythmic hum.

Roshin moved over to the woman, Ashlyn following at her heels. "You are doing so beautifully mum. Servant Granya says you are starting to feel a bit like pushing. Might I offer some pressure for the next wave?"

The woman did not cease her low hum and continued to sway, but a gentle nod of her head showed her agreement. As her humming again began to build back into the louder moaning, Roshin moved behind her and pressed her palms down onto the small of the woman's back.

As the woman's moaning grew into a louder roar Roshin turned her head smiling toward her companion, who was standing beside them looking uncertain. "Ashlyn, I think it might be good to offer some support, might you be able to help hold the lady up?" and so Ashlyn nodded eagerly, and, in a couple, quick steps stood before the laboring woman and offered her her hands.

The woman released the chair and allowed Ashlyn to take hold of her. The wave had subsided for the moment, but they all knew it would be a short reprieve. The woman began to hike up the skirt of her chemise to reach under it as if feeling for progress, but after a moment her hands returned to Ashlyn for support her face was drawn with disappointment.

Roshin continued to massage the woman's back as the next wave began to build. Ashlyn looked up at Roshin, a bit surprised, as the woman grabbed hold of her arms and squeezed. Roshin again smiled in reassurance and let out a light chuckle before addressing the woman, "Do your best to breathe into your urge, try and relax your baby down. Ashlyn here can help hold you up. Try a squat, and if that is not working for you, we can try something else."

The woman let out a roar as she bore down. Ashlyn did her best to support the woman as she squatted. Roshin bent to take a peek under the raised skirt. As the wave again subsided Roshin praised the woman. "What a great push. You let us know if you need to move."

The woman nodded and released her hold on Ashlyn, who looked a bit relieved, "I...Think.. I... Think... Maybe kneeling..." The woman worked out her words before moving back into her humming. Roshin moved the chair, turning the seat toward the woman.

"Ashlyn, grab that blanket and bring it here quickly." Roshin directed. Ashlyn grabbed the blanket and returned it to Roshin, who placed it on the seat of the chair. She stooped down to the woman who was now kneeling on her hands and knees. "You can support yourself a bit on the seat of this chair, rest your head, give it a bit of a hug for the next push. It will help support you."

No sooner had she finished talking then the woman leaned onto the seat of the chair, wrapping her arms around its legs. Her hum began to turn into a roar just as Granya came over. Suddenly there was a pop, and a rush of fluid flowed down onto the straw covered floor.

Granya handed the bowl she was holding to Roshin. "For after the birth now." And then speaking to the woman, "Try to turn your knees toward each other." The woman complied as she bore down with her urge. "Good work, let's see if we can see this baby." The old woman crouched down and pulled up the chemise to look. "I see a head!" she announced.

The woman took that as motivation gripping onto the chair hard as she roared. "Breathe lovely! Breathe" Roshin gently reminded her as the wave crashed over her body.

"You are so close now! Last one before you have your baby!" Granya announced. As if on cue the next wave came, and the woman let out her one last roar. The old woman's hands were there to catch the baby as it slipped out into the world.

The woman overcome with relief collapsed onto the chair before pivoting over to her side so that she might roll over and see the fruit of her work. The baby had begun to cry a healthy cry. "Oh settle little sir, we shall get you to your mother." Granya's voice was soothing and gentle as her hands helped unwind the cord of the baby from around his mother's legs so he could be passed to her.

The words, however, did not escape the woman's ears and like one more final wave, a sob flowed from her lungs. "A boy! Not a boy! He will be lost to me! Not a boy!" Her wailing grief shook through the women who bore witness to that moment.

Roshin knelt and clasped the woman's hand in a plea to get her attention. "He is not lost to you. Now he needs you. You are his mother, and you will define his world, no matter what is to come. Take your son, give him comfort and shelter, and let him know his mother's love."

Granya reached the crying baby toward the woman. Her breath was still cut by gasps and tears, but she let go of Roshin's hands and received him. As she drew him close to her chest he began to settle, his crying ceased. Her face looked down to him so small and helpless as tears ran down her cheek and fell onto his body.

Roshin offered to help her up. Once standing all the women helped her to remove her soiled garments. As they did new waves rolled over the woman. Ashlyn collected a large wood bowl and joined the other attendants back around the woman. With another push the woman's body birthed her placenta which Ashlyn caught into the bowl. "Your babe is truly free now."

A blanket and clean set of rags were laid over a fresh litter of straw that had been built up on the floor. The women aided the new mother with her baby over to it and guided her down. They then covered the pair in blankets. Granya brought over a candle as Roshin raised up the cord connecting the baby to the placenta.

Raising the candle's flame up to the cord, Granya began to pray, "Hulen Ahir has welcomed this child into this world, untarnished by the troubles of this age. May the light within him shine ever bright, regardless of the night around him, for it is the light of this candle that has set him free from the bounds of the womb. He may have lost that safety, but what he has gained is yet unknown. May our lord grace him and his mother with peace so that they may continue to draw on this light even if the years roll on in darkness. Praise with you."

The women around the baby knelt in reverent silence. The baby squirmed and squeaked in his mother's arms. Once the cord was burned through, they all went back to work. Soiled litter was gathered up and slowly fed into the fire to burn it away without choking the room with smoke. Once the litter was clear the fire was built up with wood and a cauldron full of water was placed over it.

Rags were added into the cauldron and Ashlyn stirred them into the water with a long wooden staff. Roshin settled beside the woman offering her the broth which at this point had cooled beyond what might have been ideal. Still the woman eagerly drank it up.

"Have you an idea of what to call him?" Roshin asked the woman.

"My father was Darren, so I have a mind to name him that, but then his father was named Angus, so I wonder if that might be a name to use since he's like to never meet the man." Her voice carried in it a deep sadness.

"Either would be an honor for him. Have both men passed?" Roshin asked with compassion in her voice as she placed a supportive hand on the woman's shoulder.

"My father, aye, he died some years back in a famine. He had refused to eat anything, saving all for myself and my sister." She paused and sighed, "As for Angus, I do not know. He may well have died, as I doubt I'll see him again since his camp has moved on."

"Had his company stayed long?" Roshin asked.

"No. He was a handsome one though." The woman smiled and her cheeks blushed. "Dark curly hair, rich brown eyes. Met him one evening when he and a small group came into the inn for drinks. He paid me special mind. Talked me into all kinds of silliness. Three days he was here, then he was gone."

Roshin knew the story. All the babies she had been present for had a similar story. Her own story was not so different. Her father was not a soldier, but a sailor, who had been captivated by her mother's beauty. She knew what it was to wonder after a man she would never meet.

Roshin sat a long while with the woman and her son. She guided the woman on how to hold the babe to feed him, and then talked to her about what to expect in the coming days. Granya and Ashlyn prepared a special tea and warm soup as a first meal, before taking the baby for a while to allow the mother some rest.

Dawn soon broke and the women gathered up their things and prepared to depart back to the cottage. "We shall be back this evening to check on you. Do you have care for the day?" Granya asked.

"Aye, my sister will no doubt be by to check me this morning, she shall bring me some food." The woman replied.

"Good," Granya declared. "Let us go then my dears. We all need our own rest and meals." And with that the women walked out the door into the light of the new day's sun.

Roshin glanced back at the door as she left. She wished she could sit longer with the woman, and she wondered what would become of them both as she had for all the births she had witnessed. But it was a new day, with so many who needed so much. "Let us rest," she affirmed.

2

The Trade

The three women returned to the cottage down the lane. It was now lit up with sunlight. They gathered around a wooden table in the center of the room. Granya led them in a simple prayer: "May our actions and service continue to reflect your truth out onto our world."

The three women in unison closed their eyes, first touching their hands to their foreheads, then to their hearts, before reaching them up to the sky in a ritualized gesture symbolizing their dedication of head, heart, and hands to their lord, Hulen Ahir.

Granya opened her eyes and looked at the other women. With a smile, she announced, "And now we eat." Ashlyn reached for a loaf of brown bread at the center of the table, and she broke off two chunks which she passed to the others, reserving what was left for herself.

With that, the women sat and ate. Granya broke the quiet that had fallen on them with a memory as she looked down at her bread. "I remember when the fields were planted full. Stalks of grains, potatoes, onions. This place was once so green and alive." Roshin and Ashlyn both turned their attention to the old woman.

"My parents were farmers, I can remember their planted fields as a small child..." Ashlyn started before trailing off, as if the rest of her memory was too painful to recall.

"I have no doubt they were beautiful, child, even if they are not anymore." Granya reached over and put a hand on her shoulder, "Those fields can be green again, and so long as you believe that, then there will be hope for you to see that day."

Ashlyn nodded and looked over to Roshin who smiled back a warm smile. Granya continued her story, "King Calder did much for the people to ensure peace and prosperity. He did not demand more than the people could pay, and he allowed our Truth Sayers and teachers to work openly in the community. His early death was a tragedy."

Granya paused and considered her next words carefully, "I wonder if it was in part grief and anger over that loss that pushed his son to war? They say it was so he could prove himself a great commander, but I do think it could be just as well that he started the war in an attempt to slash into the heart of our lord."

"But why? Our lord is good!" Ashlyn asked.

"For a man that feels he lost unjustly, that goodness is not so clear. Many suffer so much, and many die. Often those impacted feel a need to blame, and why not blame the creator of all for your pain?" Granya responded.

"I understand that, I spent a lot of time angry for the loses in my life." Roshin added, a slight waver in her voice.

"No doubt, child. It is easy to blame that which is above us for our misery. The wounded man does not wish to see that Hulen Ahir does not cause our suffering. It is in our nature to suffer; most we create for ourselves." Granya paused before finishing. "Hulen Ahir gives us a path through such pain, he can give it meaning, and that should not be discounted,"

The young women were left hanging on the old woman's words. *"She is so wise,"* Roshin thought as she finished her bread. Roshin had been following and serving as Granya's student for five years and found that even after that much time, she was still fascinated by stories her mentor shared. Listening to them gave her hope that things could again be good so long as they were.

Once the trio had finished eating, they removed their veils and aprons and settled down onto some makeshift straw mattresses laid out on the floor. The cottage had been offered to them by the lord of the town in exchange for their health services to those in the village.

They had been in the town for over a month. In this time, they had addressed an injury sustained by the aged blacksmith, treated a few cases of boils and pox, and splinted a small child's bowed leg. In addition, they had provided comfort and care to a few of the town's aged and infirmed. The birth from the night prior was the last item they had to attend to before they would be off to the next village.

"I will be sad to go tomorrow." Ashlyn commented as she laid down upon her mattress.

Roshin nodded her affirmation, "Indeed, the villagers here have been so kind, but I have no doubt we will find hospitality at our next stop as well."

"I am sure we will, but I will still miss this place," Ashlyn said, setting her head upon her arm. "Sometimes I miss having a settled home." Ashlyn had joined Granya and Roshin a year prior after the pair had come through her village. She had become fascinated with Granya and her life on the road.

"You gave up a great deal to join us. We will be back through your village likely next year. If you wish to stay, I think you will be a great asset to them," Granya reassured her.

"I am not sure there is much left there... but I do miss my mother," Ashlyn sighed.

Roshin recalled the face of Ashlyn's mother as they walked out of town. "*I imagine Ashlyn leaving hurt her more than she will ever know,"* she thought as she looked back to Ashlyn. *"Still, she is right, there was not much left of that town."*

This was the reality for most of the towns they passed through. The men in the villages were all old now as their sons and grandsons had all been taken to join the service. Most could no longer do the work that was required to maintain the communities and they had no apprentices.

The women left behind did the best they could to keep things running, but it seemed inadequate. The physicality required to properly maintain the town structures and work in many of the trades was just outside of their reach. And so, the towns slowly decayed over the years.

The cottage grew quiet as the trio laid upon their mattresses. It had been a long night, and their bodies were all exhausted. It was not long before their breaths settled into a quiet rhythm, and each followed the other into a deep and dreamless sleep.

Because of this, the knock on the cottage door sometime later failed to rouse them. The knock however, soon turned to loud pounding, and all the women quickly stirred from their sleep.

Roshin rushed over to the door, grabbing her veil and pulling it on her head as she moved briskly to answer. "It must be urgent! I hope our mum is ok!" she exclaimed as she went to reach for the handle. She was startled as the door violently flew open toward her. She staggered back in a moment of confusion.

"Some Decency!" Granya exclaimed as three men pushed in through the door.

The largest man, a rough looking monster with a long salt and pepper beard and a large, jagged scar across his face, surveyed the room. "You's the lady healers?" his words flowed out like sap in winter, slow and drawn. A coarseness in them sent the hairs on the back of Roshin's neck skyward.

"Aye, we are. Might you need assistance?" Granya responded. If she was afraid of the situation unfolding before her, her manners did not give it away. Roshin glanced over to see Ashlyn, stone faced and pale, squeezing her veil into a ball between her hands.

The large man just laughed, and his two companions soon followed. "No, No help. Just here to claim what is ours."

Roshin stood confused and blinking. Did they mean to kick them from the cottage? She had never seen these men before, and they were to leave the next day. Cold sweat began to form as she fought to banish the thought, she knew in her heart to be true, *"They are here for us."*

Before she could react each of the men had moved to a different woman in the room. The large man stood before her. She thought to whirl around and run, but before she could she was caught by the wrist and held with a grip like stone.

She squealed and squirmed and tried to pry his fingers from her. The man just laughed. She looked around to see that Ashlyn and Granya were also being held. She felt a rush of panic surge through her like lightning radiating from her center. She reached her hand around and dug her fingernails deep into his hand.

The man suddenly yelped and released her wrist. Roshin was surprised by his reaction, and she thought of it as an opportunity to run, but she was still surrounded, and her captor was still blocking the door. Before she could think of what to do, she felt a fist strike her in the face.

"Little rat!" he cursed at her. She felt herself crumple to the floor as the other two women shrieked in alarm. The world seemed to spin as she was once again grabbed around her wrists.

The next thing she knew she was moving out the door. She could hear Ashlyn crying behind her. The light of the sun hit her face, and the brightness felt overwhelming to her. She saw the villagers standing around, frozen, staring in shock. Not even one moved or said anything. "*What was happening!*" she blinked in confusion.

The three men drove and dragged the women down the lane until they reached an Ox cart, and a group of saddled horses held by two men that appeared to be little more than boys not any older than her. "*Soldiers?*" Roshin wondered, but their outfitting did not quite fit what she had seen of other soldiers on the road.

A short stocky man, not quite middle aged, hopped down from the front of the cart. He was unusual looking with curly red hair that framed his face like a mane. His rosy complexion made him look hot. His gait was slightly off as if there was a hitch somewhere up by his hip. He called out toward the women's captors, "You got them! Great!" he then paused, "Only the three?"

"Aye, only three" the large man responded.

"Just as well, easier that way to grab." The stocky man then pulled out some ropes and went to each woman in turn to bind their hands. Roshin attempted to stomp on his feet, and kick at him. "I see you have a live one!"

"No doubt, best bind their legs too," her captor responded. The red-haired man was already working to secure her legs. Roshin squirmed to make it as difficult for him as she could.

"What is this!? Where are you taking us?" she demanded.

"You are ours now, we will take you where we please." The large man responded squeezing her arms hard.

Soon all three women were bound and tossed into the back of the cart. Roshin could see the figure of a man coming down the road toward them. He had a proud and bold step. As he neared, she realized it was the lord that managed the town.

"I see you have them." The nobleman said. "I've kept my word to you. Two are even young and pretty," he said pointing to Roshin. "Now keep your deal."

"Well, aye, two are pretty, but the old one, she might not have much value," the big man said gesturing to Granya.

"Nonsense, she is a trained medicine woman, an asset despite her age. She is worth a man as much as the others." The lord retorted.

The red-haired man stroked his beard and looked hard at the women in the cart. Roshin felt his eyes bore into her. Feeling exposed she pulled her veil around her face covering more of her head. "We offer the two boys, the lads are hardy and strong. A fair trade."

"Bollycock!" The lord thundered. "I need at least one skilled man. These are skilled women. I demand the two boys and a skilled man or cut them loose!"

Roshin went to speak again, but Granya quickly raised a hand to stop her. "Hush now child, this might be over before it even starts." Roshin prayed she was right.

The two men leading the negotiations moved away from the cart. "Let's not be rash, we can reach an arrangement," the stocky man said. He placed an arm around the lord, and they walked back off toward the town.

Roshin looked around catching the eyes of one of the boys, he quickly looked away as if very uncomfortable with the situation. "They are trading us like horses," Rosin commented with a sour tone.

"It would appear as if that is the case," Granya calmly affirmed. Ashlyn began again to cry.

"Sorry mum," one of the boys said sheepishly.

"Shut your mouth," the man that had grabbed Ashlyn barked at the boy.

It seemed like hours had passed sitting in the ox cart, out in the sun. Roshin watched villagers pass, craning their necks to see what was going on. Roshin found herself growing more angry that after all they had done for the village in the last month, not one seemed to even think to help.

Eventually the three men returned. The look on their faces said that they had made a deal. The big man was outfitted with a new sword and the stocky one was wearing a new coat and was carrying a cask of something. "Darren, you go with the boys. Serve your new lord well." The big man said.

Nodding, Ashlyn's captor stepped forward and waved the two boys to follow. "Come now lads, we have work to do." And the boys rushed after him. As Roshin watched them go, she noticed the one boy look back. His face looked sad, but soon he turned and followed the lord into the town.

The next thing Roshin knew was that the cart was moving. Ashlyn was still crying. Granya spoke next, "Take heart child, we still have our lives, we must hold fast to our faith. Our freedom is found in Hulen Ahir." The words of comfort sat hollow in that moment with Roshin. All she felt was a swirling of doubt.

3

South Bound

It had been four days since Roshin and her companions had been taken from the town of Veyah. They were traveling south across a bare and muddy landscape. The clouds loomed dark overhead with the hints of more spring rains to come.

Her hands and ankles still bound; she could do little more than look out toward the back of the cart. Two horses had been tied there and were being towed along without a rider. Roshin had been watching their faces as they plodded along. They bobbed up and down in a comforting rhythm.

"*Their skin looks so soft,*" she thought to herself, marveling at the velvet fuzz that covered the end of their muzzles. She did not have much experience with horses. As far back as she could remember she had grown up alongside the docks of the great fresh sea. Goods in such places were moved by boat, barrow, or ox cart.

By the time she had set off traveling with Granya, horses were a luxury that most common folk could not afford. The Empire's forces had confiscated most from the farmers to cover tax debts. Any that remained outside of the military were owned by the nobility, "*...and slavers,*" she thought bitterly.

She turned her head to see the two horses being ridden alongside the cart. Both were bay, but the bigger of the two had a white blaze and two white stockings. "*I wonder how hard it would be to ride,*" she pictured herself climbing up on the back of one of the horses and galloping off before quickly brushing the thought away, "*I doubt I could stay on.*"

Her gaze turned to the men riding the horses. The big one who had grabbed her was Donah. Beside him rode Tahg, a tan skinned man in his thirties with coarse dark hair that seemed to cover his whole body. She had gathered their names from their conversations with each other. The red-haired man driving the cart was Cormac.

She felt a shudder of disgust run through her as Tahg turned to catch her eye, and a broad smile spread across his face as he looked hungrily at her. The leer made her want to pull her veil around her face tighter and hide.

Roshin was well accustomed to hiding from the unwanted attention of men. She was reminded of her time as an orphan in the port city of Ancalah, in the conquered southern tip of Perinthia. The city had once been a merchant and fisherman's hub, but after the war it became a host to poverty and riffraff.

The streets were not safe for young girls, so as she matured, she found it best to cut off her hair, dress in loose rags, and carry dead fish in her pockets. She acclimated to the smell, but those around her gave her a wide birth and left her alone.

That was how Granya found her, digging in the garbage piles at the edge of the docks. Somehow Granya saw through her disguise and offered her another option. Roshin reflected back on the day she first met the woman some five years past.

Roshin had not noticed her approach. "Clever disguise, I imagine most leave you alone, child," Granya mused from behind her.

Roshin turned around with a start. She tried to form words, but her surprise made it impossible to get them out, "Gah... Err... Ahh..."

"How long have you been on the streets my child?" Granya probed.

Roshin paused to count the years, but she was not sure and so in the end she just shrugged.

"A long time alone then. Would you care to come with me? I can see you get a good meal. My only ask is that you leave the fish outside," Granya said with a reassuring laugh.

Roshin was not sure why she had said yes. She had avoided people that she did not know for years on the docks, afraid of what they might do to her. Perhaps it was her plain neat dress and covered head, but somehow, Roshin knew this woman was safe and could be trusted.

Returning to the present Roshin looked over to Granya, who, at that moment, was sleeping along with Ashlyn. Each of their bodies was propping the other up. She marveled at their ability to sleep as the cart jumped and jerked on the uneven ground. "*It must be exhaustion,*" she decided.

Roshin went back to staring at the faces of the horses following the cart. She heard Cormac curse under his breath as the cart bounced over a rock and dropped hard.

"Careful, Cormac! Every bruise on their bums is a copper off our price," Tahg called out in jest.

"And how much off for that shiner on the girl's eye." Cormac shot back.

"That wasn't me! Donah's a real brute who never learned manners from his ma!" Tahg retorted, waving the end of his reins over his shoulders toward Donah who was riding behind him. "Ain't that right?"

Donah snorted before flapping his legs hard. His horse grunted from the impact and then surged forward right into the back end of Tahg's mount. Roshin whipped her head around to see what was happening as Tahg's horse squealed and kicked up in objection to the violation of its space. Tahg had to scramble to right himself after having been pitched forward from the kick.

"Knock it off, you're both bothering the ox." Cormac scolded, "I don't need no runaway beast."

A deep throaty chuckle left Donah's mouth, "No more trouble here." And the group again grew silent as the cart bounced on.

Roshin found herself dozing in and out of consciousness as the clouds cleared and sun began to make its descent back to the horizon. "Break!" Cormac called out and the cart stopped. Roshin blinked and looked around. Granya and Ashlyn were also stirring now thanks to the sudden stillness.

"Why now? I just got me rhythm back." Tahg complained

"I got-a piss. They likely need to piss too," Cormac replied, pointing his thumb at the women behind him. "Don't need ma cart soiled."

"Aye, fair enough," Tahg huffed as he swung his leg off his horse. He waved Donah over to the women.

At this point Roshin had become well acclimated to the routine. The men would come over, untie the legs of one woman at a time and then lead them out onto the ground a few paces from the cart. At that point they were expected to perform their functions right there in front of the watchful eyes of their captors before being led back to the cart and retied.

It was humiliating. "Might you look away for just a moment?" Roshin pleaded as she did her best to hike up her skirts and squat awkwardly.

Donah just gave her a devilish grin, "Naw, I don't trust you not to do something stupid like run, plus I like your pretty legs."

Roshin found herself turning red. It was Granya who interrupted and got them to avert their eyes, at least for a few seconds. "We need water here. It's been all day, and I am not sure we will make it wherever it is you are seeking to take us if we don't drink or get any food."

Cormac responded, "You will just have to wait till we camp." Upon finishing his comment, he pulled out and took a long draw from his wineskin, no doubt full of whatever he had been given from the lord's cask.

Granya let the insult go and asked, "How many more days of travel can we expect?"

Tahg began to respond, "Five more to get to—" He never finished. Donah slapped the back of his head with his enormous hand.

"You leave us to worry about that." Donah said in a gruff tone, "We will get where we will get soon enough."

The distraction was enough. Roshin had finished and had stood up to be returned to the cart. Once back she watched the men take Ashlyn. The girl was not faring well with the situation. She had said very little and had cried more than she had slept.

Roshin wished she could wrap her arms around her, but the best she could manage was to reach her bound hands over and try and hold on to her fingers once she was returned to the cart. *The not knowing is the worst part of this,"* Roshin thought.

When the cart stopped for the evening beside a river, everything unfolded as it had the three nights prior. The men unsaddled and hobbled their horses, leaving them to graze on the sparse grass that grew on the river's banks. The ox was tied around the horns with a long line that was staked into the ground.

The men left the women in the cart, and moved off a fair distance to setup a fire. *"They don't want us to hear their conversations."* Roshin assumed. Before they left, they tossed some hardtack, and a waterskin into the cart for the three to share. It was not enough. The hollow feeling Roshin had on the inside remained. "I wonder what they are eating?" She asked out loud.

Granya put her hand upon Roshin's thigh, "Don't worry about them child, save your energy. Everyone here is hungry, I have no doubt." And with that Granya invited the girls to join her in a prayer.

Roshin recited the words of thanks for the meager rations though they somehow felt hollow. She began to think on Granya's point. It was a fair observation. The land they were travelling on had been bare, and the village they left did not have much either. Hunger was something she had known well in her life.

She needed to think about something else, so she began to look around the camp. This particular stop was the greenest she had seen. Over the course of the day, they had moved closer to the Wyrmridge Mountains and the sparse tree cover of its foothills now surrounded them. "It seems like they are taking special care to avoid the open." Roshin observed.

Granya responded, "Wise choice since we are heading south. The closer we get to the capital cities, the more likely there are solders about."

Most of the trees were evergreens, but those that were not were covered in fresh leaflets that had just burst out of their buds. The new life of spring was all around them. *"If I was traveling though here in different circumstances, I would think I might like to stay."* Roshin mused to herself.

A squeaky voice broke the moment of quiet. "South. I have never been south." After days of barely a word, Ashlyn finally spoke without any tears.

It was all Roshin could do not to squeal with excitement. Granya carried on as if nothing about this was unusual, "I do believe this is one of the headwaters of the Platt River. If I am right, then we are a fortnight from our likely destination."

"Which is?" Roshin asked.

"Vargah," was all Granya said. She need not say more. Roshin knew exactly where that was.

4

The Cottage

As the days passed, it became clearer and clearer that the group was indeed traveling to Vargah. The hollowness in Roshin's stomach from the lack of food found itself replaced by a pit of dread. Roshin had been through Vargah once with Granya, shortly after she had joined her as an apprentice.

The city was a slave city. The largest slave market in all of Perinthia. "*We will not be passing through as free travelers,*" she thought.

It was the morning of their tenth day as captives. The three women were waiting in the cart as Cormac hooked up the oxen, and the other men readied their horses for the days travel. Ahead of them the Wyrmridge Mountains loomed large.

They had left the trees behind and were now angling westbound to get around the mountains. Once they were clear to go south again, Vargah would be another day or two away. "*Not much longer now.*" Roshin thought, and she leaned her body forward to try and warm herself up.

As if reading Roshin's worry, Ashlyn asked a simple question, "What is so bad about Vargah?"

Roshin responded with an uncomfortable snort, "Vargah is a slave market." She realized her response sounded harsher than she had intended.

Ashlyn blushed, "I understand that, but we are already captives. How does this place make it worse?"

"The city is a place of despair," Roshin lamented, reaching her bound hands up toward her face. "Men and women come into it as prisoners, and where they go determines the severity of their sentence."

She paused for a moment to gauge Ashlyn's mood before continuing. "They leave you tied up and chained. The streets reek of urine. There are pens full of men and women waiting to be traded like livestock."

Ashlyn's face grew pale, and her voice began to quiver, "That sounds truly awful. Why does the Emperor let this place exist?" she asked, desperate to understand.

"It's a good question, child," Granya piped in. "The city used to be a hub of trade in Sudarca before the country was conquered. It was a natural in-between for Deervar and the port of Ancalah." Granya took a deep breath before she continued.

"After the war, when Sudarca finally fell, the now Emperor Belanos had a problem. What do you do with all the loyalists and prisoners of war that no longer have a country?" Granya let the question hang for a second before continuing, "He converted Vargah into the place where this problem was dealt with."

"What do you mean 'dealt with'?" Ashlyn asked timidly.

A small chuckle left Granya as she placed her hand on Ashlyn's knee. "Fortunately, they were not all executed. Most were sold into bondage and forced to work menial or difficult jobs for the loyalists and lords in the rest of Perinthia," Granya explained.

"What kind of work?" Ashlyn asked as she balled her bound hands up into fists.

Granya nodded, "Some were forced to mine minerals and salts out of the mountains, some to work on the sea or in the lakes. A few, as an extra insult, became servants to those who were loyal to Belanos and the Empire."

Roshin quickly cut in, "But the war has long since ended? How did the markets continue?"

Granya again nodded her understanding of the question, "There have always been those who have tested the boundaries of their loyalty to the empire. Many of our sisters and brothers of the faith have been rounded up and sold at the markets. Towns could send their dissenters. Those tried and found to be criminals in the capitals are sent up the river should their sentence be anything less than death."

Roshin again broke in, frustration rising inside her, "But the men who have us are deserters and criminals themselves. How are they selling into the market..." She quieted her words to a near whisper as Donah walked past the cart. "...instead of them being sold?"

Responding in an equally hushed tone, Granya explained, "It is unlikely the younger ones will follow us all the way into Vargah, and even if they do, these men are likely some version of slaves themselves, just to a different master. The deserter who makes a deal with the traffickers is not really free. One wrong step will find him traded, just like those boys and the man now working in Veyah."

Roshin sat back against the cart. She had not ever considered that those that had abducted them might not have full agency in the situation. She looked up and out at the men who were tying bundles onto their saddle bags. They looked free, but now she was not so sure.

The cart began rolling a short time later. They were on a path straight toward the base of the mountain. Shadows loomed long and the sun would likely not make an appearance until well past midday.

As they had grown closer to the rocky peaks Roshin had noticed the wonder in Ashlyn's eyes. She had grown up near the Lakelands and had never ventured far from home. Roshin had been there the first time she had seen the Great Fresh Sea.

The wonder she was experiencing now mirrored that. "I never knew the mountains were this large!" she marveled as she craned her neck up to search for their peaks. "They seemed big before, but now? I can hardly see their tops!"

"Indeed they are wondrous," Granya affirmed, joining her in the search for the peaks.

"Do you think the stories are true? That there are dragons up there?" Ashlyn asked, still with a tone of wonder.

"I have faith that there are, though I have never seen one," Granya replied, her voice barely a whisper.

Ashlyn also replied in a whisper, "If they are, then there is still hope for us." She turned her head back to the old woman and asked, "These times, they must be like how it was before the first riders. Surely that means our prophet will be here soon?"

Granya reached over to take hold of Ashlyn's fingers, and she gave them a squeeze, "These times are indeed bad, but there is hope regardless of if we live to see the prophet or not. So long as we hold fast to the truth, then there is always hope."

Roshin just stared up at the mountains without saying a word. *"I wish I could find Granya's hope."*

Granya seemed invigorated by their conversations of dragons and prophets. She spent the day's travel recounting the stories from the sacred texts. She also wove in other lessons related to their craft as healers and their duty to serve.

Roshin listened, but she struggled to connect with anything other than the misery of the people who lived during the dark period. She had no interest in the lesson on tinctures and powders either, but all the same, she did her best to mask her sour mood for the sake of Ashlyn, who for the first time in more than a week seemed to be genuinely happy.

It had been several hours without any breaks when the cart finally ceased. Roshin prepared for another humiliating stop, but as she looked around, she realized they were now situated outside of an old stone cottage.

The walls and chimney had been built from the same limestone that made up the mountainside. Its roof was thatched with grass, and it had a few small windows without any panes. It looked cold and uninviting, especially as it was set beside a large area of loose scree that had likely fallen from the neighboring cliffside.

A sense of foreboding came over Roshin as she watched the men dismount and tie the horses to a hitching post setup in front of the cottage. Like any normal evening, she watched Cormac unhitch the Oxen, while the men untied their packs.

"It looks like we will be stopping here." She whispered to her companions, and she stared at the walls of stone that stood before her.

Tahg was first to the cart to retrieve the women. "Alright, I will take the old crone first this time," he said, reaching over to untie her restraints.

Roshin watched as the other two men entered the cottage. Granya scooted forward slowly and then allowed Tahg to assist her down. "Thank you, sir," she said, without the slightest bit of irony. Roshin had to stifle a laugh at Granya's gratitude.

If Tahg heard her, he paid it no mind. "We are going in, so if ya need to piss, best get that done now." And he proceeded to stand there and watch her as he had every day for the last 10 days. Once Granya was ready he led her through the door, and she disappeared into the dimly lit interior.

Tahg returned moments later and next took Ashlyn. It was the same routine before Ashlyn too disappeared behind the door. Roshin was not looking forward to going in there, and she chewed on her lip as she waited.

When Tahg returned for the third time he did not come alone. Donah had joined him. "Well, hello again, m'lady!" Tahg proclaimed. "I've brought our large grumbling friend here in case you decide to stage a daring escape." He gestured at Donah, who stood with his thick arms crossed, glaring sternly at Roshin.

Part of her wished to make their show worth it by trying to fight or run, but she was also tired, hungry, and ready for all of this to be done with, so she said nothing and let Tahg untie her legs and lead her off the cart. She made no issue as they watched her squat, and instead, like a horse that had just been broken, she let them lead her right through the weathered wooden door into the cold grey cottage.

It took a minute of blinking for her eyes to adjust to the dimness of the interior. It was as grim as she expected. The place was dark and damp. A moldy smell hung in the air that she guessed was coming from the rotten-looking beams above her head. The floor was mostly stone with some litter laid out to try and collect some of the moisture.

There were some old plain wooden chairs, and a roughhewn table set in the middle of the single room, there were shelves on the wall with jars and pots of various sizes, there was a mantle hung above the fireplace. The last thing Roshin saw were a few dirty looking straw mattresses laid out onto the floor.

Cormac stooped over the fireplace, striking a flint in hopes of lighting his pile of sticks. Roshin's companions had been tucked into a corner on a pile of litter. Donah had walked past her and pulled out one of the chairs to park his large frame. As he did Roshin half expected it to break.

Tahg gave her a shove forward toward Ashlyn and Granya, and soon she too found herself sitting upon the floor in the far corner of the room. Her legs were again tied before Tahg moved over to one of the shelves to retrieve a pot which he used as a scoop for the contents of a burlap bag that was set upon the floor.

Soon a fire was going, and the cottage, now lit with a warm orange glow, began to feel drier and more comfortable. All the men seemed to be quite happy to be in this place. Donah had leaned back and closed his eyes, Cormac used a long grass he had placed in the fire to light a pipe before he too sat down, puffing out rings of smoke.

Tahg seemed to be in the highest of spirits. He had added water to his pot before hanging it on a hook that was set in the stone over the fire. He then moved over to retrieve some of the jars on the shelves and hummed a tune as he returned to the fire to sprinkle the contents of the jars into the pot that had already begun to simmer.

Roshin felt her stomach grumble as the smell of culinary herbs filled the small space. Cormac set his pipe down and sniffed the air around him. "Smells a damn sight better than those moldy biscuits we have been eating for the last fortnight."

Donah grunted in agreement; his eyes still closed.

Cormac let out a throaty chuckle. "So, if I recall right, you learned your cooking skills in service. Who taught you to use them spices? It sure wasn't the head cook!"

Tahg laughed brightly as he stirred the bubbling mixture in the pot. "If I said I learned it from the officers' meals, I know you all would believe it! We got the gruel that we could 'fancy up' with crumbled brown bread, and they got the spices."

"Remember how Darren used to try and fancy his rations up by crumbling those moldy biscuits into that swamp water broth?" Cormac asked the group. "The smug bastard is probably eating steak in Veyah."

"Given how much that Lord wanted him," Tahg replied, shaking his head, "I have no doubt he'll be fed proper in no time. Mark my words, next time we pass through, Darren'll be a married man with a little 'un on the way!"

Even Donah let out a gravelly chuckle before adding, "and here we are acting like fools over a few coppers and a bowl full of beans."

"Them coppers will sure be nice though. Just need to get back to where we can spend um." Tahg commented as he ladled the contents of the pot into several bowls. He passed them out to his companions before looking over to the corner and catching Roshin's eye. He smiled at her before turning back and grabbing another large bowl and a wooden spoon.

Filling it until it was heaping, he walked over and offered it to her. "Here ma lady, we all will eat well tonight." Roshin took the bowl and with a slight bow Tahg turned on his heel to find his spot at the table.

"What did you do that for!? Cormac scolded Tahg in a lighthearted way.

"It's them that is the reason we will be getting those coppers, they should enjoy the bounty too!" Tahg defended.

"Let um eat." Donah agreed before tucking into his food.

Roshin just held the bowl, as if paralyzed by her surprise. It was Granya who tapped her on the wrist as a way to draw her attention back to the women on the floor. "It is a true kindness that we should get to eat as much as them. Let us enjoy and be grateful, and nothing more."

Roshin looked at Granya before nodding and holding out the bowl for Granya to eat from. "You first, take what you need. There is more than enough for us all." And with that the room grew quiet, as everyone enjoyed the meal.

5

The Switch

In the morning, Tahg again prepared the entire group a meal of spiced beans. *"It feels like we are lambs before the slaughter,"* Roshin thought as she ate.

Despite the pleasantness of her full stomach the night before, she could not shake the feeling that the cottage was the harbinger of bad things to come. She had struggled to fall asleep, even as everyone else did, and she spent the night staring at the fire until it burned down to nothing more than embers.

It was then, in the pitch black, that she was finally able to sleep. It was not long before the light of morning trickled through the window holes, and the men stirred from their slumber. She too stirred, even though she still felt exhausted from her vigilance.

The men spent the morning planning how to spend their coppers. They seemed eager to head back north, hoping to pick up some more work along the way. It was clear now to the women that Granya had been right and that these men would not be going any closer to Vargah.

"I wonder who will be taking us?" Ashlyn asked with an uncomfortable timidity in her voice.

Granya replied, "It will likely be older men who have a regular presence in the city. Most likely men who have been there since the slave market started."

Roshin felt the pit return to her stomach. "So characters we really do not want to meet."

"You are likely right on that, my child, but let's just handle it with composure and soon we will be there and hopefully done with them," Granya tried her best to reassure them. "Vargah is likely only another day or two away."

Ashlyn grew pale as those words sank in. "But then what will happen to us?" Her voice grew more frantic. "What if they separate us?"

Granya placed her bound hands upon the girls. "I know it feels impossible not to worry about such things, but that has not happened, so let us just pray that our lord has his eyes on us and will keep us together."

No sooner had Granya finished than the door of the cottage swung open. A blast of cold air whirled into the room, scattering the litter about, and fanning the embers that remained in the hearth into a warm glow.

The men in the room jumped to attention. Donah knocked over his chair but stood ready to draw his sword, depending on who was about to come in.

Two men entered the room. Their appearance took Roshin aback. She had expected the slavers to be greasy, unkempt, and ugly. Her mind had painted a picture of old men with thinning hair and lips fixed in a permanent scowl, giving them a mean, almost rat-like appearance.

What stood before her in the dark room, backlit by the light of the morning, were two regal and proud-looking men. They were older, for sure, but they looked strong, healthy, and clean. "*These are the slavers?*" she thought, feeling confused.

The first man was tall with a graying beard and salt and pepper hair that Roshin could tell had once been quite dark. His mustache was groomed so that each side was styled into a point that he then rolled up into a neat coil. His face had the lines of age, but his skin was tanned and warm looking, his eyes were a rich brown.

The second man had a reddish hue to his hair; a few white strands could be seen in his beard, but overall, it was still rich and full of color. His beard and mustache were trimmed short, and his eyes were a piercing blue. Like his companion he had lines on his face indicating his age, but he too looked strong and proud.

Both men were richly adorned. The first man was wearing a clean white tunic, over which he had a tight-fitting and intricately embroidered burgundy surcoat. Its fasteners were large and ornate, with garnets encrusted into them.

His companion was wearing a blue-colored tunic that reached all the way down to his ankles. Over it was a leather jerkin and a rich-looking fur-collared cloak. He preferred his adornments to be hanging from his neck with large metal showpieces that were rimmed some hefty blue-colored jewels.

Their legs were both covered with long padded chausses, and their feet were covered with smooth leather shoes that came to a point at the toe. They looked like lords, completely out of place in this dark and dingy cottage.

The first man spoke, "I am Bryan, and this is my partner Liam. We understand you have brought down some goods from Veyah to be taken to the market."

"Aye, we have," Cormac noted, pointing over to the women in the corner.

"Good then, let's bring them out so I can see them better," Bryan replied.

Donah and Tahg both stepped away from their chairs and over to the corner where the women were. The slavers had turned and gone out the door. Donah stooped to untie Roshin's legs, and Tahg did the same for Ashlyn.

Once free of the restraints, the men helped the women to their feet and walked them to the door. As they cleared the way, Cormac stepped forward to untie and walk out Granya. As Roshin reached the door she tried to stop, Donah pushed her through.

Before her were the slavers, who were looking even more extravagant in the full light of the day. She looked around to see that they had ridden in on a couple of beautiful palfreys. One was grey with dapples, and the other had a golden-colored coat and a light blonde mane and tail.

Near them was a heavily laden pack mule being held by a man whom Roshin assumed to be a slave. He was an older man as well, tall and thin. He was wearing a simple rough-spun tunic with breeches and leather boots. He had no sword, no other armaments. His skin was tanned and chapped, and his hair looked ungroomed.

She noticed that they did not have a wagon. Tahg seemed to notice this as well, and he made an inquiry, "Pardon me, my lord, but you have no cart for the ladies here?"

Bryan seemed surprised that the man had spoken to him, but he responded all the same, "No cart. They will walk."

Roshin looked back over at Tahg, who again caught her eyes. He looked nervous and uncomfortable. "But sirs, the one lady is old, and this is rocky ground. We have a couple of spare horses; maybe you could take one for them to switch off and ride?"

Cormac struck him from behind and cursed, "Shut up, we are not going to give them one of our horses. It's likely worth more than the old bag."

Bryan and Liam both laughed. "The women can walk. I have seen older and sicker make it farther. Now let's dispense with this nonsense; I wish to see what I am buying."

After a moment of hesitation, Tahg stepped aside, and the other men did the same, leaving the women standing alone on the stones in front of the cottage. Liam stroked his chin in consideration as he studied them, and then suddenly he walked forward toward Roshin.

"I cannot tell what we have here with this ridiculous cover." And with that, Liam reached out and grabbed Roshin's veil. She had worn it through the entirety of their travel; it offered her a sense of privacy and security. None of the men had seen her hair in the ten days they had spent together.

As the cloth was pulled over her head, it felt like time had slowed down. She tried to reach up and grab it with her hands, but she was not fast enough. A moment later, as long auburn locks fell around her head, she felt completely exposed.

"Now that is much better, and look, she is much prettier now too," Liam commented as he walked backward. After a minute of feeling his piercing blue eyes boring into her, he turned toward Bryan and whispered something into his ear.

Roshin just stared in a state of shock as Bryan looked toward her and smiled. She felt so cold. "*I could run,*" she thought. "*I might not make it far, but I could run.*" She looked off, down the mountainside. She then looked up into the cliffs and imagined a dragon coming down to take them all away.

She returned her attention to the scene unfolding before her. Tahg once again caught her eyes. "*He looks angry,*" she thought.

Bryan brought her back to the moment by calling out to Cormac, "The old one... well, she is what she is. You can take her away for now."

Cormac nodded before returning to Granya. Taking hold of her arm, he said, "Come on, mum, let's get you back inside."

"What do you mean to do with the girls?" Granya called out as she was being led away, but Cormac didn't give her a moment to hear the response. Instead, he just shoved her back into the cottage and disappeared behind the door.

Liam laughed. "It's as if she does not realize she is a slave."

"Indeed," Bryan agreed before pointing to Donah. "You," he said, turning his finger to Roshin, "strip that one down. I want to see what we have here."

Roshin felt her heart leap up into her chest as Tahg burst in, "Now wait a minute, surely that is not necessary. Anyone with eyes can see she is a pretty woman!"

"A pretty one, to be sure," Liam remarked with an appraising look, "but beauty is more common than you might expect on the auction block. That fiery hair, though, that's a rare trait. It could fetch a higher price from the right buyer."

He furrowed his brow, considering the possibilities. "Of course, we'll need to verify she's free of any imperfections that would negate that added value."

"Free of imperfections?" Roshin repeated in her mind. *"Do they mean to strip me bare?"*

"Hold on now," Tahg burst out, grabbing Roshin's other arm. "Surely gentlemen like yourselves don't need to be treating a lady this way?"

He tried to subtly move between Donah and Roshin. "Why not just take her as she is? No need for all this mess." He forced an easy smile, though his jaw was tight.

"Yous look like proper men of status. The woman's beauty speaks for itself without peeling her clothes off in front of gods and all," Tahg said, doing his best to keep his tone measured and reasonable.

"You'd do well to remember your place," Bryan said, his voice slow and sharp like the edge of a blade. "There's a reason you're hauling cargo and not selling in the market. I'd suggest you mind your station." Bryan pointed a stern finger toward Tahg. "Or you might just find yourself joining us on the road to Vargah...as more product."

He lingered on those last words, letting their meaning sink in. Tahg was treading in very dangerous water. Roshin watched as Donah put a hand on his companion, "Easy Tahg, the girl's not worth your freedom. Let us just finish here, get our coppers, and go."

"It's like Granya said, they are not really free either," Roshin thought as she watched Tahg's face fall. She felt his fingers loosen from around her arm, and for the first time, she wished that he would not let her go. *"If they stood together, they could stop this,"* she mused as she watched his hand slip away.

Liam smiled and responded in a jovial tone. "Smart man. Now back to the girl."

Ashlyn had broken down into tears. "This is wrong!" Tahg gave as a final protest before pumping his fists in anger and turning to walk back through the cottage door. Roshin craned her head to watch him. As he disappeared into the cottage, Cormac came out.

"Alright, let's get this over with," Donah grumbled. He grabbed Roshin's arm in his steely grip. She tensed, squirming away, but he held firm. "Hold still now, girl," he rasped low in her ear. "Don't make me fight you on this. I don't like it no more than you do."

Cormac looked at Donah. "What's wrong with Tahg?" he asked.

Bryan laughed. "That was the man you should have traded in Veyah. All he is is trouble for you."

Cormac mostly ignored the response and gestured to Ashlyn, who had dropped to the ground. "Why is the girl so upset?"

"It appears she fears an evaluation. Your companion here is helping us inspect the goods," Bryan noted, pointing over to Donah.

"Now hold on, that ain't part of our deal," Cormac grumbled, holding up his hands. "We brought you the goods, fair and square. Don't matter to us what you can sell 'em for. We're owed those coppers either way."

He hitched up his belt, thumb resting casually on the pommel of his sword. "So pay up and me and my men will be on our way. Leave you to handle your business however you see fit. Ain't no concern of ours."

Bryan's face flashed with frustration, but he quickly switched over to formality. "As you wish." He pulled out his coin belt and waved over to the enslaved man still holding the mule. "Pull off their sacks and put them in the carts." He counted out a number of coppers and then waved Cormac over.

Cormac moved with a slight hesitation in his step, as if Bryan were a snake that was liable to bite him should he not be careful. Once he was within arm's reach, he held out his hand, and Bryan poured the coins into it.

Cormac began counting them and then, with a nod, he announced, "And so we are done now." He looked over to Donah. "Get Tahg and saddle the horses."

Donah's firm grip released from Roshin's arm. As he moved off, he muttered over his shoulder, "Sorry, lass," before stomping away toward the cottage door, his shoulders slumped. Roshin continued to watch the door for a few moments before he emerged with an armful of bundles and Tahg trailing behind him.

Roshin could see that Tahg's shoulders were tense. His mouth was fixed in a hard line, and his eyes seemed to be smoldering. *"Strange for a man who seemed to turn everything into a joke,"* she thought as she watched him.

His face was flushed. He kept stealing glances her way, shaking his head and clenching his jaw before wrenching his gaze away. *"He doesn't want to go* and leave us. *Good,"* she assured herself. *"Maybe he will decide the coppers are not worth it."*

The two slavers had moved back to their horses to discuss something. The enslaved man had delivered several bundles and a cask from the back of the mule into the smugglers' cart. She and Ashlyn remained there, standing on the pile of loose stones that made up the front of the cottage.

It was only a few more minutes before Cormac climbed up onto the front of the ox cart and called out to the others, "Off we are!" Donah and Tahg mounted up and followed. Not one word was spoken, but Roshin caught sight of Bryan offering a salute to the men as they rode back up the path from which they had come.

Tahg looked back at her one more time before he kicked his heels into his mount, shooting forward into a gallop and out ahead of the rest of the group. Just like that, they were gone, and now Roshin, Ashlyn, and Granya were left with the slavers.

6

The Road to Vargah

It was now the afternoon of their second day of walking. The increased traffic on the road told her that they must be getting close to Vargah. The afternoon before, they had peeled away from the mountains and begun to again head south over the open countryside.

At first, she was surprised when the slavers horses had merged onto a road, given the care her previous captors had taken to avoid them. *"They are in fact free men, no need to hide,"* she remembered.

The road, like so many she had traveled with Granya, was uneven and rutted, filled with muddy potholes left by the spring rains. Even so, it provided easier passage than the rocky mountain terrain, which was a blessing for one traveling on foot.

The slavers' horses moved smoothly across the uneven ground, and Roshin marveled at them. The riders barely bounced at all in the saddles. *"Smooth as the morning waters. These look like horses even I could ride,"* Roshin thought to herself.

They were clearly animals of high value between their coloring, and their gait. Even at a faster pace the horses seemed to glide. Their ambling provided a steady four beats without a moment of suspension in the air, as was the case with a common horse.

She watched them for a time, wishing she could sit up on their backs and float along like a queen, but eventually she lost her focus and began to look around her. Like the landscape outside of Veyah, the fields here were mostly bare, with sparse weeds and hardy grasses holding fast to the hard-packed ground.

Surprisingly, they had traveled past some small houses and huts that appeared to be occupied. As they neared them, Roshin had noticed that a few sat before fields that looked to have been plowed up and planted.

She had pointed this out to Ashlyn and Granya. Ashlyn had looked out longingly toward them, as if reminded of the farm that her parents once tended. Roshin could feel the young girl's despair as the plots faded back into the distance.

Looking out ahead past the horses, Roshin noticed what looked to be a dark blotch out on the horizon. "*Vargah,*" she thought, but she did not bother saying the word aloud. None of the women had spoken much since they had started walking.

After what the slavers had done to them at the cottage, Roshin felt too afraid to say anything that might draw their eyes back to her. A flush of shame and disgust flared up from her chest and into her face before she did her best to chase the memory away with more menial observations.

The enslaved man was walking alongside the mule as it followed behind the horses. While he was holding a lead that connected to a halter on the mule's head, Roshin wagered that the mule was really being led by the horses.

"That mule would happily drag us all with him if the slavers picked up the pace." She thought. Suddenly, she felt a jerk from behind her, and she turned to see that a pale-faced Ashlyn had tripped on a hole and stumbled.

Granya was now walking alongside her, trying to help steady her as best she could. "Here now, girl," the old woman said, stuffing her bound hands under Ashlyn's elbow to help lift her. "You have your feet again. Just keep walking."

The three women were bound together with a rough rope that looped around their wrist restraints. The rope was attached to a thick collar that hung around the neck of the mule. Roshin began to strategize how she might find a way to move back in the line to help, should one of the others fall.

She turned again to look ahead toward the slavers, the feeling of disgust renewing in her chest. "We can't get away from them soon enough," she decided, and with that declaration, the growing spot on the horizon began to feel more exciting.

Again, her mind moved back to the cottage after the others had gone. "*Stop. Don't think about that. Stop,*" she scolded herself, but it seemed useless; the memory had a foothold and was impossible to shake away.

She turned her head down to look at the road, but every stone she passed just made her think of the cold stone floor of that cottage. "*It's over,*" she reminded herself, but it wasn't really over. She was still following them; her eyes flickered up to the backs of Bryan and Liam.

"*They didn't need to do it,*" she knew. "*They just wanted to because they could.*" A tress of her hair blew into her face, and she found she needed to fight back the tears. "*They made sure to see all of me,*" she thought as her emotions began to well up in the corners of her eyes.

The memory overtook her resistance, and she found herself back in the cottage. Liam had ordered the enslaved man to take her and Ashlyn back inside and rebind their feet. He then ordered the man to build a fire and boil a kettle of water. The slavers sat at the table for what felt like an eternity, waiting for the water to heat.

At the time, she wondered if they had decided to forgo their inspection now that they had lost the help of Donah. She turned to the weepy Ashlyn and whispered, "Perhaps they will simply rest a spell and then we will head out." Ashlyn sniffed and lifted her chin to look up at the men.

The kettle was finally hissing, and the enslaved man took it down from the fire and set it onto the thick wooden table. He dropped into it a satchel of something, likely spices for a tea, and then left it to steep.

He left the room and brought in a meal of dried meat, cheese, and bread. Roshin remembered Liam's eyes, which she could not seem to cast away. She blushed and tried to shrink down, but it was no use. *"He liked what he saw,"* she thought bitterly, fighting to shake off her humiliation.

At some point while they were eating, Liam turned to Bryan and asked him, "Shall we inspect them now?"

Bryan, stern-faced and professional, nodded before waving the enslaved man over. He instructed the man, "Go to the cart and get the travel dresses, then strip them down. You can cut the garments off if that is easier; they have no need for them anymore." Then he handed the man a small knife.

The enslaved man just stood there, staring at the knife. It was not until Bryan placed his hand on the hilt of his sword that the man nodded and ran out the door. That was when Granya broke in, "Please, sirs, these are young women of virtue. We are healers and sisters of Hulen Ahir. This is not necessary."

Liam and Bryan simply ignored her and continued to discuss something that Roshin could not understand. Granya grew more agitated. "Have you no mothers, sisters, wives, or daughters to defend? Have you—"

Liam cut her off. "My wife was the finest purchase I made in the market, a jewel like no other. This is simply business, dear woman, and nothing more. I benefit not should I defile my own goods." And with that, he stood.

"If this is too much for you to handle, we shall simply take you out, but know this, good woman: no harm or violation will come to either girl by my hand." And with that, he waved the enslaved man over, took from him the linen dresses, and bade him to take Granya outside.

Roshin could hear her prayer as she was dragged from the room:

"Hulen Ahir, grant me strength in this time of darkness. They cannot touch our spirits. Help us find light even now. Keep your daughters safe from harm and despair. Remind us that no chains can bind a soul that puts its trust in you. May your prophet rise again."

"No violation," Roshin muttered bitterly. "What else does one call an unwanted inspection?"

Ashlyn had cried as their cold fingers touched her body. They made comments on her brown eyes and her dark hair. They liked the fact that it had some waves in it. They commented that her face seemed plain and her arms seemed soft. They made other comments as well, but Roshin did her best to blot them out of her mind. A shudder ran over her as she recalled how helpless she had felt to do anything to stop them.

Roshin then remembered her own fear and shame as she found herself stripped bare in front of them. She remembered how Liam had noted her green eyes and the freckles that painted her nose as a selling feature, but then when he pulled back her hair to expose her ears, he could not help but chuckle.

"Well, I found at least one defect here," he had announced to Bryan, waving him over to come and see. "Her ears are far too large," he noted in a matter-of-fact tone.

Bryan took hold of one of them, inspecting their shape. "No matter," he assured him. "She has enough hair; we can just make sure they stay covered up when she is presented to buyers, perhaps a nice loose braid and some flowers in her hair to emphasize the good parts." Bryan gestured to the rest of her exposed body. "She has plenty of other valuable qualities. I say this one for sure could sell as a bride."

"A bride to whom?" Roshin pondered as she stared hard at the floor, willing herself not to cry. After the inspection, the slavers left them and walked out the door. The enslaved man came over and gently helped the girls up without a word.

He untied their wrists and offered them the travel shifts to slip into. "I will have to bind you back up, but I can give you a moment to stretch and scratch," he paused and then looked up into Roshin's eyes. "I am sorry you are here," his words were a whisper, and his own eyes were full of sorrow.

"I wonder who he is and how he got here?" she remembered thinking. As she again became aware of her feet, she looked back at the man holding on to the mule. "I am sorry you are here," she repeated in a voice he was unlikely to hear.

The spot on the horizon was now much clearer. A walled city stood before them at the end of the road. Within the hour, they would have arrived at Vargah, and their future path would be set without any of their input.

It felt so unjust. Roshin could not help but think back to her childhood. "So much of my life has been outside of my control," she whispered to herself. Somehow, being a slave seemed a fitting destiny for an orphan girl from across the sea.

Her first concrete memory was being on the boat that would take her from the place of her birth to Perinthia and the city of Ancalah. As it was, she could not even remember the name of the land on which she was born. She cursed her mother under her breath. "Why did you even leave there and come here?"

It was a question Roshin had asked so much that it had left tracks on her mind. Her mother had died not too long after their arrival, and Roshin had found herself a child trying to survive alone on the streets. She would have surely starved had it not been for the fish markets, the fishermen, and warmer weather by the sea.

Becoming an apprentice to Granya was the first time she finally felt as though she had any agency and control over her life. She had freely chosen to follow her and freely chosen to learn the art of healing and the faith of Hulen Ahir.

Now, as she stood before the gates of Vargah, a commodity to be traded, she wondered what it was all for if she was just to be the bride of some old man who would purchase her out of a pen like a prized horse.

The gates loomed large now, and before them was a dock with a slave-run ferry that would take them across the churning river and onto their fate. Roshin looked behind her and gave a soft smile to Ashlyn and Granya. "Let's face this together," she said with a deep breath.

7

City of Slaves

The women huddled close together as they wove around the people on the crowded streets of Vargah. They had just entered the gates behind the dock where a large flat-bottomed ferry had deposited them.

The crossing had been unnerving to the women, especially to Ashlyn, who did not have much experience on boats. The river was swollen as it had taken in the meltwater and rain that accompanied the season. The muddy water was moving fast toward the west.

The dock across from Vargah was positioned to the east of the city gates, but all the same the slave oarsmen had to fight hard against the current to stay on course. Roshin wondered how they managed to return, given that they would have to fight the forces of the water even more to get back to the dock on the other side.

"They must carry less cargo out," she thought. The weight being less on the return trip would certainly make the job easier. She hoped, for their sake, that the water settled as the season progressed. Given the traffic on the road she assumed that the ferry would make at least a dozen more runs before the day was out.

Once they had passed through the city gates, the Slavers stopped and dropped off their animals in the livery. The enslaved man went with them. Roshin watched him, with his slumped shoulders, as he followed the mule into the stables to be unpacked.

The women were now alone with Bryan and Liam. It was not what Roshin would have preferred. Liam had boldly drawn his sword and had headed to a position behind the women, while Bryan took the front of the rope to tow them along.

Bryan called out to them, "I shall have you follow me. Do not attempt to flee." He paused and pointed up to a tall stone-sided watchtower that connected to the outer wall. "There are guards all about, and you will be quickly retrieved." Roshin felt a shudder as she glanced up to see the soldier standing vigil at his post.

It was not clear for whom the display of steel from Liam was intended. If it was as Bryan said, there was no hope for them to run off. "*So why the threat?*" Roshin wondered. She imagined that perhaps it was to dissuade the others around them from trying to sample the merchandise before the sale.

Regardless the trio bunched together and followed Bryan as he made his way down the central thoroughfare. It looked to Roshin that the city was more crowded than it had been when she had last passed through.

For Ashlyn, the sights around her were completely new. Like with the sea, and the mountains before, the sheltered girl had never seen a proper city. "There are so many people," she observed with wonder. Roshin took the girl's hand and offered her a squeeze for reassurance.

"It seems the business of trading in men is doing quite well." Granya observed, "May Hulen Ahir watch over them all," and with that, the old woman bowed her head so that she might be able to reach her forehead to perform the blessing ritual.

The smells were hard for Roshin to take. The odor of refuse and urine hung heavy all around them, but at different points it would mix with perfumes, the faint smells of baked goods, or cured meats. It triggered hunger and revulsion all at the same time, which left her stomach lurching about as confused as the rest of her felt.

Bryan and Liam turned down a crowded side street. Stone buildings seemed to lean in around them. In front of the looming structures were dozens of street vendors. Some stood alone with armfuls of goods, but most were manning wooden carts or barrels as they hawked their wares.

The merchants carefully observed the women and their bound wrists before turning and stretching their arms out toward Bryan and Liam. They were laden with an assortment of items: strings of beads, scarves, linen, and other fine fabrics. Another vender waved around hats and hairpieces.

"Fine cloths to sell a fine lady!" an old man with thin hair and missing teeth called out to Bryan, who simply waved him away. Roshin wondered if the entirety of this marketplace was based around a need to make a slave woman attractive for a sale. "Surely there are free women who may want these things?" she asked Granya.

"The peddlers clearly know their audience," Granya replied, raising up the rope that tied them all together.

Bryan suddenly stopped in front of a cart selling flowers. He searched through the wrapped bouquets, picking out one that was to his liking. Once in hand, he flipped a copper to the vendor. It was more than such a thing should be worth, but fresh flowers were in short supply.

Roshin watched as the merchant failed to catch it, and the coin dropped to the ground. He immediately fell to his knees, searching frantically in the dirt until the metal was firmly in his hands.

 "The things done for a slaver's coin," Roshin stated to nobody in particular.

Their captors continued on, turning onto different streets. "I couldn't find the gates again even if I wanted to," Roshin commented to the others after the fourth turn. Yet the men seemed to know exactly where they were going.

After one more turn, the street opened up, and before them was a sprawling courtyard. "The market," Ashlyn whispered, tension in her voice. It was indeed the market. Bryan stopped for a minute to talk to another man giving the women a chance to take it all in.

Roshin had never seen the market before. It was larger than she expected, ringed with what looked like weathered wooden houses stacked on top of each other. In the center were several different raised platforms. Two of which were actively being used.

Bound men stood beside the stage waiting to be brought up on and sold. A flamboyant man with a dark leather coat and hat, from which sprouted several large feathers, stood in the middle of the platform. He was holding up the bound wrists of a thin man in a worn linen tunic.

The face of the man being sold was grim, but the auctioneer, ever the showman, was singing the praises of this fine worker with many years of service left. In his free hand the auctioneer held a whip, which he waved in different directions to acknowledge a bid from one of the dozen or so men clustered around the stage.

Bryan and Liam paid no mind to the activities in the market center, and instead made a straight line to one of the wooden houses. As they moved along the edge of the courtyard it was impossible not to see the pens and ties setup and full of people, men, women, and even children.

As if sensing their concern, Liam broke in, "You need not worry about the pens. We keep our stock in a market house. It's much safer that way. There are thieves all about."

"*Maybe a thief is just what we need to get out of this city,*" Roshin thought as Bryan pulled them along toward the men's market house. All the buildings looked similar. Roshin was not sure how to tell them apart.

They reached one of the houses in the southwestern corner of the square. It was old but fairly well maintained. "*A city full of slaves does not lack for men to perform repairs,*" she thought. The windows in the front of the house were dark. The wooden door was solid with a heavy iron lock.

As they approached, Bryan fished around in one of his leather pouches and pulled out a ring of keys. He placed the key in the lock, and it clicked. The door was then pushed open. The women were pulled down a dark hallway, lit with only a few candles stuck into cutouts along the wall. They passed several doors before they finally stopped before one.

This door was also locked, and Bryan opened it with another key. The women were pushed in by Liam, who stood in the opening, sword in hand. Bryan, who had come into the room with them, began to untie the bindings on their wrists. As he worked, Roshin looked about the room.

A few shafts of daylight filtered through two small windows on the far side, opposite the door. The windows were covered with bars and were set high on the wall. Looking through all Roshin could see was the side of another building nearby. It was unlikely they could squeeze through them. *"I am not sure why I expected otherwise,"* Roshin scolded herself.

The floors of the room were unfinished wooden planks, as were the walls. A simple table and two rickety chairs were the only furnishings. In one corner lay a pile of wool blankets that looked serviceable enough. There was a chamber pot, and a few candlesticks though no way to light them. The room looked gloomy and was full of dust.

Bryan finished releasing their bindings and moved to the door. "We will have our servant bring you food and water in a few hours. I bid you rest in the meantime."

Liam continued for him, "You will be bathed in the morning and dressed for the sale. Don't expect to stay long." With that, the men departed, and the door was closed and locked behind them.

It felt to Roshin as if they had just been enclosed in a large crate with all the wood around them. All the same, after two weeks of having near-constant supervision, it felt liberating to move about and to not have to carefully mind their tongues.

Roshin rubbed her chafed wrists and turned to the others. "It seems we are to be sold tomorrow, then."

She watched as Ashlyn shrank down onto the floor and pulled her knees up to her chest. "What do we do now?" she asked, her voice little more than a whisper, as tears welled up in her eyes.

Roshin sat down beside her and wrapped her arms around her. "I have wanted to do this for weeks," she said, doing her best to keep back her own tears.

Ashlyn leaned in close to her friend. "They say that you may be a bride, but what does that mean for me? I am not especially pretty or unusual in any way," she said as she stroked her long, dark brown hair

"The fate of a bride is not guaranteed to be any better than any other, depending on the groom," Granya noted. "I say, child, that the best you can do is hold yourself tall and embrace your fate. This is what I will do."

Granya sat down upon one of the chairs. "Do you recall the tale of Leina?"

Both Ashlyn and Roshin shook their heads.

Granya smiled and scooted her chair so that she was seated before the women huddled on the floor. Then she began to tell the story: "Leina was sold to be one of the forty concubines to King Janux. When she first faced her fate, she burned with rage and sorrow. She did not wish for this life. It was not what she desired..."

The story continued, and the two girls held each other as they listened to Granya describe a situation that reminded them of their own.

"Leina found her anger at the injustice did naught to make her life better, so instead she sought to be more than a slave through the goodness of her words and actions." As Granya spoke, she waved her hands, bringing the tale to life.

She continued, "Her sisters in the harem came to love her, and the king admired her the most out of all the women in his company. She gained power and influence over her lord's household, and she was able to free many from a life of bondage."

Pausing, Granya reached for Ashlyn's hand. "Darkness cannot drive out darkness; only light can do that.

"How can I find light in this situation? What does that even mean?" Ashlyn asked.

"We are called to live our lives in truth and service. The rewards for our work are not guaranteed in this life, but so long as we act with integrity, and as long as we keep hold of our hope and faith, we shall see our reward when our time here has ended.

Ashlyn let out a soft sob. "I should have stayed with my mother."

"We cannot go back, child, so there is no sense in dwelling on such things," Granya explained, placing a warm hand on her shoulder. "There is no way to know if that different choice would have been better. Think instead of what you have seen and learned, and hold fast to the family you have made here while you still have it."

8

The Market

A rush of cold water cascaded down Roshin's head and onto her bare shoulders. She was folded up in a narrow wooden wash barrel, being soaped and scrubbed by a middle-aged slave woman. "*It might be nice if they bothered to warm it,*" she thought as she shivered.

Ashlyn sat in a different barrel beside her, teeth chattering and eyes wide. Where the water was sourced from, she did not know; all she knew was that it was cold. One woman had been coming in and out of the room with buckets, while the other used a stiff sisal brush to scrub the dirt from under her nails.

When the morning came the young women had been retrieved from the room where they had been locked the day before. They were brought down the hall by two older male slaves to this room, with a gravel floor and big bright windows. The wash tubs were set down in the middle, with wooden stools set beside them.

The men left, and three women came in wearing simple brown linen dresses and white aprons. The women did not really address the girls; one just pointed and barked out assignments for the others to direct their actions. The girls were stripped down and placed into the tubs.

At least they were being attended to by women. Under a different circumstance the experience might be reminiscent of what it would be like for a lord's lady to be tended to and washed by servants. The reality here, however, was that neither Roshin nor Ashlyn had a better station or prospect than any of the three attendants.

Roshin wondered about what had been done with Granya. The old women had not joined them for a bath and this fact made her uncomfortable. *"They don't see that she has enough value to bother washing,"* Roshin concluded, though the thought made her sad.

The washer woman moved on to Roshin's hair. She used an oily soap and rubbed it into her scalp. This part Roshin had to admit felt quite nice. The two buckets of water that followed, however, erased away any of the pleasure she had experienced.

"Up now, girl," the old woman barked at her, and Roshin stood dripping wet. "Out ya get!" Another short command followed by a pat on the bottom, as the washer woman turned to retrieve a rough-spun towel with which she patted Roshin dry.

Around the same time, the other woman was also helping Ashlyn from the tub. Roshin had a small moment of relief to think that the girl had been spared the gruff washer. "*Any kindness today will do her good,*" she concluded.

Despite the hours of talking the night before, Ashlyn still seemed to be struggling to put on a brave face. She looked like a scared ball of nerves, tight and tired. "*Hulen Ahir, I beg you give her some courage when she gets to that stage,*" Roshin prayed.

If the girl could not get it together, Roshin feared her fate might be made all the worse. Cruelty seemed to find fear attractive. She had learned this from her life on the streets. Those around her that cowered were summarily crushed. She had learned to act bigger than she felt, and in this moment, she hoped it would serve her well.

Ashlyn, however, came from a different world. A family of farmers in a quiet village. She had lost like everyone else, but she always had her home, and people that cared for her. The adventure of following Granya had been a trial for her already. This was a trial of a different kind, and Roshin was uncertain she was persevering through it.

"If our lord truly is good, then I will find a way for us to stay together," she whispered under her breath.

"Sit." It was an order followed by a firm hand pushing her down to the stool. The washer woman was behind her with a bottle of perfumed oil and a comb. Next, Roshin was subjected to the tugging and pulling of her hair as the old woman struggled to put its waves in order.

It seemed a long while, but eventually it was all brushed, braided and bundled. The old woman pulled her to her feet and then waved one of her companions over with a clean chemise. What came next was her dressing.

With an under layer on, the women next pulled on an overdress with puffy, lacey sleeves. A greenish blue skirt was next, and then a corset laced up tight from behind. The last thing the women added were some of the flowers from the bouquet Bryan had selected the day before. They were tucked in amongst the braids and bindings.

It was the finest thing Roshin had ever worn. The dress of a proper lady, "Or a bride," she thought, a tightness forming in her stomach. She turned her head to look at Ashlyn, who was also dressed, just a bit more simply.

Ashlyn's hair had also been combed, braided, and set with flowers. Her skirt and corset were more earthy in tone and less decorative. Though it was clean and flattering all the same. "You look beautiful," the girl said to Roshin as she caught her eye, but her tone held a distinct sadness, and it weighed heavily on Roshin.

What followed came as a rush, The girls were fitted with delicate looking shoes and then pushed out of the room back into the hall. The male slaves were outside the door waiting, and each one took the arm of one of the girls and led them through the door across the way.

It was a sitting room, with the same wooden walls as all the others, but this room housed shelves, covered in books, a rare sight in a country where few even knew the written language. Granya had taught her to read so she could study the sacred texts, but the four books that Granya had carried with her were the only ones Roshin had ever seen.

Before her, seated in padded chairs, were Brian and Liam. Both had books in one hand, and a pipe in the other, which were both set down as the women entered the room. "Phenomenal!" Liam exclaimed.

"What fine work, fit to fetch a King's ransom no doubt."

Bryan stood up and proceeded to walk a circle around the women. He paused near Roshin's side and reached out toward her hair, grabbing hold of the petal of a delicate pink rose. He congratulated himself. "The flowers truly add a finishing touch,"

Just then the toll of bells rang out. "Ah, just in time as well." Liam looked to the girls. "Your prospects will be much improved if you do not step onto the stage in bindings," he looked hard at Roshin, "...however, I will let that be your choice with how you compose yourself."

Roshin bristled at his insult and stood up tall and proud. "I shall go on my own accord."

"Wonderful!" Liam announced and then he turned to Ashlyn, "Dry your tears girl, look to your companion and follow her lead. You will determine the buyers you attract."

Roshin looked over her shoulder to see Ashlyn, wiping her tear-streaked cheeks and sniffling. Her stomach dropped *"Please help her,"* was the thought she sent out as a prayer, before turning back to the men. "What about Granya?"

"I suppose you mean the old woman," Bryan replied. "She is set to run through the standard sale this afternoon. You ladies will be first, but depending on your buyer I might offer her as a maid to you," Bryan smiled. "Think of it as a good will offering for your performance."

"*My maid. We could stay together,*" she pondered the thought, trying to think of how she might be able to improve those odds. Not wanting to miss a moment she blurted out, "That would be well, she is a fine woman."

Roshin looked around until her eyes settled on the books the men had set down on the table and she gestured over to them, "she even taught me to read. It would be a shame for her to sell alone this afternoon."

"To read? You are full of surprises!" Liam called out with a chuckle, "I will remember this detail."

Roshin nodded before glancing back toward Ashlyn. The girl still had red, teary eyes, and tight balled up hands. She reached over to try and squeeze the girl's shoulder, but found her hand quickly grabbed by the slave man at her back, "No touching," he huffed.

Bryan and Liam both retrieved their pipes and had moved to open the door. "Take them out," Liam ordered calmly, and with that the slave man grabbed tightly onto Roshin's forearm before turning around and leading her out the door.

If the courtyard had seemed busy the day before, it was now flooded with people. There were military men, as well as merchants, and those like her captors, that were dressed like nobility. A few finely dressed women followed the men through the market.

The pens she had seen the day before were even more crowded. Soldiers were being used to grab people out of them. The people who were grabbed then got hooked onto a tie, their arms pulled up above their heads. Men would gather around and inspect them.

A shiver ran down Roshin's spine at the sight, but she did her best to steel her resolve and walk forward as a lady of value. Her heart sank again, however, when she realized the weeping, she had heard behind her was not from one of the pens. It was coming from Ashlyn.

She turned her head to try and project her voice over her shoulder. "Ashlyn, you must stay your tears." The market was so loud she had no way of knowing if the girl had heard her.

The man holding her arm gave it a gentle squeeze and spoke, "She has to find it in herself to stop ma lady. You can't do it for her." She looked up at him and saw him for the first time. He had sad dark eyes that told of a difficult life, and a scar down his cheek that spoke of war.

Roshin remembered the story of how Granya said the market started. Sudarcan loyalists were turned into slaves under Perinthian masters as punishment for their patriotism. She wondered if he might be one of those men.

"I know." She replied, and her chin fell.

The man spoke with gentle words, "Chin up ma lady, set her an example to follow."

He was right. Roshin pressed her eyes closed for but an instant, and then with a breath as big as she could manage in her finery, she raised her chin and walked confidently onward.

The man stopped when they reached the center stage, it was set up higher than the others, right out in the gleaming sun. A crowd had gathered in front of it and she saw before her several other clean and well-dressed young women.

Some of the girls had bound wrists. All had some kind of escort. She began to count them. She and Ashlyn made nine. It made her feel a bit better to see that Ashlyn was not the only girl who was crying. In fact, most of the girls were crying. She began to feel like the rarity for not.

A man walked up onto the stage from the other side. She recognized him. He was the same one who she had seen the day before on the auction stage. He announced to the crowd, "Who is ready to see the fine ladies?!" His voice boomed out over all the chatter and cries.

He then turned toward the women, "Bring up the first girl!" and with that a finely dressed man dragged a bound woman onto the stage. Roshin watched as the woman pulled back and fought him. The man cursed before he struck her. The girl then grew still and stood red faced on the stage.

The auctioneer shouted, "We have here a handful! But it looks that she can be tamed." He turned to the man who brought her up, "What do you know of this one?"

The man spoke, "Aye, she's sixteen and from outside Deervar. A worker's daughter, she can clean and cook. A bit spirited, but with some discipline, she will make a fine house maid."

"And there you have it!" The auctioneer grabbed the girls' wrists and spun her around, "Maybe this one is worth a gold piece?" He paused and looked around, "Maybe we start with seven silvers?" It went on like that until in the end the girl had been sold for four silver coins, about the value that a fat hog might sell for.

Roshin had focused so much on the selling, she realized that she did not even see who the buyer was. More girls were pulled up onto the stage. A dark-haired maid of eighteen sold for seven silvers, a blonde-haired girl of fifteen sold for five.

It did seem to be true that the more fighting and tears the girls put on display the lower the winning bid would be. Roshin did her best to ground herself in the moment and push back her grief. "*I must find my own Leina,*" she thought as she remembered Granya's story.

It was finally her turn. Liam went to take hold of her arm, but she caught his eye and instead offered him her hand. A grin spread across the man's face as he gently took it, and together they walked up onto the stage.

Roshin stood tall and poised. She tried her best to embody the ladies she had seen walking about the markets though she herself had had no formal training. The Auctioneer broke in, "My my! What a jewel we have here! Look at that fine fiery hair!" He moved in close and locked eyes with her, "And I dare say she has striking green eyes as well."

Liam then spoke to offer her details, "She is a maid of nineteen, and I guarantee her virtue is intact." He looked at Roshin with a nod as his arm gracefully cast her away from him and around as if she was an elegant dancer.

The crowd was quiet. "She came from Veyah where she was serving as a traveling nurse. She is trained up in the healing arts and is literate as well." Chatter broke out amongst the audience at that last point.

With that she looked out into the crowd and awaited her fate. "Shall we start this fine lady out at a gold piece?" the auctioneer inquired. No sooner had he said it than he received a bid. "Two gold?" another bid. The bidders got animated as more offers flew.

In the end she received three gold and five silvers. Liam leaned in and whispered in her ear, "Fine job my lady." Roshin looked off to the side of the stage to see Ashlyn waiting to come on. Without so much as thinking she ran over and took the girls hand and pulled her on the stage.

"I want my buyer to take her too!" She called out to the crowd. She had not seen who won, but she was hopeful that if they had the money for her, they might be able to take Ashlyn too.

"Unusual indeed," the auctioneer introjected. "Do I have an offer for the other girl?"

The buyer called back, "No deal!"

Roshin did not let that sit "All I wish for my happiness are my companions."

"Yer not for me!" the buyer barked back.

"Surely for what you agreed to pay, whoever I am for would find it I fine deal for my companions to join me." Roshin proclaimed

With a huff the buyer called out, "Eh bother, I will give another four silvers for other."

The Auctioneer scanned the crowd, "Do I have any other offers?" but all he was greeted with was silence. "Then there we have it, four silvers for the other girl, A fine deal indeed!" and with that Ashlyn fell weeping into Roshin's arms, until the two were taken down from the stage by Bryan and Liam.

Clever girl you are," Bryan said. "You fetched far more than I expected, the other one less, but all the same we got more than we hoped. I will see about making sure the old woman joins you as well, you have earned that much." And with that the man bowed to her before walking off to meet with the buyer.

9

Detour

"*I have kept us together!*" Roshin's thoughts were bright as she and Ashlyn were removed from the central square. The misery around her became a blur as she floated on her feelings of success.

As they reached the door of the market house, however, a new feeling of nervousness took root in her gut. "*Would Granya be included too?*" she worried.

She had confidence that Bryan and Liam would do honest advocacy to see that the old woman went with them, but that did not mean that the buyer would be wanting a third mouth to feed. It was then, as they all waited for the transaction to be finalized, that she had a new thought: "*And to whom are we now bound?*"

It was then that the door opened, and Liam stepped out with two other men. Liam introduced them, "This is Delvin, he is your buyer. His companion here is Toran, they are agents acting at the behest of Officer..." Liam looked over to Delvin, having forgotten the name.

"Randyll, m'lord. Officer Randyll," Delvin finished bowing his shoulder down in deference.

"That's right," Liam nodded before continuing, "These men will be your charges to take you to meet Officer Randyll at his current camp." Liam stepped forward toward Roshin and extended his hand to receive hers. She slipped her fingers into it as he leaned down to kiss them. "It is my sincerest wish that you ladies have good fortune on the road ahead."

Just then Bryan came through the door with Granya. "Ah yes, and Delvin has agreed to take your nurse along as well." He stepped aside to allow Granya to join them. She had a perplexed look on her face that said she was owed a story later.

"The deal is done then! They are yours to take," Liam trumpeted, and with that both men turned and walked back into the door of the market house. The slave escorts that had been standing with the girls peeled away to follow them.

Roshin looked over to her new masters. Toran was hard to miss, he towered over Delvin and most likely over all the other men in the city. He was clean shaven with short cropped hair, his limbs were thick and his shoulders broad. *"I would sooner believe his parents to be oxen than a man and a woman,"* she thought.

In comparison Delvin looked small, but in fact he was not. He had nearly a head on Roshin, and by the looks of it was plenty strong. His wide smile projected warmth and confidence. His sandy blonde hair fell around his face, which was framed by long sideburns. His chin and upper lip were shaved clean, emphasizing his mouth and giving him a roguish charm. He appeared to be a man near 30, if not slightly older.

She could tell the men were soldiers, though something about their appearance was a bit off. They wore military issued tunics, surcoats, and boots. They had military issued swords and belts, but they each had a unique looking dagger, and Delvin had several distinctly personal looking bags and pouches hanging from him.

"Right then, let's be off," Delvin declared with a stomp of his foot. "We've been stuck in this cursed pisspot of a city for a month, can't leave it soon enough."

Toran said nothing, he just walked forward away from the house. Roshin was expecting him to come over and bind their hands and string them to a rope, but he did not. She looked over at Ashlyn and then to Granya with a puzzled expression.

"It seems we are walking on our own accord for this next journey," Granya said in a tone that told Roshin to call no further attention to it. Roshin understood and with a smile she took Ashlyn's hand and started off after Delvin and Toran. Granya followed last of all.

They again found themselves weaving through the crowded streets, she recognized nothing. After a while they made it to the outer wall and were standing before a gate, but it looked different. Toran turned and disappeared for a while. Delvin stood there, straight-backed yet relaxed, looking between them with an easy smile before scanning their surroundings.

It felt as if ages had passed when Toran finally emerged from around one of the side streets. He was leading a donkey that was strapped to a little wooden cart. Delvin grunted, "Took ya long enough. I was thinkin' I might need to get another room!"

He turned and looked back to the women, "Weren't part of my plan to have three ladies as company on this trek." He gestured to the cart. "It ain't no royal carriage, it ain't even much of a cart, but I think ya can each trade out to save your feet some."

Roshin was a bit surprised, "You will be walking too?" she asked.

Delvin slapped his leg with a chuckle and smiled wide, "Horses are for lords, outlanders, and outlaws. We soldiers were made for walkin'." He stepped over and patted the neck of the donkey, "This ole thing makes the load lighter and can help you a bit, but we will get where we get on foot."

With that he turned back toward the gate and waved to the man at the watch. The man waved back and then with a groan from the iron hinges, the gates opened before them.

Roshin was surprised to see that there was no river on the other side of the wall. "I thought this looked wrong," she whispered to Ashlyn. Instead, a rough and rocky road, like the one they arrived on stretched off to the horizon. Roshin enquired to her new charges, "This is not the same gate we arrived though?"

Delvin's lips curved into a disarming smile as he rubbed his chin. "Aye, no, it's likely not. I have me some unfinished business that needs tending to." He noticed Roshin's nervous expression and waved his hand reassuringly. "No worry lass. I even sent a letter to our master letting him know I secured his bride. Once I wrap up my affairs, we'll be headed back north in no time."

Delvin slapped one of the brown sacks in the cart. "We picked up extra rations. Even with the three of yous, we have enough to go an extra week, no problem!" He flashed a confident grin.

Roshin was still unsure, "*I almost rather go straight there*," she thought, but she didn't voice her concerns for fear of chasing away Ashlyn's smile. She instead offered Delvin her own smile and a nod.

"Right then," Delvin said, turning toward the open gate. "There is a river crossing a half a day's journey from here with a small settlement and an inn beside it. I am hoping to make it that far before we stop for the evening." And so, they walked out from the gate and down the road.

They were only a few hours into the trek when Roshin began thinking of nothing more than liberating herself from her dress and corset. The sun was beating down and the weather was warm. The road had turned to the west after heading south for a while.

The landscape around them hinted that they were nearing a lake or the sea. The soil had become sandier, and she began to see gulls overhead. "Lake Sirona," she thought. If that was indeed where this road was taking them, then she had an idea as to where they might be heading.

She was walking just behind Toran and the donkey, beside the cart. With a few long paces she caught up beside him and touched his shoulder to ask, "Are we on the road to Ancalah?"

The big man just turned his head toward her and smiled. "He won't answer ya. Got no tongue to speak!" Delvin exclaimed as if he had just told a joke. The big man opened his mouth and to Roshin's horror she realized Delvin was telling the truth.

With a hardy laugh he continued, "Don't worry 'bout it none. Things for my friend here only got better once his tongue was out of the way and not causing him trouble." He winked back at her and flashed a broad grin, "To answer your question, that is exactly where we are going! You know the place?"

"I've passed through." Roshin said with a distant tone as her mind rolled back to the boats and the docks that she roamed as a child.

Ashlyn picked up on the conversation excitedly and exclaimed "I will get to see your home then!" before catching a side eye glance for Roshin and quickly shutting her mouth.

"Home ah? Well, how about that for luck!" Delvin replied.

Granya put her hands on Roshin's shoulders. "You are not the same girl whom I found there. Do not be afraid to see the place again."

Roshin just nodded. It was not clear as to why the idea of going back in the town gave her such pause, after all it was the closest thing to a home she had, but it was also the place where she watched her mother die. Once she had left, she had made a promise to herself to never go back.

"I guess I did not expect to find myself in a position where I didn't have a choice," she thought bitterly.

The group walked on for several more hours before they reached the settlement. The girls had insisted that Granya ride in the cart when it became clear she was starting to fall behind. They were all tired and the sun was beginning to sink low in the sky. Reaching their destination was a welcome sight for tired feet and empty stomachs.

The settlement was small. It had been built around the river crossing after the war to serve as a resting place for those traveling between Vargah and Ancalah. The bridge was the only crossing north of Lake Sirona and it was key given the lake butted up against the bottom of the Wyrmridge Mountains to the south.

The buildings in the settlement were made mostly of wood from a forest that had long since been cleared from the land. Everything looked weathered, but in good repair. The largest buildings in the little town were the inn, and a mill that was set up next to the river to support the big waterwheel that spun round and round with the current. Aside from that were a few small docks that parked little boats, and a dozen or so small cottages.

Roshin remembered passing through this village with Granya several years prior. They had even stayed for a couple weeks to provide care services to the residence. "Things have changed," she remarked to Granya as they neared the inn.

Like so many of the other towns it looked like it had aged and was struggling to function. The proximity to the slave market no doubt helped keep the money flowing, and she guessed they were not short on labor, but they could not bring the forests back to replace the wood that was damaged or rotted.

Delvin waved the group toward the inn, "Come now! I have a need to try the local brew, and we can get you all a warm meal and a room for the night. I don't suppose you ladies mind if we all stay together then. Can't have you running off in the dark of night now!"

It was the first reminder all day that they were not there of their own accord. "We will be happy for any accommodations that is more than a camp outside," Granya replied.

"I say so!" Delvin exclained before walking into the door of the inn. "Time for a drink."

10

The Drinker

Roshin looked out over Lake Sirona. There were lakes in the Lakelands that were larger, but to Roshin, this one was especially beautiful. It was cool and deep, with crystal-clear turquoise waters, and bright sandy beaches. The thing that made it stand out to her, however, was how the mountains seemed to sprout out of the eastern horizon line.

The group had followed the road up to the top of a hill, and then had moved off the road to make their camp on a ridgeline overlooking the water. The sun was hanging low, casting an orange glow over the rippling waves below, and soon it would be dark. It was the third night of their journey to Ancalah and the second night they had spent out on the land.

"*At least this night it is not raining,*" she thought, remembering how the sky had opened a few hours before they had intended to stop the day before. It had been a cold and wet night. The men had attempted to create a crude tent using a sheet of canvas that they had in the cart, but it had not worked, and they all laid out beside each other in the drizzle, draped in the canvas.

That night had made Roshin appreciate the opportunity she had had to sleep on a straw mattress at the inn. She thought back to the room. There were only four beds for five travelers, so Toran had spent the night propped up against the door so that the others might sleep well. "And so that we might not escape," Roshin muttered to herself as she scratched at the ground with a stick.

While she felt far closer to a free woman with this group than she had since leaving Veyah, there were reminders to her that that was not the case. The men seemed to sleep in shifts, and they were never too far off. Toran especially seemed to keep a watchful eye on Roshin, and between that and his silence she found it unnerving.

The weather this day was pleasant, and travel went smoothly once they had dried out in the sun. After the longest day of walking they had done yet, the men had selected this spot at the top of a ridge to camp. It seemed an odd choice to Roshin as it was quite exposed, "*At least it has a view,*" she thought.

Delvin had not been dishonest about his provisions, at least at this point. For the first time in the weeks since they had been taken from Veyah, everyone was eating well. They had cracked grains to make a morning porridge, and dried beans for the evening.

This part of the country made it hard to set a fire to cook, but the men had managed by gathering dry dung from the road, and the branches off several dead shrubs along the way. This was enough to boil the beans for their dinner since the men had been wise enough to soak them starting the night before.

After dinner they would scoop a healthy helping of the dried beans into a pot, then cover them with water, and set it in the cart. The beans would soak and sprout overnight, and this gave them a softer and richer flavor than Roshin had been used to when a long boil over a fire was not possible.

One of the pouches Delvin carried, she had discovered, was full of a beautiful red salt. It was a common practice for people in this country to do, as salt was rare within the landscape, yet essential to good health, and beneficial to flavor food.

Delvin's salt had been sourced from the mountain mines and was rich in minerals that were hard to get elsewhere. The salt greatly improved the taste of the otherwise bland fare, and Delvin was liberal with his sharing, which she found to be a welcome quality in comparison to her prior captors.

She still found the man to be strange and was not sure how much she should trust in him. After they had arrived at the inn, Delvin had invited them all to sit and share a meal. He had bought for them meat and cheese, which was fare that she had not had in any capacity for at least a month.

He had also ordered them all cider, which seemed a kindness, but she noticed that his tankard never seemed to run dry. The man was jovial no doubt, and as the night wore on his tongue had gotten looser, until finally Toran took hold of the mug when the maid came by to fill it, and shook his head to her.

Still, the situation had offered her a chance to learn more about him, the officer she was to marry, and exactly why he had selected her. She could remember some of their conversation. She had asked him how he ended up in Vargah in the first place.

"Us fellows like me, we ain't exactly prime soldier material," Delvin sneered at himself as he spoke. "But I always managed to find myself a good game of dice." A broad smile spread across his face. "Usually, it's just the guards and officers who play, but I figured out how to get me in to one of the player's tents."

He leaned in and lowered his voice, forcing Roshin to lean in as well. "So I spent a few weeks beatin' this one officer at every throw. Took 'im for nearly every copper he had! Well, he wasn't much for losing, especially to a lot like me."

Delvin laughed and banged his mug on the table "I told 'im, I told 'im 'This here's an honest game, fair and square.' I expected proper compensation for winning!"

He paused to take another swig of his cider. "He told me he had just the thing, an outing of sorts to get me out and away from the gruel – told me it was a chance of a lifetime!"

Delvin leaned back and chuckled again before pointing at Toran, "He gave me this brute to keep me in line, and sent me to Vargah, said I was to find him a 'unique woman'."

He looked Roshin in the eyes and then raised his voice, "I spent a month in that city, attending every maid sale. Had to put up with the uptight prissy dealers and traders until finally you walked yourself up there, danced around like a fairy, and then I learned you could even read. Let me tell you, not much is more unique than that. I wasn't about to mess it up."

Delvin leaned back, red-faced and panting. Everyone at the table was staring at him, but he just banged his mug looking for another round. Roshin did not fail to notice that the big man had done much to help him up the stairs and into the room that night.

They had a late start the next morning as Delvin failed to wake early. When he finally crawled his way out of his bedroll, his mood seemed decidedly more sour. As everyone was getting ready to leave, he disappeared back into the inn. When he met them at the donkey cart with a small cask from inside, it was clear he was feeling better.

"I am not sure he is as good a man as he seems," Roshin whispered to herself, and she glanced over to watch him as he rocked and laughed with Ashlyn near what remained of the fire.

That was another thing she had noticed. Outside of that first night at the inn he treated her with an almost courtly formality. He was polite and deferential, maintaining a careful distance, but he was a lot less restrained with his charm when it came to his interactions with Ashlyn.

It started with simple glances sent back to her, catching her eye and smiling. Any chance he got he would pay her a complement, and this included subtle and gentle touches to her arms, hair, and face. He had even picked her some flowers. The girl could not seem to get enough of this attention from this debonair charmer. Roshin thought it was dangerous, but it had been Granya that had discouraged her from voicing her concerns with Ashlyn. "Right now, it is just harmless fun. Watch them, yes, but the girl has been through so much. Imagine how it must feel to have that kind of caring attention."

She understood where the old woman was coming from, and it was true that the girl had come to life in a way she had not seen since their capture. Still, she had an uneasy feeling about this relationship that she could not seem to shake.

Night was now upon them. Ashlyn was still leaning in, eagerly listening to Delvin's stories, Toran had been sharpening his blade, but had seemingly fallen asleep with it on his lap. Granya was busy sitting on the back of the cart separating the leaves from the stems of some medicinal herbs she had found along the road.

All seemed quiet and in order. Roshin was worn out from the day's walking, so she laid down upon the sand and closed her eyes. The next thing she knew she was dreaming about the docks of Ancalah. It was as if she was a child again, but she was not a child in this dream.

She was running from someone, and she was confused and feeling lost. She ducked into a boat to hide, but one of the sailors found her and spoke to her, "You are a sailor's get. The sea is in your blood. Don't you hide, get out! The water is where you belong."

She was confused, there was something out there that she was afraid of, she didn't want to leave, but he told her again to get out. She rose and looked around. The docks were dark; whoever was after her must have gone. It was then that she heard it, a scream!

It was a girl's scream, the girl was crying, so she turned to look for the girl, and began searching the docks, following the cries and sobs. "She is in trouble! She needs me! Something is wrong." She ran until she saw a girl crying on the edge of a dock.

The girl was just sitting there, her legs dangling off the dock and splashing in the water. She found herself approaching cautiously. For some reason the girl made her nervous. Still, she went to her. When she reached out to touch her, the girl turned. She found herself staring right into her own eyes. The girl was herself.

With that Roshin was jolted awake. Her mind reeling with confusion. "What was that dream?" she wondered, but the thought was broken by the cries, they were the same ones from the dream, she looked around confused, it was so dark.

She wanted to get up and run, but she remembered they were on the top of a ravine. She did not know where it was, and she did not want to fall. So she got up on her hands and knees and slowly began to crawl in her skirts toward the sound.

She was stopped. A massive hand set down upon her shoulder, it gave her a squeeze as a warning, as if telling her she had gone far enough. The cries turned to soft sobs. "Ashlyn!" she called out, but another large hand covered her mouth. She thought to try and bite it, but she did not. "Let me go!" she tried to yell, but it came out all garbled.

It felt like an eternity that she was held there in place, listening to the tears of her friend. Eventually the crying stopped and the big man released her and lumbered off somewhere else. Roshin was off again, and she crawled around in the dark searching for Ashlyn.

She finally found her, lying on her side. Roshin creeped up beside her, when she touched her the girl recoiled and let out a moan of distress. Roshin did not know what was wrong, "Are you hurt?" she asked in little more than a whisper.

Ashlyn just sniffled and then reached out a hand. Roshin took it and held it in hers and she laid down beside the girl. Something had happened, and it was not good.

11

Silence

The dawn took a long time to break. It seemed to Roshin that she had been awake for the entire night, but she was not sure. She felt tired, but not as tired as she would have expected, and she had strange memories that felt a bit like dreams.

She was vaguely aware that both men had woken and were working to repack the cart and prepare a breakfast. She looked over at Ashlyn, relieved to see her sleeping. Roshin was loath to disturb her, so she just stayed where she was, holding her hand, still as stone.

When Granya woke sometime later she seemed to know right away that something was wrong. Likely it was the fact that both girls were lying some distance from the rest of the camp. The old woman came over to sit beside them. As she stooped, she saw Roshin was awake and she asked in a whisper, "What is wrong child?"

Roshin croaked out a response, "I am not sure." She paused to swallow and try to wet her throat. "I was asleep. Dreaming. I heard screaming. I woke up and she was crying. I tried to get to her." Roshin stopped as her voice cracked with tears, "Toran stopped me. I couldn't get to her!"

"I see." The old woman murmured as she looked up to search for the men. Once she had sight of them, the old woman put her hand on her thigh and pushed herself up. She turned and stormed over to them, and then with a roar she asked, "What have you done here?!" It was spoken with a force that Roshin had never heard from the old healer.

Both men stopped and regarded her. Roshin sat up, as Ashlyn's eyes opened. The scene before her seemed to play out in almost slow motion. Delvin's face turned red, and at first, he closed his eyes as if grief-stricken, before taking a swig from his water skin.

His face changed quickly, and the grief that was there was suddenly replaced with anger. He staggered a few steps forward, pointing an accusatory finger at Granya, "You better get a mind to quit your yammering, this ain't none of your concern, I will not put up with this, ya hear?" His speech seemed slurred, and his balance seemed off.

"It does concern me," Granya retorted sharply. "It concerns us all. What. Did you do. To the girl?"

Delvin rolled back his eyes and went to turn away from her, "I don't owe you nothin'. I bought you with my own coppers, you are mine by right. I can leave you right here if I want. Same with the girl, she was MY four silvers."

He was swaying around as if standing on the deck of a boat in rough seas. Toran walked over to Granya and handed her a bowl of porridge without a sound. She did not take it, so he just stood there, looming over her and blocking her view.

Granya looked up at him, "And what do you think to be doing? You think this is a help? Look at her!" she barked, pointing back toward Ashlyn, who was still laying on her side, but was now blinking back tears.

Toran stood still as stone, aside from his fingers which opened, dropping the bowl of porridge. It fell unceremoniously onto the ground, splashing out of the bowl and onto the sandy soil. He then walked over to Ashlyn, stooped down, and with his big arms he scooped her up from the ground.

Granya and Roshin just watched him as he took the girl and walked her over to the cart. He set her down gently in the back, propped up against the bags of grain. He then grunted to Delvin as he pulled the donkey's line free from where it had been staked. With that he started walking forward.

"Right then," Delvin steamed, and he struggled to grab a few of the items still scattered around the camp before stumbling off after him. Toran then stopped and turned. He pointed his thick finger at Roshin and gave her a look that told her it was best if she started walking.

She looked over at the cart, and Ashlyn who was laying in it, curled up in a ball, arms wrapped around her knees. She then looked over to Granya, whose expression was waves of fear, anger, and distress.

Roshin took a deep breath, and she started walking after them, her shoulders slumped, and her head bowed low. Granya too began to follow, and the party began their walk in silence.

It remained unsaid, but all knew what had happened. As they walked toward the south on the road to Ancalah, Roshin cursed herself in a soundless torrent, "*It's my fault, I am why she is here,*" Roshin fought back another wave of tears, her mind still reeling, "*I knew it was no good, I should have said something. Hulen Ahir, how can I ever forgive myself for not doing more to keep her safe?*"

Her silent prayers continued as she pored over every detail of the prior days, every opportunity where she could have done or said something different. "*Why did I fall asleep and leave them alone?*" she wondered

She had grown up around the sailors on the docks. She knew better that to trust a drunken man. After her mother died, she was left alone, kicked out of the small, rented room, and turned out onto the streets.

She naturally went down to the docks in a desperate search to find her father, a man who she only knew from her mother's stories. She had never seen him, and it was a good possibility he was dead or gone far away. Still, she searched.

Her innocent questions about her father gained her sympathy. Many of the older men on the boats began to treat her as a daughter, and they looked out for her. They would go off to sea and when they came back to port, they would give her food and offer her a bed in the safety of their little fishing vessels.

"They told me I was a daughter of the sea," she reminded herself. It was how they addressed her, and how they saw her. It was their good will and charity that kept her alive, but not all the men were good, and for every kind one, there was another to watch out for.

She learned to be wary of the man who spent all his coin in the taverns and stumbled back to the docks. As she grew, these men would leer at her and make comments that sent shivers down her spine.

The men that cared for her told her to watch out. They pointed out the places to not go, and the men she was best to steer clear of. She recalled one time as a girl of 10, that she had been wandering late at night around a place called "The Blind Gull."

It was busy and the kitchen would dump food scraps out the back door. She was hungry and it seemed a perfect opportunity to get a free meal. A man came staggering out the door and caught sight of her. He was a hulking man with a wild white beard. He spotted her and called out, "Hey girl, how bouts I be your pop tonight?"

He came over and attempted to grab her, she squirmed away and ran back against the wall of the tavern. The man moved to go after her, but he was thwarted by Boden, one of the men that cared for her. Boden grabbed the man on the shoulder, "Leave the girl," he said in a firm tone.

"And who be yous to tell me what to do?" the man slurred in reply as he went to try and grab Boden's hand and push him away.

Boden did not hesitate, he pulled back and punched the man right in his crooked nose, "I am her father," he said in a serious tone before turning to Roshin and calling out, "Come girl!" with his hand extended.

She darted past the drunken man who was stooped over, hands clasping at his bleeding nose, and she followed Boden back to the relative safety of his boat.

It was an awkward talk that followed. Boden told her that she was getting older and soon enough she would get a woman's body. He warned her to stay far from the taverns, and never go near the drunken men.

Boden's advice had been sage. As she grew to be a maid, the attention she drew made her feel so unsafe that she cut off her hair and dressed in men's rags. The fish in her pockets was the last thing she tried to keep them all away.

Ashlyn had no such experience. She was from a quiet village and lived with kind parents. She had been part of a family, with siblings, and neighbors, and friends. She didn't know how to be cautious; she didn't get the lessons Roshin did.

Roshin could have taught her, but she had let herself forget the lessons because she was desperate to trust someone, and desperate to see goodness in her situation. "It has been so hard. How will we get through this," she wept quietly to herself.

Granya, too, seemed to be struggling with her guilt. The old woman had also let her kindness and goodwill cloud her judgement. The first several hours of the walk she had spent in silent reflection, now she had moved on to ritualistic recitation of the sacred texts, prayers, and the singing of hymns.

As the old woman sung her voice cracked, but Roshin knew the songs as well, so she joined in to lift up her voice. They sang in harmony as they held on to each other's hands. Ashlyn had stopped crying and was now listening to the song. Delvin began to grow agitated.

"Can't you stop that blasted singing?!" he turned and barked. "All I hear is singing, singing, singing. It's liable to make a man go mad!" At this outburst everyone stopped. "Good," Delvin mumbled as he tried to take another drink from his skin, but it was dry.

"I'm out m'drink," he muttered in frustration, before looking over at the cart. He shook his head and then extended his skin back to Toran, "Fill it up!" he demanded, but the big man just crossed his arms and stared at him. "I said fill it up!" he stomped his foot in anger as the big man did not move.

Delvin cursed, "FINE," and he walked back to the cart. Ashlyn shrank down into a tighter ball at his approach. He hesitated as he neared the side, but then he reached his hand in and pulled out the entire cask of cider with a grunt, before shouldering it and walking off.

Everyone left behind seemed to need a moment to shake off the tension. Toran was the first to start to move after him, the donkey and cart trailing behind him. The rest of the walk was again in silence, aside from the angry mutterings of Delvin as he drank, and walked, and drank some more.

It was nearing sunset, and the landscape had begun to change. The terrain all around them became hilly and covered in large craggy boulders. It was as if a giant had swatted the peak of one of the nearby mountains scattering its remains all about.

Roshin knew what this meant, however; they were getting close to Ancalah. As the group crested one of the hills, they got their first look at the sea. "There it is," she whispered, staring down the road to a mess of wooden structures along the shoreline.

Catching sight of the town, the docks, and the boats in the harbor felt oddly comforting to Roshin. She had felt lost and out of control for weeks at this point, but here was a place she knew, with people she knew.

She looked around to the rest of the party. The mood was still grim. A tension hung over them, like they were walking in a thick fog. There did not seem to be much excitement at the fact that they had arrived.

She thought about how this was just one detour on a much longer journey. "We can't go on like this," she muttered to herself. She looked ahead to Delvin and watched as he stumbled forward down the hill toward the city.

"*He doesn't want this anymore than we do,*" she thought before setting off at a jog to catch up to him. "Listen here," she started as she reached his side. She stretched her hand out and caught his shoulder to try and get him to stop.

"Don't you touch me." He barked back, ducking away from her fingers and stumbling on.

Roshin persisted, "I'm the bride you bought, remember? You don't need the others." She again tried to catch his arm, desperate to get him to face her, "Let them go and be done with it." Her voice was racked with pain and desperation.

Delvin's body tightened and then he whirled around in a rage. He took his hand, still holding the water skin, and extended his finger out right into her face. She could hear the sloshing of the contents as he jabbed at her, "Don't tell me what I need!" he slurred. "I paid good coin for those wretches. They're mine to do with as I please."

Roshin shrank back away from him. The waft of alcohol from his mouth was all she could smell.

"I'll take them back to Vargah and sell them again," he spat. "Make back every copper I spent, and then some," he paused and looked up before turning his body away from her, "Now get away from me, girl, 'fore I knock ya flat."

Roshins felt her face flush as she stopped to let him get some distance. She had hoped to find in him some compassion, but the drink had drowned any that he might possess. Delvin turned and charged hard onward toward Ancalah.

Toran walked past her with the donkey cart, and grunted. She decided that was his way of offering respect for her efforts. Granya came up and put an arm around her shoulder, "It was a good attempt child." She then signed, "Maybe once the cask runs dry, he will be able to hear reason."

She turned her tear-soaked face and looked Granya in the eyes. "Will that cask ever be dry?"

12

Harbor Lights

It was now twilight. Shadows covered the land around the party. The large rocks that encircled them felt like an eerie presence, reminding Roshin of hulking, stooped guards keeping a watchful eye on them.

The party did not make it to Ancalah. Toran had stopped walking shortly after Roshin's attempt to negotiate for the others' freedom had failed. Delvin did not take kindly to this. He had turned back in a rage and now he seemed fit to fight Toran over it.

Seeing the drunk man make an uncoordinated charge toward Toran and the donkey, Roshin decided she needed to remove Ashlyn and get her far from whatever was about to transpire. She crept up, careful not to draw too much attention and helped Ashlyn down from the cart.

Together, the pair edged their way over toward Granya, who had seated herself upon one of the large boulders. It was just off the road and offered a clear view of the cart, the men, and even the sea. As they seated themselves beside her, the one-sided argument reached a boiling point.

 "What are you doing, you mute fool?" Delvin brayed as he kicked stones toward Toran's legs. "The city's right there!" he slurred, pointing down the hill.

The city, like the rest of the land had been cast in darkness. Roshin could make out specs of light around the doors and windows of the buildings and the burning glow of torches moving about the city to light the braziers in the streets and around the bay.

Soon, flickering firelights could be seen all along the shores as the harbor lights were lit to protect any wayward ships that might be out at night. This also helped illuminate the waters below and made visible the bobbing outlines of several moored boats rocking with the waves. The bay around Ancalah was ready for the darkness.

Back beside the road, Toran just stared at Delvin, his arms crossed defiantly as the drunken man unleashed his fury upon him. Curses flew, and Delvin's hands waved wildly in what seemed like poor attempts to swing at Toran. Delvin had to stop to catch his breath.

It was then that Toran made a gesture. He took two fingers and pressed them against his forehead and then pointed those same fingers to the ground.

"I think he is telling Delvin he will be staying right here," Roshin murmured to Ashlyn and Granya.

This was not received well by Delvin, who protested, "No reason not to go in town and lock um up in a room while I manage my affairs."

The big man shook his head no and then again pointed to the ground.

"We are here for my business!" Delvin shouted at Toran, waving his balled-up fists as if to hammer the air. "I will not have you run off and leave me to take credit for my purchase." He pointed to Roshin and then sucked in another breath, "This was not the agreement, you were to come with me to the city!"

There was a long pause as the men again, just starred at each other, as if waiting to see who would break first. It was Delvin. Unable to handle the silence, he continued, "I don't need you! I don't need any of you!" He spat angrily, before throwing a fist toward Toran.

Toran caught it and then pushed the man back hard before reaching his hand over to the hilt of his sword. Delvin stumbled and nearly fell over. There was a thick tension in the air as Toran drew enough of his sword for Delvin to get a good look at the steel.

With that Delvin finally threw up his hands, "Fine! Stay here and sleep on the rocks. I will go tend my own matters alone." With that Delvin cursed, picked up the cask he had been carrying most of the day, and stumbled away down the road toward Ancalah.

Roshin let out a relieved sigh. She had half expected the man to pull out his own sword in response and attempt to fight Toran for his defiance, but thankfully even in his current state, Delvin had the judgment to avoid such a physical altercation with the monster of a man who stood before him.

She leaned over to Granya, "Why do you think Toran does not want to go into Ancalah?"

Granya hummed with consideration, "Delvin's mind is not exactly clear; he is likely heading into more trouble than he anticipates." The old woman rubbed her chin, "Toran is here on behalf of the officer's interests, which are to see you safely back to his camp. That city does nothing to serve those interests."

Roshin nodded, "That would make sense. Do you think Toran means to leave him there as he said?" She asked and she watched Toran begin to set the camp.

"It certainly does not seem so," Granya replied pointing toward the man as he unhitched the cart from the donkey. "I do think he is tired of letting Delvin lead," Granya sighed, "It is clear that Delvin is in no state to tend to any business, including even business found at the bottom of a tankard.

Roshin nodded, "No he is not."

"I pray that he does not find more trouble than he can manage, and if he does, that it stays in that city," Granya whispered as she reached over and grabbed a hand from both Roshin and Ashlyn.

With Delvin gone, a sense of calm fell over the camp. The day had been so difficult, and emotional. Even though Roshin was angry at Toran for holding her back the night before, she could at least appreciate that his quiet presence was a welcome contrast to Delvin's drunken outbursts.

He went about his business paying little mind to the women. He staked the donkey next to a patch of tall coarse grasses. He assembled a fire lay, lit the fire, and began to cook the evening's ration of beans. He prepared a bedroll, and sat down beside the fire, again pulling out his sword and his sharpening stone.

"I cannot imagine that sword could get much sharper." Roshin mused as she watched him. Granya chuckled. Some of the tension began to leave her shoulders, but it soon returned when she glanced to her side and got a look at Ashlyn.

The girl, like her, was seated on the rock beside Granya. Her face was dark from the shadows of the twilight, and she was staring off toward the sea as if transfixed by the harbor lights and rolling waves. Her cheeks however had shiny streaks. "*She is crying,*" Roshin realized.

Her whole expression seemed far off and distant. She had not said a single word all day. Roshin bowed her head and closed her eyes. "*Hulen Ahir, help me find the words to say to help her through this,*" it was a silent prayer.

She looked back over to the girl who still seemed so lost and far away. Roshin felt her anger begin to rise, but then she looked over to Granya, who was just sitting there quietly, holding the girl's hands. She stuffed down her indignation and decided what she really needed was to speak to the old woman alone.

Roshin rose up off the rock before taking a step away and then turning back. She asked the old woman, "Would you help me see if we might find some purslane?"

The old woman nodded, stood, and walked some ways off with Roshin, leaving Ashlyn to sit and watch the waves.

Looking for greens was hardly the right thing to do in the dark of night, but she had needed an excuse to pull Granya away, and that was what entered her mind. As such Roshin knelt down upon the sandy ground and began to pick through the different weeds. The old woman joined her and did not speak a word.

"Granya?" Roshin finally asked gently.

The old woman looked up at her, "Yes child?"

"I know we are living in a dark time, but how much more must we bear? Why must Ashlyn suffer so much?" Roshin felt the tears well up in her eyes, "I don't know what to do!" her fingers dug into the sand, and she squeezed it as if trying to extract water from the grains.

Granya reached down and laid her hand upon Roshin's, "Evil is often hard for the good to understand." The old woman set back down onto her bottom before continuing, "A man's nature is often jealous and selfish. We often fail to see our own vises and limitations, and we believe we know more than we do."

Roshin wiped at her tears, "but Ashlyn is so good and kind."

She paused to catch Roshin's eyes, "We live around and with others. Some of those others cast long shadows that can easily consume people who had nothing to do with their creation. That is what Delvin has done to Ashlyn."

Roshin looked back toward Ashlyn, tears again streaming down her face, "So what do we do when the shadows are everywhere?"

Granya pointed out to the harbor lights that circled the bay, "You be the light in the darkness, no matter how faint, and if enough bring forth that light, then we can help protect others from the dangers of the shadows."

Roshin closed her eyes and crumpled her shoulders, "But what about Ashlyn who has already been hurt?"

The old woman also looked back at the girl. "Show her love. We will care for her, feed her, sit with her so long as we can, and even should our circumstances be such where we are apart, let us not forget each other in our thoughts and prayers." The old woman took Roshin's hands and offered them a squeeze.

"It is not fair," Roshin whispered. Her observation extending far beyond what had happened to Ashlyn. "Is it wrong I am wishing for Delvin not to return? Even knowing what that might mean?"

Granya looked down the road and then shook her head. "I understand your thoughts. It would be dishonest for me to say I have not shared them." She paused and gave Roshin a gentle smile, "The road before us looks quite treacherous, and it is only natural to want to take a path that seems smoother," The old woman pulled out a weed and handed it to Roshin, " but that path may not be what you think it is either, so I say it is better to wish that the man's heart can one day be reached."

Roshin received the plant, a healthy bit of purslane. "Then that is what I shall do, pray for a change of heart," and with that Roshin rose and moved off toward Toran and the cookfire.

13

A Poor Gamble

The cookfire was still flickering several hours after Delvin had left. Toran had been busy pacing around looking for fuel to feed it. The dung supply on the road had been sizable, and he had pulled up a few dead shrubs that had failed to survive on tops of the boulders to aid in his efforts.

The women had settled not too far from the fire on the sandy ground. None of them seemed able to sleep; they had hardly been able to eat. Granya was sitting beside Roshin watching the fire, and Ashlyn had lain down, setting her head on Roshin's lap.

There was a quiet comfort in the act of combing through Ashlyn's long, dark hair, and the activity seemed to calm the girl. As she watched Toran however, that comfort began to fall away, replaced by a nervous pit in her stomach. "It seems he has an eye out for trouble," Roshin whispered toward Granya.

After sharpening his sword, he did not put it away. He carried it with him, in his hand, even when he was snapping twigs and tossing cow pies into the flames. It was as if he was prepared to fight. Granya gave her shoulders a squeeze, but she did not say anything. Roshin was left to mull over her anxiety.

The town seemed quiet. The braziers were still lit as were many of the lanterns around the doors. A few of the candles in the windows had been snuffed. Roshin could hear the sound of the waves lapping on the shore.

It was the barking of dogs from inside the city that broke the quiet of the night. Their yips and howls rung out, disturbing the silence. Roshin watched as Toran froze and stared off into the darkness toward the town.

His back was lit by the fire light revealing tense shoulders and a ready posture. Roshin felt her mouth go dry. A shadowy figure approached fast up the road, shrouded by the darkness. Toran put his other hand upon his sword and raised it up, ready to strike.

Delvin appeared before the fire. His face shone in the glow as if wet with sweat. "Get back off the road and gather our things!" he barked in a breathless panic. Toran relaxed his stance slightly but did not move.

The women all sat up in attention as Delvin grunted, "Useless as ever!" before jogging over to the donkey and pulling up the stake. He turned to the women, "Grab what you can carry from the cart, we will leave it!" and then he began to try and drag the donkey away from the grass.

The donkey too refused, digging its heels, uninterested in being led away, into the dark. Delvin howled "AH COME ON, MOVE!" and he pulled hard against the line. It did not move. "Useless Ass! Useless man!" He dropped the line and turned to Roshin, "You!" he waved her toward him. "Come with me now."

Roshin looked around at everyone and then turned back to him and said, "No." She was scared and had no idea what was happening. It seemed he was trying to run away from something, and if so, she had no interest in following him.

Delvin grabbed hold of his sword and pulled it from its scabbard and took a step toward Roshin. She stepped back and gasped as Toran came up from behind him. The big man seized Delvin's shoulder and pulled him around with a great force that set him whirling.

With the cover of Toran's intervention, Roshin made a run for one of the boulders, grabbing Ashlyn's hand as she did. Granya joined them and together the three women ducked back behind the stone and watched the confrontation play out.

Delvin howled and dropped his sword from the force of Toran's pull. As the big man released him, he staggered for balance and cried, "No! You don't understand!" He began to search the ground to retrieve his fallen arms, but Toran put his sword to his throat.

Delvin froze. A laugh rang out from behind them. Several new shadowy figures appeared from the road. They were illuminated slightly by the light of the fire. A couple of the men were carrying torches.

Roshin squinted to try to make out who they were, or at least how many there might be, but they crowded together, and their faces were masked by shadows. All she knew was that they were likely who Delvin was trying to avoid. She ducked down further behind the rock, hoping to stay out of view.

"Find another 'friend' on the road, Delvin?" the lead man called out.

"Seems like he's tryin' to swindle this one as well," came the voice of another as he walked over to retrieve the loose donkey.

Toran turned toward the voices. "Yeah! A big one I see!" noted the lead man, "Delvin must be REALLY drunk!" he finished with a laugh. Toran stiffened and Roshin could see him grip his fingers back around his sword.

Delvin took advantage of Toran's change in attention and began to crawl around the ground searching for his sword. When he found it, he yipped and jumped back up onto his feet.

"So? What da ya have to say for yourself then?" the lead man asked Toran, "He your friend, or foe?"

Toran was obviously not able to respond, but Delvin did for him. It seemed unclear to Roshin in that moment, if Toran agreed with the answer, "He's my partner."

"Is that so?" the first man sneered. "Well then maybe he can cover your debts without turning to weighted dice."

Toran grunted and looked sourly to Delvin.

Delvin began to nervously stammer, "I don't know where you found that but it's not mine," he waved a free hand in front of himself as if shaking away the accusation. "I play fair games; all mines are honest earnings."

The men collectively laughed before the leader stepped forward toward Delvin, "You are a good cheat, I give you that." He paused and pulled out what Roshin assumed to be a die and rolled it around between his fingers.

" Usually, you're more... disciplined and careful with the timing of your drinking." He looked straight at the die and then, with a chuckle, continued, "Seems you got ahead of yourself today, Delvin. You weren't so careful."

The man returned the object to his pocket and took another step toward Delvin with his hand extended, "So where is it friend?" his voice lingered on the last word, "Will you hand over the coins, or will I have to cut them off you? "

Delvin was clearly in a state of panic. "I told you, I don't have my own coins," he continued, waving his hands and backing away from the man. "All I got is m'lord's money; he gave it to me for procuring his bride."

"I see" said the group leader. "THAT, is not my problem. You can figure out how to pay him back if you ever slink back to your camp." The man reached down to the hilt of his sword and drew the blade up enough to flash the steel, "I expect payment now," his words were sharp and cold.

At the mention of taking the officer's coin, Toran growled and stepped forward.

The leader seemed surprised and looked up at Toran, "Seems you have a problem with that soldier?" he queried slyly before drawing out his sword the rest of the way.

In an instant the situation went from a conversation to the clashing of steel, as Toran met the man's threat with a swift back swing. Roshin almost squealed in surprise, but she caught herself. The leader of the group managed to parry back the blow, but it knocked him off his guard and he staggered back a few paces.

The sound of drawn steel rang out as the other men prepared to join in and fight, "Two against how many? Five, six?" Roshin though. She turned to the other women and whispered, "This is going to be a disaster for them."

As the swords clashed, Ashlyn reached for cover and wrapped her arms around Roshin's waist. Roshin, for her part, could not draw her eyes away from the scene. Toran was a terrifying fighter. He swung his sword as if he was a giant troll welding a club.

Several men charged him but with a few strong blows he successfully knocked the swords out of the hands of two of his attackers. Once disarmed he grabbed one and tossed him into the donkey cart. The other he kicked back into the bodies of the other men.

Delvin had slunk back behind him, using Toran's hulking frame as a human shield. Two men were engaging him at the front before a third man tried to engage Toran from the side. Toran saw him and swung hard in an arc to meet him.

The man failed to block, and Toran's blade cut deep into his shoulder. There was a terrible scream and Roshin watched the man's now limp body shake like a doll as Toran ripped his blade from the flesh and bone. Once he did the man collapsed on the ground without another movement.

For an instant all the men froze, staring in disbelief at the brutal execution of their companion.

Roshin found herself feeling faint and nauseous as she watched Toran engage the leader of the group. At first it seemed like he finally had a match. Their blades met, gleaming in the firelight, and for a moment Toran even lost some ground.

It was short lived, however, and the big man recovered and came back at him with a set of savage blows, one after the other. The leader stumbled back and for a moment left himself open. Toran seized the opportunity and skewered him.

She had to look away, and when she did, she caught sight of Delvin, who had started creeping off into the darkness. One of the men saw him however and left Toran to give chase.

"We need to go," Roshin whispered.

Granya nodded and then turned away from the camp to head down the hill toward the city. Roshin crouched low, holding Ashlyn's hand and leading her along as she followed Granya. Another scream of pain pierced the air, and Roshin closed her eyes trying to put out of her mind the image of the man's limp body.

They needed to pick up the pace if they were to get away. Toran was making short work of eliminating the attackers, and if they were not quick enough, they would simply be recaught. Cold fear hit Roshin at that idea, nothing good would come from being caught by a man fevered with blood lust, "We have to run." She whispered with increasing intensity.

Another cry pierced the air, this time it sounded much like Delvin. There was a curse that followed and a roar from the big man. Roshin was not sure what had happened, but she suddenly realized the Granya had stopped and was looking back.

She turned back around and rushed over to her side, trying to grab her hand to ferry her along. The old woman seemed rooted. "I cannot go with you child."

"What do you mean you cannot go?" Roshin demanded with a tone of desperation.

"There are men back there that need aid," her tone was calm and measured, "If not dead then they are injured or dying," The old woman took Roshin's hand and squeezed it. "I am a healer. I cannot leave them."

"But if we stay, then we are still slaves" Roshin howled, "We may never get another chance to escape!"

"I said I cannot go child, not that you cannot go," The old woman smiled back at her, and released her hand.

Roshin found herself stammering, tears welling up in her eyes. "B-but we can't just leave you!"

"You are not leaving me," Granya pressed a hand on her chest, "I am staying on my own accord to perform my service," Granya spoke gently, as she used her hand to push Roshin back toward Ancalah. "Take Ashlyn to the docks, find one of the boats to take you out to sea," She directed firmly, "they cannot possibly follow you there."

Tears streamed down Roshin's cheeks, "But-" she started, before Granya held up her hand.

"May Hulen Ahir watch over you" she paused and then in a serious tone, "but go now!"

Roshin found herself overcome with despair. She could not remember much of her own mother, and so Granya had been the only mother she really knew. The idea of leaving her, especially with as brutal of a monster as Toran tore her apart.

She looked to the shadowy silhouette of Ashlyn, cowering behind another boulder and took a deep breath, "I will go then." And with that Roshin turned, retrieved Ashlyn and sprinted toward Ancalah.

Section 2
The Fresh Sea

14

The Blue Tales

They reached the streets out of breath and panting. Ashlyn tried to stop beside one of the braziers. "No. We must keep going," Roshin gasped. She dragged Ashlyn on, in the direction of the docks.

Familiarity became her guide. As she moved between the worn wooden structures, part of her felt as if she had never left the city. The streets here were dark and still. This part of the town was primarily occupied by those who made it their home, and they were all bedded down for the night.

Roshin looked up; the little two-story wooden buildings seemed to have aged since she was last here. Many of the shutters hung askew or were missing entirely. There were a few broken windows stuffed with rags to keep out the breeze from the sea. "Soon this place too will be ruins," she thought bitterly.

When she caught sight of it, she felt a pang of sadness, "That is where my mother died," she whispered mostly to herself. The building looked much like the others, the wood had grayed, and the shutters were gone.

She remembered waking and finding her mother face down on the floor. The woman had been ill for what seemed like months, but had reassured her daughter that it would pass, and soon she would be fine. Roshin did not understand what was wrong, or what had made her sick, just that one day she stopped breathing.

Tears began to well in her eyes. The painful memory felt all the more acute for having just left Granya behind. "*I have known so much loss,*" she thought grimly. She took a breath to shake off the sadness and return to the present.

As she led Ashlyn around the buildings, she remembered the winding streets of Vargah, and imagined that the girl was likely feeling lost, "Just a little more and we will make it to the docks," she whispered before making another cut down an ally between the buildings.

They passed a set of market stalls, all empty and covered for the night, "This is the fish market, we are almost there." She nearly tripped over a crate left out beside one of the stalls, but she caught herself and weaved around it. The smell of the sea was now so heavy, she might as well be walking into it.

The stench of the water here was not a pleasant one and she heard Ashlyn gag beside her. The waters right near town were dark and dirty from the dumping of refuse from the markets and thus had a distinct odor, *"Dead fish and garbage,"* she thought as her stomach turned. "You get use to it," she told Ashlyn with a squeeze of the hand.

"There they are!" Her voice was quiet but excited. The docks laid out before them. Worn, long wooden decking stretched out into the water, moonlight was reflecting off the bay, casting shadows on the boats that were moored there.

They bobbed up and down on the gentle waves, which she could hear lapping against the sea wall at the edge of the street. During a storm or rough weather, the waves would sometimes splash over the wall, but at the moment things seemed quite calm. "Good," she thought, imagining herself out in the sea on a little fishing boat.

"Watch out for the edge," she instructed as she helped Ashlyn down onto the wooden platform that formed the base of the docks. Ashlyn was careful and she stayed close to Roshin, silent as a mouse. "I am going to look for a boat of someone I know," she offered as she selected one of the extensions to walk down.

She passed several little fishing vessels. Most were occupied by one or two white-haired men sleeping in the bottoms. She read the names of the boats painted on the front, "The Bold Mariner, The White Gull, Summer Song," none of these were names she knew.

When she was five, she had sailed across the fresh sea on a ship called *The Dauntless*. It had seemed to her to be a massive ship. In reality, it was a good size cog that had a lower deck and was designed for a crew to spend weeks at sea. Many cogs like that had once been moored here, but not anymore.

Over the years the larger ships were replaced with smaller sailing vessels that could be manned by a crew of one or two. They no longer went out very far and if they spent many days on the water, it was usually after anchoring and possibly after setting up a camp on the shores.

There was one cog that still occupied the bay, it had run aground due to poor operation and was simply left there to rot after nobody could get it free. It now sits out in the harbor, a marker for the city to the incoming fishermen, and a warning to not get in over your head.

"There are not enough young men to man the big ships now," she thought as she turned back around to return to the platform and try the next dock.

It went like this for awhile. It was not until the third extension that she finally saw the name of a boat that she knew. She read, "Lady Swift, that's Neil's boat!" She excitedly released Ashlyn's hand and crept over to the side of the vessel, peering over and see if anyone was inside.

Curled up on a bed of nets was Neil. Covered up and sleeping like all the rest, his face was obscured by the shadows of the night, but she would recognize his round red nose anywhere even though his hair was greyer, and the lines of his face looked deeper.

Reaching her hand over the side of the boat and onto his shoulders, she softly called out to him. "Neil?" She gave his boney shoulders a gentle shake which was enough to stir him from his slumber.

His eyes shot open, and he blinked in confusion. "Eh? Who's there?" he grumbled, before rolling to his side to get an arm under him. He slowly levered himself into a sitting position and squinted in Roshin's direction.

She leaned her face closer for him to see her, "Neil, it's Roshin." Her tone grew hopeful.

"Roshin?" the old man sat for a minute combing through his memory.

"I'm the daughter of the sea!" she exclaimed hoping to remind him.

"Roshin, ah yes Roshin, the dock girl!" Recognition slowly dawned upon him as the corners of his mouth drew up into a broad smile. "Is that really you? Let me get my light." And with that the old man fumbled around trying to light a lantern.

Once it was lit, he held it up to the girl, "My eyesight isn't what it used to be." He paused, studying her through squinting eyes obscured by bushy eyebrows, "Ah yes, I do believe I see the girl in your face," he pinched her cheek affectionately, "but you're a proper woman now, and a pretty one at that!" again he smiled.

"I can't believe it!" he announced with a slap to his thigh "What brought you back here? And in the middle of the night no less?" he queried; his curiosity peaked.

Roshin nodded and smiled gently back at him. "I had not planned to come back but providence has found me here." She gestured over to to Ashlyn. "This is my dear companion, Ashlyn. We've found ourselves in urgent need of passage out of Ancalah."

Neil stared back at her with a look of surprise. He then cast his eyes up to the night sky, which was steadily filling with clouds now partially obscuring the moon and stars. "You wish to leave now?"

Roshin nodded, "Yes, it is not safe for us," she said before looking back nervously toward the town.

"I am sorry, but I cannot take you, not now anyways." He shook his head and gestured up, "The signs this evening all tells of a storm coming. It would not be wise to take to sea just now."

"I see." Roshin replied somberly.

Neil moved to stand. "Let me take you girls to the inn, I can see you accommodated and safe for the night. In a day or so I would be able to take you wherever you need." At that moment Roshin again heard the barking of the dogs, signaling a disturbance, Neil heard it too and looked off toward it.

Roshin felt her face drain and a rush of dread wash over her. "No bother, we will find our own safety for this night," She spoke quickly and began to back away from the boat, "It was good to see you again old friend," as she finished the words she turned and began to run back down the docks toward the platform.

She heard Neil call out after her, but she ignored him. They would need to leave, with or without the help of a fisherman. As they got a bit of distance from Niel, Ashlyn piped in, "Do you think those dogs were..." The girl trailed off.

"I do not intend to find out," she said in a rush as she ran down the platform with Ashlyn toward the end of the dock. She turned down the last row, about four or so extensions from Neil's boat. "He should not see us here," she willed out loud, as she again read the names of the boats and peeked inside.

Most of the boats had occupants and a sense of despair started to take hold. They were nearing the end of the dock with only a few boats left when she read another name, "The Blue Tales." It was a small vessel with a single mast wrapped with a tightly furled sail and a sturdy looking set of oars.

"This would be ideal," she thought. It resembled the type of boat that she had learned to sail on as a girl. Her heart was pounding with nerves as she peaked cautiously over the side. To her relief, all she saw were sacks and nets, "No fisherman!" she announced quietly.

Ashlyn tugged on her arm, "You don't mean to steal this boat, do you?"

Roshin began to climb over the side. "I would like for someone to take us, but if we cannot find someone then I don't know what else to do but take ourselves," she said, her tone full of righteous indignation.

Ashlyn however had scratched in her a bit of doubt. "The sailor is not here, so he was either on that road dying by Toran's hand, or he is still in the tavern drunk," she continued, working to reassure herself of her decision.

"...but what about the storm?" Ashlyn asked cautiously as she stepped over the side after Roshin.

Roshin looked up to the sky, "We will need to take our chances, storm or no storm, we can't stay here." The dogs were still barking, and Roshin caught sight of what looked like torchlight from the streets

A hush fell over both of them and Roshin began to move about the boat, checking it over to look for any signs it would not sail, "How can I help?" Ashlyn asked

Roshin pointed to the ropes that were tied around the dock supports, "Release those and then push us off away from the dock." Roshin handed the girl an oar, "You can use this to help push."

Roshin took the other oar and placed it down into the oarlock. She then helped Ashlyn to secure her own oar. "We will need to row out of here before we can set up the sail. Sit there and I will help you row.

After a brief demonstration to Ashlyn on the movement needed to row, Roshin sat down and grabbed the other oar. "Together. Stroke. Raise. Back. Stroke. Raise. Back," she repeated over and over, and the girls worked together to move the boat forward and away from the docks.

Roshin and Ashlyn continued rowing the small boat for what felt like an eternity. She had no idea how they had kept going. Roshin's arms felt weak, and the muscles had begun to cramp up. She had no doubt Ashlyn too was likely exhausted. Thankfully the lights of Ancalah had faded into the distance.

The moon had been covered by clouds, and the waters were eerily dark, but the sky was starting to lighten, and she felt a strong comfort in their current location, especially after having seen the light from a couple torches run up and down the platform of the dock shortly after their departure.

"We made it, we are free!" she thought with jubilation. Nobody could easily meet them where they were, but they still needed to get out of the bay. She shipped the oars and moved carefully over to the middle of the boat. "I need to raise the sail," she announced to Ashlyn.

At first, she just stared at the bundled sail set down on the hull boards. "How am I going to do this?" she asked herself. She closed her eyes and tried to remember her lessons. She took a deep breath before attempting to raise the sail.

At first, she struggled. Her arms had so little left after the rowing. Her mind struggled to hold a thought due to fatigue, but Ashlyn had stepped over to her, and offered to help, and together they pulled with their combined body weight and were able to get the sail up.

She had to fight the stiff canvas to fasten the corners to the wooden yardarm, but soon the sail was finally raised. She sighed with relief and walked to the rear of the boat to take the steering oar just as the first winds billowed the fabric taut.

She adjusted her setting and then collapsed down into the boat, exhaustion threatening to overtake her. "Where are we going?" Ashlyn asked her from her spot beside the mast.

"We need to get out of the bay, and then I think we should follow the western shore," Roshin proposed. "I am not sure how far we will realistically make it in such a small boat, but I would like to get as far from here as possible."

Ashlyn looked out over the water. "I think I might like to go home," she stated with a hint of sadness in her words.

Roshin looked over to her, "Then maybe that is where we are now headed." She nodded and joined Ashlyn in looking out over the water. Dawn had come, the sky was covered in fluffy gray clouds and the edge of the bay was in view. "Now how do we get from the south to the Lakelands with no provisions?" she wondered, but she kept her doubts to herself.

15

Beside the Harbor Light

A large wave knocked into the side of the little boat, causing it to roll hard. Roshin startled awake, adrenaline coursing through her body. She had not realized she had fallen asleep, and she jumped up to see where they were.

The wind had picked up tremendously, and the water had come to life with churning, rolling waves that broke over themselves forming tips of white foam. "The storm," Roshin thought in a rush of panic.

She looked out for the shore and to her great relief they were not far from it. The details of the rocky shoreline were easily visible even in the gathering darkness. "I need to get the sail down and then head us in to shore!" she exclaimed, rushing over to the mast.

At this point, the blowing wind was battering the canvas sail, causing the small boat to list hard to starboard. Roshin knew she needed to get the sail down to prevent the boat from capsizing. Her hands fumbled with the slick ropes, and she struggled to pick the knots loose after they had been pulled tight from the force of the wind.

"I might have used the wrong knot," she cursed herself through gritted teeth. "I need help!" Roshin shouted out to Ashlyn, who had also woken and was sitting frozen in place. "We have to get the boat to shore, or we are liable to capsize as the waves grow," Roshin called out.

"What can I do?" the girl asked, her face looking quite pale as the boards beneath her rolled hard back and forth with each passing wave.

"Get over to the rudder and see if you can turn us to the beach." She grabbed Ashlyn's arm and then made a gesture with her hands, "Turn it this way until we are facing the shoreline, and then straighten it up."

Roshin continued to struggle with the knots, but she persisted, and the rigging came loose. As she tried to pull the sail down, the loose canvas began to flap wildly in the wind. She couldn't get control. The sail threatened to rip from her grasp.

The boat had turned, and the rolling had stopped. Instead, it began to pitch and ride the waves toward the shore. The movement change made it easier for Roshin to hold the sail and finally it dropped.

Thunder boomed overhead as Roshin watched the coastline grow before them. She prayed that they would strike no rocks on the way that would prevent them from being able to pull the boat far enough up on the shore to not be lost to the raging sea.

By the time they struck the ground, the rain had begun to fall heavily upon them. Roshin grabbed a rope that was tied to the bow of the boat and jumped over the side into the water. Ashlyn followed and together they strained and struggled to pull the boat up onto the shore.

The water was frigid. It was early summer now, but it had not been warm enough to see the temperatures of the sea rise to a tolerable level. Roshin sucked in a breath as the water hit her stomach. Ashlyn cried out in distress as she stumbled on a rock and nearly fell in.

Roshin turned and grabbed her arm for support. Once the girl was stable, they worked together with each surge of a wave to move the boat further and further up onto the shore. "A sandy beach would be nice," Roshin muttered, and she tugged her weight against the line.

When she felt like she could pull it no further she began to look around for something to tie the rope to. Two large rocks sat next to each other nearby. She tied a knot in the end of the rope and then jammed it between the two rocks until it seemed well lodged.

"Hopefully that won't pull free," she said in an attempt to reassure herself, and then she scrambled up the beach looking for any place they might be able to shelter. Providence smiled upon them as she could see a nearby stone tower, "A harbor light!" she exclaimed pointing off toward the structure. Roshin took Ashlyn's hand, and the pair rushed off toward the tower.

Roshin looked up with wonder as they reached the harbor light. The tapered stone structure towered above them. "Imagine building that!" she remarked in awe. As the girls walked around to the back of the tower they saw an opening cut into the side. The opening led to a spiraling staircase which wound up the tower to the brazier at the top.

It was the sturdy stone structure behind the harbor light, however, that interested them. "This would be where the light keepers store the fuel for the brazier." Roshin explained, "We can shelter inside."

The building was larger than she would have expected to just store fuel. It had a wood door and no windows. Roshin made a quick walk around it to look for any signs of occupancy before creeping toward the door. It had a latch on the outside which she removed. "Do you think there is anything else in there?" Ashlyn asked as she peered cautiously around.

"Aside from fuel? I am not sure," she answered as she pulled open the door. Inside sacks of charcoal were piled up on the floor. The pair stepped into the building. Without any windows Roshin knew that if they closed the door they would be swallowed up in darkness.

She turned to Ashlyn. "Leave the door open so we can see whatever else is in here." She looked around. There were several other items lying about that she thought might be useful, a shovel, candlesticks and a few wood boxes and crates.

Her eyes lit up when she saw a lantern hanging from a hook on the wall. Hanging with it was a thin rope from which hung a small piece of flint and steel. "Just what we need!" she exclaimed excitedly.

She grabbed them from the hook and then set the lantern on the floor. She opened the little window and then began striking the flint against the steel near the wick. She managed to make a spark, but it took several minutes of striking to finally get a flame. The warm glow was welcome as it meant they could finally shut the door.

Roshin returned the lantern to the hook, but she put the flint and steel over her head, *"You will likely be a lifeline for us,"* she thought. Their clothes were soaked, and she found herself shivering with cold.

She again began to look around, aided by lantern light, and that is when she noticed the stack of blankets in the corner. "Look Ashlyn!" she caught the girl's shoulder and pointed to the blankets. They were likely there to support a light keeper who might, like them, find himself stuck beside this light.

Regardless of why they were there, it was welcome to them now. The girls helped each other out of their soaked dresses before tossing them in the corner of the building. It felt freeing to be out from under the layered fabric that was so heavy from the rains and the sea, but they were also now really freezing.

Teeth chattering, they wrapped themselves in the blankets and huddled against each other in the corner of the room. Warmth began to return to them, and for the first time in many weeks, they were somewhere that felt safe.

"Now if only one of these boxes had some food in it," Roshin mused, kicking one open with her toe to reveal only emptiness.

The storm raged on around them. They could hear the thunder, and even see the impact of the rain, as drips of water infiltrated the thatched roof and fell onto the dirt floor. They sat a long while in silence.

Ashlyn was the first to speak, "I can't believe we got away." Her voice held a tired sadness, as if the escape itself was weighing on her. She paused for a moment then asked, "Do you think Granya survived?"

Roshin turned to meet her eyes, and with a smile answered, "I have no doubt she spent the evening tending wounds and is likely now in the city."

Ashlyn turned her body toward Roshin, "Yes, but, do you think they let her go? Or..." Ashlyn trailed off, and Roshin knew she was thinking of something awful.

She pulled her arms free of her blanket and wrapped them around her friend, "I don't know, but I like to think they would." Her words were spoken in a quiet and reassuring manner. She did hope that if Granya had indeed helped them with their injuries, the men would have understood her mission and let her go.

All the same she harbored plenty of doubts as to if that was the case, especially after the old woman told them to run away. She decided not to share her doubts with Ashlyn at that moment. Ashlyn however seemed eager to explore her doubts, "I would like to think that too, but I am not so sure."

Roshin did not know what to say, so she just gave the girl a comforting squeeze.

Ashlyn continued, this time tears welling up in her eyes as she spoke, "I had wanted so badly to believe they were good." She drew her knees up to her chin and took a few sniffing breaths, "Delvin had been so kind to me."

"I wanted to see that too," Roshin responded, turning her head to look at her feet, reminded of her own guilt for not having said anything to Ashlyn when she had started to worry.

Ashlyn broke down into heavy sobs. A moment later, with a quaking voice, she wailed, "I feel so foolish!"

Roshin just closed her eyes and held onto her friend while her pain and emotion spilled out over her. As Ashlyn began to calm her cries she continued in a quiet self-reflective voice, "I can't blame anyone but myself for what happened."

At this Roshin felt a strong need to object, "No, we all wanted to see the good in them! I know I did, and so did Granya," She had a desperation in her voice to make Ashlyn see it was not her fault. "We all wanted to forget the truth of our situation."

Ashlyn cut in quickly, "but it was me who let him…" she trailed off before starting again, "He just made me feel so special." The younger girl looked up at Roshin, "I needed to be special. You were the one everyone wanted, not me. For the first time someone wanted me!"

The admission felt crushing to Roshin. Ashlyn was not wrong, and she did not blame the girl for wanting to feel special. She felt her own tears begin to well up, and she tried to blink them back to keep a strong face. "It's over now," she whispered.

 "I don't know if it will ever be over," the young girl whimpered. "I don't think I will ever be able to forget it."

"You don't need to forget it to move forward," Roshin whispered to her with a squeeze. "Granya would tell you that to move forward what you need to do is forgive."

Ashlyn shook her head, "I don't understand how to do that. How can I forgive him for such a terrible thing?"

"I struggled to with forgiveness too." Roshin said with a nod, thinking back to how angry she was with her mother, her father, and all the others who seemed to have hurt her. "The way she explained it to me was that the things that happen to us, well, we carry them around with us like a debt owed. A debt that the debtor can't pay. When we keep the debt, we bind ourselves to the person that hurt us."

She combed her fingers through Ashlyn's hair, "Forgiveness doesn't excuse or dismiss what happened. You don't forget it, it simply allows us to cut those ties that bind us to those that hurt us in the past"

"So forgiveness is freedom." Ashlyn asserted.

"Forgiveness is freedom." Roshin agreed.

With that the tone of their conversation changed. A small light kindled back in Ashlyn. She asked Roshin to tell her more about Neil and the other fishermen who cared for her, and more about her years in Ancalah

The girl was especially curious to understand how Roshin had learned to sail, to which Roshin replied with a laugh, "You can't be a daughter of the sea and not know how to be part of it." The girls talked for hours more. After a long while they finally grew quiet and fell into a deep and settled sleep, long after the storm had passed, and the lamp burned out.

16

Daughter of the Sea

The sail had been dropped, and the boat had slowed markedly as the drag from the net behind it cut away at its momentum. Once they were at a near crawl, the women worked together to pull in the ropes and bring the net onboard.

It had been over a week since they had taken to the sea. The pair had found a rhythm in its navigation, but it had not been without struggle. The day after the storm, they had spent what felt like hours bailing out the water from the bottom of the boat.

The nature of their escape meant they were not exactly prepared for a long journey. Fortunately, the shack had a few supplies they could use to help improve their odds of survival. Ashlyn had been uncomfortable with the idea of taking from the little harbor light shack. "These things are here for the light keepers, and to protect the ships in the bay," she lamented.

Roshin was also uncomfortable as well, but more pragmatic about the situation, "We may be weeks at sea, and all our boat has in it are nets! We are not likely to survive with that alone," she argued.

"Let us at least take the blankets, and we should also bring some fuel, there will still be a dozen bags of fuel," she pleaded to her friend.

Ashlyn seemed still unconvinced, so Roshin continued, "The blankets were here to help someone in need, it seems to me we could be that someone. When the keeper does his inventory, he will see them missing and replace them."

Ashlyn finally relented. They decided to bring two of the blankets, leaving the third, one of the sacks filled with charcoal to aid them in fire making, as well as a flat piece of steel and a small bowl they hoped could be useful in preparing any fish they may catch.

Once they packed these items in the boat and were ready to go, they found they were unable to free it from the rocks that they had used to secure the boat during the storm. They next ended up having to search through the shack, and then the boat to find a way to cut the rope as they could not get it dislodged any other way.

It was a great relief when they found a small box under the nets that contained a couple of different knives. The knives were designed for the cutting and scaling of fish. Cutting a rope was not the ideal usage, but after a long while of sawing on the thick rope, cutting it cord by cord, the boat was finally free.

The next challenge was to push it off the beach after the storm surge had receded. They shoved, and pushed and wiggled it free and got it out into the water, once there however they needed to get in themselves.

This had seemed impossible, as they did not have the arm strength to pull themselves up over the side. Instead, they led the boat through the shallows until they found a large rock that came near out of the water.

The height the rock afforded helped them make it over the side and into the boat, but the required wading in the water meant their skirts were again soaked and they were once more freezing.

They removed their skirts, squeezing them out as best they could before hanging them over the side of the boat, praying that a rogue wave would not wash them overboard and carry them out to sea. They then each wrapped themselves in a blanket and did their best to get warm.

"Can you see if we caught anything?" Ashlyn asked as she continued reeling in the net.

Roshin grunted as she pulled, "Not yet, but judging by the weight, I would have to think we have something in there!"

This was their only net, as they had lost another in the water when they lacked the strength to pull it up. The net had been weighted and was designed to be left out and retrieved later. The women had been able to set it and then row ashore to make a camp on the sandy beach for the night.

When they rowed back and tried to pull it in, they ended up near to tears in frustration. The net had likely caught some fish, but they were not strong enough to pull it back into the boat with the added resistance.

"I could jump in and swim along the net to see if I could get any fish free." Roshin proposed.

Ashlyn brought her back to reality pretty quickly. "But how would you get back over the side? I can't row back to the shore on my own!" The girl was right, so they had no real choice but to leave the net behind.

This had stung. The idea of their independence and survival depended on their ability to feed themselves. The loss of the net marked the third day without any food. The coastline had little to forage, and they had tried but failed to dig around for clams on the beach the night before.

The sea itself should have plenty to feed them, but they would need to be able to procure it. The losing of the net made that ability all the more tenuous. Fortunately, they had another option.

There was a second smaller net that was designed to be dragged from behind the boat. The likelihood of a single catch from this kind of net was less, but the smaller size and method of deployment made it easier for them to manage.

It was the use of this net on the fourth day that had broken their fast, and they had been able to eat well after the successful catching of three larger fish. One thing Roshin knew she could manage was the gutting and filleting of fish.

She taught the skill to Ashlyn, who for her part had eaten more of the forest than of the sea. "I thought your village was on a river?" Roshin asked her.

"It is, and we did eat some fish" The girl explained, "My brothers and father would fish, my mother mostly would just gut them and put them in a cook pot to stretch the meal. The river fish were mostly quite small compared to what we have already caught."

It made sense to Roshin; there wasn't much benefit to filleting a small fish compared to dropping it into a cook pot. All the same Ashlyn had been a good student, and fast learner, wielding her knife with some skill.

When the net was finally drawn in the girls howled with victory, they had made a catch. And a large one at that. Five fish in total. "It looks like we should try and build a smoker tonight," Roshin commented.

Smoking the fillets would help them store longer, as would salting them. The box with the knives had a small bag of salt for just this purpose, but with the quantity of fish Roshin felt it better to try smoking instead.

One thing Ashlyn did know was how to construct a smoker. Her father used to smoke meat on their farm for longer storage and Ashlyn had been curious about how it worked.

"We can certainly try, so long as there is enough green matter and stones," Ashlyn said casting her eyes doubtfully to the rolling dunes on the shore.

Roshin looked at them as well before concluding, "Salt then?"

"Salt," Ashlyn nodded in agreement.

They had cleared Ancalah's bay and had been traveling northwest along the coastline, trying to stay not too far from the shore. The rocky shoreline had given way to a long line of massive dunes that stretched ahead of them as far as the eye could see.

Aside from the storm on that first night, the weather had been favorable, and the water had been relatively calm. This was a good thing, for as the pair soon found out, Ashlyn did not have much tolerance for the motion of the boat.

She had spent several days retching over the side at midday when the waves tended to be at their peak. The little boat could not really cut through them, so it was left to pitch and roll along with the movement of the water.

Roshin would hold back her hair and rub her wrists to try and alleviate the nausea, but it was only calm seas or time on the beach that would see her able to settle and eat. This was tricky to manage as when the water was calm the sail was at its least effective.

The pair decided the best they could do about it was just camp on shore each night so Ashlyn could at least eat one meal and have it all stay down. "We just need to get past the capitals," Roshin tried to reassure her.

Staying busy seemed to help. Hauling in nets and helping Roshin with the sail or the rudder could at least give her something to do to keep her mind off the queasiness. Despite her discomfort she did her best to keep her spirit bright, after all, they were trying to get her home.

"How much longer do you think we will be out here?" Ashlyn asked.

Roshin did not know the answer. She had no idea where they were, or how much distance they had covered. She could recall from maps that the capital cities were set in the southwest corner of a large bay called Loch Da Crun.

There was a long rocky peninsula that jutted out on the south side of the bay, and at its point was a village called Ardvar. She had been looking for the village to serve as a marker, but so long as she saw sand dunes, she knew they were still some ways off.

Still, she felt she needed to reassure her friend, who was looking a bit green again, now that they had pulled the net in. "I would say four days for us to get on the other side of the capitals and to leave the water."

Ashlyn nodded, appearing reassured, "Four days. I can do four days."

The pair rowed into shore a while before sunset. They had fish to clean and work to do. As they reached the sandy beach Roshin removed her skirts and jumped down into the water. She was already feeling as though she was becoming stronger, and better able to drag the boat around.

Ashlyn followed behind her, and together they pulled the boat up onto the sand. Once it was pulled up and well settled on the beach the pair climbed back in to ready their camp. Roshin took the bowl and with a few passes, scooped out enough charcoal to get a good cookfire going.

Ashlyn got to work gutting, scaling, and fileting the fish, flinging the guts out of the boat toward the hungry beaks of excited gulls. The chatter and commotion from the birds seemed to delight the girl, who may have offered more of the fish to them than she should have.

With their efforts it was not long before they were sitting on their blankets upon the sand before a glowing cook fire, the fish fillets sizzled on the steel plate, filling the air with the delicious aroma of their successful effort to feed themselves.

The girls settled down and watched out over the water as the sun sank toward the horizon, turning the sky into a brilliant tapestry of colors. Roshin thought of all they had been through and let out a contented sigh.

She then said a prayer, "This day is a good day, and I would ask for it not to be our last. Darkness gathers again for the evening, Hulen Ahir guide our destiny and help us be a light that can hold us until morning."

17

The Tempest

"I don't think I have seen a sunrise like that before," Ashlyn exclaimed, wide-eyed with wonder. The women had made their camp on the northernmost tip of the southern peninsula that led into Loch Da Crun.

"I don't believe I have either," agreed Roshin. The sky was awash in colors, mostly rich and beautiful reds, with some more subtle oranges and pinks. It reminded Roshin of so many sunsets, but never a sunrise.

When she thought about it she had rarely been in a place where she could see a sunrise. The water stretched out before her all the way to the horizon in the east. "Usually the mountains block the sunrise," she thought to herself.

At this location the Fresh Sea was all around them, it looked like endless waves stretching out to the horizon in the north, the east, and the west. It was a rare treat to see such a sunrise indeed. The morning air was humid, and they were packing up and getting ready to head out for the day.

They had reached a pivotal point in their journey toward the Lake Lands. Roshin had guessed right, and the night before that had sailed past Ardvar, four days after Ashlyn had asked Roshin how much further they had left to go.

"Now we just need to get across Loch Da Crun," Roshin thought to herself as she cast her eyes out to the north.

Loch Da Crun was a tremendous bay with two lobes, north and south. To the south was the inlet that led straight into the heart of the Capital Cities. To the north, the women had a direct line to get to the Lake Lands and Ashlyn's hometown.

They had to get across it. A journey along the coast to the south would take them into the busiest harbor of the empire. "Too close to the slavers and soldiers in a stolen boat," Roshin thought to reassure herself of their next steps.

This was a hard truth. Not only would continuing to follow the coast add another week or more to their already long journey, but women were not fishermen, and two women in a fishing boat would get all the wrong attention. "We have to cut across," Roshin felt settled in her plan.

Standing next to Ashlyn, she squinted and looked hard at the northern horizon. "Do you see that spot way out there?" she asked pointing out into the water.

Ashlyn gazed out and nodded, "I think I do," Her tone seemed to harbor a nervousness within it.

Roshin drew a circle around it with her finger as if confirming its location. "That is the Gateway Island. It sits in the center of the bay and marks the halfway point across."

"It is so far away, Is it a large island?" Ashlyn looked back at Roshin, her eyes wide, and her tone uncertain.

"Large enough. I believe it once had a small village on it, but no more," Roshin confirmed before continuing. "We will use that as our marker and set sail toward it. We can then follow it around and into the northern lobe of the bay."

"Are you sure we can make it that far?" Ashlyn asked, the fear in her question was palpable, "The water is all so open." Ashlyn looked around her at the vastness of the sea.

Roshin sighed. She too shared the girl's nervousness, but she could not see another option. "I don't know that we have much choice," she said with resignation. "We can't go to the south along the coast."

Ashlyn pushed back, "Is there not another way to avoid them? I thought the capitals were along a river"

"They are," Roshin confirmed, "but the settlement stretches to the sea, and the harbor will be full of ships."

"What is so bad about the ships?" Ashlyn asked.

Roshin looked out toward the east, "Some might be the boats of slavers, some soldiers, regardless a couple of women alone in a fishing boat is liable to get attention." Roshin had her own fear in her voice, "I am worried we will end up taken again, and this time we might not get away."

Ashlyn cast her gaze back off to the speck on the horizon, "If you think we can make it that far, then I guess that is our best option." She slumped her shoulders, "I certainly don't want to end up back in a slaver's market."

Roshin turned to the girl, "*She can't know your doubts,*" she counseled herself and then she stood up straight and picked up the rope to lead the boat off the beach, "Then let us not waste any more time! The waves will only grow by the hour."

The women set off shortly after. Roshin had been quick to raise the sail and set the rudder toward the Gateway Island. Ashlyn sat low in the back of the boat watching the shore grow further and further off.

The waves this morning were choppy right from the start, and Roshin could already see that the girl appeared to be growing pale and clammy. "Would I but wish for calm seas," she whispered, and she looked out toward their destination.

The sky was cloudy and gray, and the breeze was strongly filling their sail. At their current speed Roshin thought they may make it to the island faster than she expected, "*maybe before midday even,*" she hoped.

That hope became more of a prayer as the little boat began to be challenged by the growing waves of the open water. The boat pitched and yawed as it rode along the top of the rolling sea.

Ashlyn began to grow distressed, and she even cried out as the boat was lifted upward and then rolled forcefully as it came down. Roshin felt helpless as she watched the girl creep over to the edge of the boat and lean over the side as her body physically objected to their current situation.

Roshin did her best to keep the boat true toward the shadow of the island ahead of them. She decided to dare not look back toward the shore they left and instead fix her attention on their destination. "If we can get to the island, then we can stop," she reassured herself.

But the sky began to grow darker, and the spot she had fixed on ahead of them soon found itself erased in a milky white covering of clouds. Roshin glanced off toward the west and the direction the waves were coming from and felt her heart sink.

Dark clouds were gathering on the horizon, and the wind was beginning to pick up along with the waves. "A storm," she whispered to herself with dread. She finally turned to look for the shore behind her, but it too seemed to disappear behind a veil for white.

The waves became massive swells, shot toward them from the storm to the west. Roshin fought the rudder and prayed, "May we stay true toward the island."

Everything seemed to be happening so fast. Ashlyn had collapsed and was lying prone in the bottom of the boat, gripping on in vain to the net underneath her. Water from the waves was now spraying up over the sides of the boat.

Roshin remembered the first storm they had faced after they had set out and she had a thought, "I need to lower the sail." The fabric was pulling hard away from the mast, and the boat was still moving rapidly forward despite the being shaken so from the rising swells.

Roshin looked out around them and for a moment felt herself panic. "*There is nothing out here.*" If she lowered the sail now than they would be stuck. There only movement set by the course of the waves.

They could get lucky and end up washed into the bay, or they might not make it and end up sunk or capsized. "If I can keep us moving forward, we just might make it to that island," she thought.

A huge wave broke over the side of the boat and it violently rolled in response. Roshin noticed that the boat now had a list to starboard, and the wind in the sail seemed to be making it worse.

The black clouds were growing closer, and lightning cut through the sky, lighting it up for an instance before being chased off by a crack of thunder. The sky had darkened markedly, and fat raindrops splattered down upon them, slow at first but with gathering intensity.

Ashlyn had willed herself off the boards and shouted out to Roshin, "What do we do?" her cries were pleading and full of fear, "I cannot swim!"

Roshin had a dark thought, "It matters not, there is nowhere to swim too," but she pushed it aside and tried to refocus on what she needed to do. She heard a groan from the mast, and she found herself reminded that the sail needed to come down.

"We will have to take our chances," she thought as she staggered over to the mast. She found her fingers again fumbling with the ropes. Another wave struck the boat hard and washed over the side. She called out to Ashlyn, "Get a rope and tie yourself to the boat!"

Ashlyn began to look around searching for a rope she could wrap around herself, "What do I tie?" she cried out to Roshin, trying to raise her voice above the tempest winds and booming thunder.

"Your waist, and then wrap your hands around it. Keep it short," she called back. Roshin was still fumbling with the sail. She managed to get part of it loose and with the release of the pressure on the full sail the canvas began to violently whip out before them.

Roshin wondered if that might be just enough of a release to ease the stress on the mast but still drive them forward. Another grown from somewhere in the boat told her it was not. She looked around her for another rope to wrap around her waist just as another swell came over the side and nearly knocked her from her feet.

Again the boat began to list hard and Roshin was terrified that they were one more hit away from capsizing. She ran for the rope at the bow of the boat and quickly tied it around herself just as she heard it.

A terrifying crack that sent a vibration through her feet caused her to look up, just in time to see the mast coming down toward her, the wind in what remained of the sail seemed to quicky pull it down and forward.

The mast struck the boat and was enough to exacerbate the current lean. "Hold on to something!" she cried out to Ashlyn as she dove for the port side of the boat. Another wave sealed the fate of the little boat, as its starboard side was finally forced below the waves.

Ashlyn screamed and rolled back into the water. Roshin gasped and then pushed off away from her hold toward the girl. Fortunately Ashlyn had tied herself short to one of the ropes on the port side, and Roshin was able to help her get her head above water.

The girl bobbed and gasped and she frantically searched for the side of the boat. Another wave shot the them upward and another crack found the mast free of the rest to the boat, the loss of the sail to the churning waters allowed the boat to tip back and the starboard side again rose above the water.

The boat was still listing terribly, and it was completely swamped but the waves seemed to be lessening, and they found themselves being knocked around far less. The lightning and thunder grew further apart, and Roshin prayed that this meant the worst of the storm had passed over them.

Roshin looked about the deck for something to bail out the water that was up to their knees. Ashlyn gripped the port side with most of her upper body, her fingers white from the force of her hold.

Roshin found a box she could use to bail that had gotten caught up under the net, but to her great distress she could not find the starboard oar. It too must have been lost with the mast. "We have nothing to propel us," she thought bitterly, "It was my fault for not taking down the sail."

She felt her stomach tie itself in a knot over the idea that they may find themselves drifting aimlessly for some unknown length of time. They may find themselves lost out in the bay for days, "We may wash up on the shores of the capitals," she thought as her anger seethed at her failure.

She took her frustration out on the water at her feet and began to scoop and dump it over the side. It felt like a long while had passed before the waves seemed to calm to match what they had known before.

It was then that Ashlyn finally spoke, She peeled her side body off of the boards and looked over to Roshin who had collapsed down into the water, "We survived," she said.

"We survived," Roshin confirmed, though for just how long that would be true she was not sure. "Can you help me bail?" she asked the girl. She knew the longer they sat in the cold water, the less likely the observation would stay true. Already her fingers felt numb, and her body had taken to shivering.

Ashlyn nodded and Roshin tossed the box over to her to take over the effort. Roshin looked out over the side of the boat, expecting to see nothing but water as far as the eyes could see. Before them however she could make out a beach.

"Ashlyn! Look!" she called out in excitement. They were slowly moving toward its shores.

"Do you think that is the Gateway Island?" Ashlyn asked.

Roshin smiled and shrugged, "I honestly don't care what it is, I just want to get my feet onto it!"

18

The Settlement

It felt like hours before the boat finally got pushed close enough to shore for the girls to jump out. They had to huddle together and cover themselves with a wet blanket to try to keep their bodies warm.

Roshin had thought about jumping into the sea and swimming with a rope to try and pull the boat in faster. She decided against it, as she was already finding herself cramping up with the cold. "That shoreline might be farther off than I think it is too," she told herself.

When the boat finally brushed the bottom of a sandbar maybe fifty paces from the shore, she jumped over the side with her rope and began to tug it in. The water reminded her that their priority would need to be getting warm.

Ashlyn soon joined her in the waist-deep water, letting out a little yelp as the cold hit her stomach. Together they pulled the boat up onto the beach, though with the loss of the sail, and also an oar, they were not sure if there was any point in trying to preserve it.

Once firmly on the beach, Roshin stopped and looked around. The island before her had a wilder look than most of what she had seen across Perinthia. They looked to have landed on the western shore judging by the sandy beaches and dunes.

She suspected they ended up off course to the west when she lost sight of the island and, by providence, they had made it far enough that the waves simply redirected them back toward the east once they were no longer going forward.

The landscape beyond the dunes appeared to be mostly sturdy young trees. The bigger ones, she figured, were likely logged, but it's too much work to pile up the saplings to take them back to the mainland. As a result, they had been able to grow up for likely more than a decade undisturbed, reinvigorating the wildlands.

She turned to Ashlyn, "If this is indeed the Gateway Island, then there should be an old settlement somewhere nearby," She looked around to gauge the landscape and get her bearings, "If I recall correctly, it was on the western side, nearer to the south of the island."

"So that way?" Ashlyn said pointing down the beach to the south.

With a nod, Roshin turned in the direction of Ashlyn's finger and started to walk. "Let's move, lest we stand here and freeze."

The weather that followed the storm was at least warmer, albeit humid. It did not matter much, however. After a long while sitting in a boat swamped with the frigid water of the sea, the women needed more than pleasant weather to regain their body heat.

They walked down the beach for a while until they reached the southernmost tip, at which point the island shore began to cut around to the northeast. A familiar sight caught their eye, it was another harbor light.

Like the light they stayed at near Ancalah, this light was a tall stone tower that tapered toward the top. It had a narrow entry that led to what seemed like an even narrower staircase. Roshin popped her head in to look around.

This light did not have a supply shed behind it to host the fuel, instead there was a small trail with two worn tracks in the sand that led off to the northeast at an angle just a bit more north than the coastline.

She called Ashlyn's attention to the trail, "I bet there is a building this way, or maybe the settlement." Her tone was hopeful.

From what she understood, the settlement had been abandoned after the empire cleared the resources off the island. The state of the trail, however, made her second-guess this and wonder if perhaps a keeper might be stationed here to man the harbor light's brazier.

Regardless she hoped that there might be a structure that was serviceable enough, with a fireplace, and blankets. A rumble of thunder in the distance caught her attention. A second band of storms seemed to be forming on the western horizon.

"It looks like we are not done yet," she told Ashlyn, pointing out to the clouds.

The girl looked out, and her eyes grew wide. "I hope you are right; I can't think of being out in another storm right now," Ashlyn said as she wrapped her arms around herself and shuddered.

The pair made haste down the trail, which wove into the forest and up what felt like a mountain of a hill. As they reached the top a sense of relief came over them as they saw what looked to be the settlement just up ahead.

The sky was again beginning to darken, and the fat raindrops from the storm clouds had just begun to fall as they reached the first of the buildings. Their hearts sank. As Roshin suspected, the settlement looked to have been built and then abandoned some time ago.

It was mostly an assortment of small wood cottages, that were slowly being consumed back into the surrounding landscape. Grasses, weeds, and vines all encroached in on the walls that themselves were punky and covered in fungus.

Shutters and doors were knocked off their hinges or missing entirely, and some of the walls seemed to be missing their cladding, making them look skeletal and open to the elements. "It's as if their walls have been scavenged," Roshin thought to herself.

"I am not sure we will find shelter here," Ashlyn commented as she reached out to touch a vine that had snaked its way through the wall boards and out through the roof of the first cottage.

"I fear you may be right." Roshin agreed. The roofs on these first set of cottages had collapsed in on themselves. "But let's keep looking, all we need is one that still has most of a roof. They must keep the charcoal for the harbor light somewhere here, right?"

"Assuming that light is still used," Ashlyn added doubtfully. They moved forward toward the next set of buildings. These too seemed to be in poor repair, but a few looked more solid with their walls constructed from whole logs rather than boards.

Roshin began to cast her eyes around the sturdier cottages, looking for one that still had most of a roof. The rain began to fall heavier and thunder coming up behind them made her search all the more desperate.

Finally, her eyes found what she was looking for, "Ashlyn, Look!" she said pointing over toward one of the log structures near the center of the little village. A trail of smoke was coming through the chimney. The roof was intact, and appeared to have been recently patched with dune grasses.

Ashlyn gasped in surprise, "The light keeper?"

"That seems the most likely," Roshin replied.

The cottage had a door, and shutters that hung in alignment to the windows, the walls appeared to be patched with extra boards, likely pried from the other cottages to cover gaps between the logs where the mortar likely flaked away.

There were vines crawling up the side, but they did not appear to have made it through to the inside of the little house. The path toward the door was clear and well-traveled. "Someone is definitely there," she said in a near whisper.

A feeling of trepidation came over her at the idea of encountering a stranger, but they did not have much choice. "*We are freezing out here,*" she thought to herself as a chill ran down her body.

Ashlyn walked over and put a hand on her shoulder, "We have to take the chance, and hope that whoever it is will be willing to help."

Roshin nodded, knowing that the girl was right. As the pair began their brisk walk over to the door of the cottage, Roshin kept looking around to see if maybe there was another option that would not need to take them into the home of a stranger.

What she found were three more cottages that looked to have been repaired and seemed to have occupants. "There are more," she whispered to Ashlyn, pointing out to the trails of smoke emanating from the other structures.

"Well, we saw this one first so let's try it first." Ashlyn seemed to have a surprisingly cool confidence about approaching the homes. Roshin imagined it was because she had grown up in a little village not so unlike this one.

Roshin had to remind herself that for five years she had served little towns like these as a nurse, and all but the last had received her well. "*They are not slavers, and they are not soldiers,*" she assured herself.

As they neared the door Ashlyn asked, "What should we say?"

"We were washed up in the storm, I would tell that one true, perhaps we offer our services as healers to the town?"

"I like that," Ashlyn replied as her hand reached out to knock upon the door.

It took a few knocks, but moments later the door opened just a bit, and a nervous eye looked out at them from the crack. It appraised them quickly before apparently deciding they were not a threat, and whoever it was opened the door enough to pop a head out.

The head was that of a woman, and she looked surprised. She was wearing a clean cream-colored veil and had rich brown eyes; her face looked youthful but had a few fine lines indicating a woman around thirty.

She wasted no time, "Oh my! You look a right mess! As if plucked from the sea!" She looked up to the clouds overhead and the rain coming down and then pulled the door open and stepped aside. "Come in now, come in," she spoke in a quick but quiet tone.

The girls stepped past her and entered the cottage. The first thing they noticed was the warmth, and then the smell. A fire was burning in the hearth and above it hung what looked to be a cauldron, likely full of some kind of rich stew.

The smell of the food dominated the space, masking an otherwise earthy undertone from the old lumber that made up the walls. The woman before her, Roshin noticed, was visibly pregnant. She was also not alone. Around them she saw several others had all stopped what they were doing to stare at her.

There was a small dark-haired girl of maybe three, clinging to the skirts of the woman, who Roshin deduced must be her mother. Two older boys, maybe five and eight were standing near a seated figure, who was turned toward the fire. At the commotion of the door, the figure turned toward them, and then shot up in surprise.

It was a man, and in his hand was a smoking pipe. The man looked strong with long brown hair tied back into a bun. Like most men she had seen outside of the military, he sported a beard, though it was short and well-trimmed.

It was his youthful appearance that surprised Roshin the most. He, like the woman looked to be around thirty. How he had come to be here she did not know. The age of the children spoke to a man that would have somehow escaped service some years past.

"*A deserter,*" she thought. The idea brought a sense of relief to her, as a deserter with a family was not likely to turn around and see them shipped down to the capitals.

Roshin suddenly became aware of her own presence. She felt as though she must resemble a drowned rat with her hair plastered to her cheeks and her clothing soaked and hanging heavy. She looked over to Ashlyn, who looked similarly miserable.

Once they were inside and the door closed behind them, the woman ushered them over to the hearth. "To the fire with you, you look a proper mess!" and with that she pushed on their backs and directed them forward toward the hearth.

As she pushed them, Roshin decided she should probably introduce herself and give them an idea as to why they were there. "I apologize for the loss of my manners, I am Roshin," she said by way of introduction, before turning to Ashlyn, "This is my companion, Ashlyn. We were shipwrecked and drifted here."

"Shipwrecked?" the man announced in surprise, "Two women out upon the sea in a storm?"

"There was no storm when we set out. We were seeking to cross Loch Da Crun, and about halfway out to Gateway Island the storm came up."

"And you lived!" the woman exclaimed, "Hulen Ahir is good!"

Roshin was surprised to hear the mention of her god. Followers of the faith were exceedingly rare and often practiced in secret. She decided to cautiously enquire, "Are you followers of the faith?"

The woman seemed the shrink a bit and blush as if she realized she had said something she likely should not. The man answered for her, "We keep to the teachings of Hulen Ahir, yes, do you know of the faith?"

It was Ashlyn who answered with excitement this time, "Yes! We are believers and servants of the faith. We had been serving as sisters and healers around the Empire before..." she trailed off as if realizing that she may be saying too much.

Roshin helped her, "Before one of our hosts sold us into bondage for the purchase of some men."

"I see," the man gave as a reply, his face studying them. "I am Lochlan, this is my wife, Deirdre."

"Might I ask if this place has a name?" Roshin enquired, "Are we on the Gateway Island?"

Deirdre answered, "You are, and we call this settlement, The Light."

19

The Light

The families from the settlement—men, women, and children—had descended the hill and gathered, hands joined in a circle around the base of the harbor light. A chant rose up and filled the air along with the golden rays of the sunrise over the sea,

"Oh Hulen Ahir, Keeper of the Light,
Guide us across seas and over the land.

Lead us through darkness, toward the light of truth,
Until the dragon rider returns to guide our way.

Fill our hearts with mercy, our minds with knowledge,
That we may honor the gifts of land and sea.

Open our eyes to beauty, our ears to nature's song,
Fill our souls with hope for the prophet's return.

Radiant Hulen Ahir, shine your light upon us,
That we reflect your grace while we await.

Bound as one body beside our glistening sea,
A light in the darkness until your servant's return."

The light keeper had ascended the stairs and, upon completion of the chant, poured a bucket of water over the remaining glowing coals of the brazier. They hissed as steam rose up into the cloudless sky.

The light keeper called down to those gathered below, "We still our light, for the darkness has passed, and we welcome forth the light of the new day. Let us be reminded that the dark always gives way to the light of a new dawn."

And with that those encircling the harbor light bowed their heads and hummed as the light keeper made his way back down the spiraling stairs. "Thank you for this day," Roshin whispered to herself, as the hands she was holding released their hold.

It was the morning after the storm had left them wrecked upon the Gateway Island. This was Ashlyn and Roshin's first opportunity to meet the rest of the settlers and learn their story, but it was the light keeper that was especially interesting to Roshin as he had an unusual presence.

As he emerged from the small opening on the side of the tower, he was greeted by the welcoming chatter of his followers. The man was old, his head was almost entirely bald though somehow, he still managed to keep a long white beard.

He wore a plain, hooded robe that had a rough-spun look to it, with a rope belt tied around his waist. On his feet were simple sandals that could be seen occasionally swinging out from under the bottom of his robes.

The man had a warm and kindly expression, his honey-colored eyes held a depth that spoke to his vast experience, and deep wisdom. Roshin had been taken by him in their first meeting. She understood why the settlers seemed to be drawn to him.

After their arrival at the cottage, Lochlan had taken the boys to find the light keeper while Deirdre stayed and ensured that the women were dried and changed out of their wet garments. It was a great comfort for Roshin to find herself again wearing a simple linen dress.

Deirdre had even helped them brush and braid their hair, and then had given them each a light-colored snood and veil to cover their head. Roshin had felt like herself again, put together and proper. She would not miss the layered skirts, and the tightness of the corset that had been given to her before the sale.

Ashlyn too looked to be feeling quite bright about the situation. Her eyes, while tired, for the first time in some weeks, seemed relaxed. "Thank you for this." She had told Deirdre, "You don't know what it means."

After a quick convergence with Ashlyn, Roshin told Deirdre that she could keep their dresses. Deirdre seemed confused and tried to object to the gift of such finery, but Roshin explained, "To us they were not gifts but a sign of our bondage. They can be a gift to you, or whoever you see fit to offer them to." The woman seemed to understand this.

Once dressed and dried, Deirdre offered them bowls of the stew that was hanging over the hearth. It was a rich broth, filled with wild garlic, bullrush roots, and wild turkey. Its warmth was the final thing Roshin felt she needed to shake off the cold from their ordeal.

As they ate, Deirdre asked them for their story. Perhaps without the caution they should have observed for being in a stranger's home they recounted the details. They told her of how they had been sold in the village where they had been serving as healers. Traded for young and able-bodied men.

They told her of the slavers and the market for men, how they were dressed up and run through the auction, sold to the highest bidder. When they got to Delvin and Toran, the details began to grow thin, but the woman seemed sensitive not to pry, and she just continued to listen.

For the recounting of fight on the road and the escape to the docks, Deirdre had moved to perch herself on the edge of her seat, "So you took the boat despite the warning?"

"We had no other real choice, less we risk being retaken," Roshin explained.

From there it was a simple recounting of the journey, how they survived on fish and determination to see Ashlyn back to her home with her mother. Finally, they told of the harrowing trip across the bay. Deirdre stood up and then offered them another ladle from the stew.

"I am sure the light keeper would bid you to stay here as long as you like. As followers of the faith and healers, this community would be happy to have you," she explained.

Roshin nodded, "We look forward to meeting him." She did not want to disappoint the woman, but looking over to Ashlyn, it seemed plain that this would not to be their final destination. It was at that moment that the door of the cottage opened, and a now wet Lochlan returned with the hooded old man they all called the light keeper.

The man dropped his hood revealing his lined face and bald head. His kind eyes looked them over, "When Lochlan told me two women had washed in from the storm, I did not at first think to believe him," the old man commented with a chuckle, "it seems Hulen Ahir must have had a hand in directing those waves for you to find yourselves here."

The women just stood before him and shyly nodded, "It was truly good fortune," Ashlyn commented.

The old man again laughed, "I would say it is likely more than good fortune my dear, but that is because I have learned to see providence from coincidence." He winked at them and smiled, "So tell me, my daughters, what of your story sent you across the bay in a storm?"

For the second time that evening, the women wove the tale of their journey. The light keeper stood and listened carefully to them as they spoke. Once they finished with the recounting of their drifting to the island the man erupted in jubilation, "Then this does indeed seem to be providence that has joined us here, we welcome you to stay for as long as you wish."

With that the man seemed to shift "I see our dear Deirdre has done well to see you warm and provisioned. Lochlan has bid his sons to ready a fire for you in one of our cottages, I will walk you over and you can stay the night there."

"That would be well," Roshin replied and together the girls and the light keeper slipped back out into the rain and off to a nearby cottage that had come to life thanks to a fire in the hearth.

The light keeper did not stay, but he welcomed them to join the morning prayer at sunrise around the harbor light. The women settled into the cottage, sitting themselves down upon a fur that had been laid out before the hearth.

They had been provided blankets, and wood to keep the fire going. The cottage, like the others was built of solid logs. It had an old and earthy smell, but it was well thatched, and the sides were patched to keep out any drafts.

There was one simple table with a kettle full of water, and a jar full of dried herbs that they could use for a tea. The fur and the blankets would make their bed. It had no mattresses, no chairs, and no other comforts, but it was warm and dry, and quiet.

The women said a blessing and then fell asleep before the nightfall as the exhaustion from their ordeal was finally able to settle over them.

The early night saw them awake well before dawn. They gathered themselves and then made their way down to the harbor light. This had been their first chance to see the other residence as the families all made their way down shortly after them.

There were three families in total, husbands, wives, and children of various ages. All energetic and full of life. The other men and women appeared to be similarly aged to Lochlan and Deirdre. Roshin wondered their story.

After the ritual prayer, the families had all gathered around them, introducing each member, and welcoming them to their settlement. There was Eadin who was the wife of Brian, and Shanon who was the wife of Garrett.

They each had four children, infant babies, and older children up to nine years of age. After the introductions the oldest of the children all ran off to the beach to play and climb up the hills of sand. The women seemed most interested in the girls, and for a third time Roshin and Ashlyn found themselves recounting their story.

The light keeper interjected upon the completion of their tale, "Let us all gather for a joint meal this morning. Our guests have recounted to you their story, but they know not of ours." The women nodded and soon all had turned to head back up the hill toward the settlement.

Roshin took notice of Ashlyn as she struggled to make the climb, "Are you alright?" she asked with worry in her voice.

"I feel as though I am still on the boat," she responded. "I think it is being down around the waves. The sound, it is as if I am out on the water."

Roshin noticed that she looked pale and clammy, "Here let me help you, we can return to the settlement and be away from here."

The men gathered tables and collected them in an open area behind the cottages. The boys brought out chairs and benches. The women put upon the tables bowls and spoons, kettles of stew, and baskets of berries they had gathered from around the island.

The families all gathered around the tables with the lightkeeper at the head. He led them in a prayer of thanks for the food and their visitors, and then they all sat and ate, breaking their fast for the new day together.

Roshin was hungry, but she could not help but notice that Ashlyn had barely touched her bowl. "*It seems she is still feeling ill,*" she worried to herself.

As everyone else finished eating, the light keeper stood and announced over the tables, "Hulen Ahir has given us a blessing in seeing our guests safely to our community. They have shared with us their story, but they do not yet know ours."

He paused and looked about to ensure all eyes had fallen upon him, "I have been the lightkeeper on this island for near on 50 years. I was here when this was a vibrant community, I saw it exploited, and I watched it fall as the Empire took from it all we had."

He paused to let the gravity of his words settle on them. "I stayed here in reflective solitude, long after the last man left these shores," he said, his words somber and heavy. "For years I stayed, tending the light, and praying for greater understanding. That time taught me much, but it, like all things was to be temporary."

With that he smiled brightly to Ashlyn and Roshin and then gestured to the men and women who sat around the table, "Some ten years past the men and women you see here landed a boat on these shores."

"These men, like all the others, were once soldiers, but love and a desire for more saw them free of that bondage," he finished his speech before gesturing to Lochlan to rise.

"We were sea folk, having grown up along the northern coast." Lochlan explained, "We knew our best chance for survival was to find a quiet Island outside the empire."

Lochlan continued, "We had sought one of the larger islands, but landed here as a stopover on our journey." He smiled back at the light keeper, "We met the light keeper, who showed us what remained of the settlement."

The light keeper interjected, "It was Hulen Ahir that directed them here as I was servicing the light. I invited them to stay and shelter for a while. I offered them food, but most of all I offered them truth and purpose."

"We all chose to stay and make our life here," Lochlan finished, "and that choice has seen us truly blessed."

The girls received more details as to how the settlement was rehabilitated. It had been a conscious choice to leave the first cottages off the trail in a dilapidated state. They also chose to keep their own accommodations only moderately repaired.

The hope was if anyone from the empire was to stop on the island, they would write the community off as abandon without much further investigation, and so far, it had worked. "Once the empire falls, we will restore this place," Lochlan affirmed.

Once the meal was done Ashlyn excused herself to walk off behind one of the cottages. Roshin had followed her out of concern at her hasty departure and found her retching behind one of the buildings. "Oh my, perhaps you should go inside and lay down?" Roshin asked her.

The girl rose, looking as sad and pale as she had on the boat so many of the days they had sailed together. Ashlyn nodded, and together they walked back to their accommodations. Once Ashlyn had been settled inside, Roshin returned to the tables to help the women clean and wash up after the meal.

Deirdre asked after Ashlyn, and Roshin gave her a look of concern. "I don't understand it. Ashlyn had been sick nearly every day from the boat, but she is off the boat now and yet she still seems to be sick." She paused and slumped her shoulders, "I have never known of sea sickness to persist so long after being out of the water, and yet hers has."

The woman simply listened and then put a hand on Roshin's shoulder, "It is not my place to pry into the details for your ordeal, but I might suggest that it seems to me she may not be ill at all." Deirdre placed her hand on her swollen belly and gave her a gentle smile.

"This has been my fifth time being with child, so I speak with experience on this matter. Often the first sign of expectancy comes as a queasiness of stomach, and weakness in appetite." She gestured back toward the cottage, "The boat may have masked it until now. The true question is how long has it been since she has last bled."

Roshin simply stared at Deirdre, her mouth agape in a state of surprise. She somehow had never thought about this as a possible outcome, and her first reaction was of dread and sadness for the girl.

"Could this not have been spared for her? Has she not suffered enough for this travesty?" she asked up to the sky, and then she followed the women, with her arm full of dirty bowls.

20

A Different Destiny

One week had passed since the storm. Roshin and Ashlyn stood on the northern shore of the Gateway Island as Brian and Lochlan passed a few more bags into the hull of a sturdy-looking wooden sailing skiff.

The boat was the one that the men had used to bring themselves and their wives to the island some ten years prior. It had required a few days' worth of effort on the part of the men to see it back in working order to make the trip up the northern channel of Loch Da Crun and then back to the island.

They had been able to cannibalize much of the wood and parts from the girls' washed-up fishing boat to make the repairs, and they had already taken it out into the channel for a test run to ensure it was seaworthy.

"It's been so long since we have been out to sea! I am looking forward to this," Brian announced jovially, as he patted Lochlan on the back.

"Indeed! The breeze looks favorable, this should be a good trip," Lochland replied.

Roshin looked behind her nervously to see the crowd of women and children gathered to send them off. The lightkeeper stepped forward to offer a blessing and say his formal goodbyes.

"It has been a pleasure, my children, to serve as your way station on the journey toward your destiny. I am hopeful that this is not the last time that our paths will cross, but for now I will wish you fair weather, and smooth sailing toward the next stop on your journey." With that the old man opened his arms and offered a warm embrace to each of the girls in turn

It took all Roshin had to put on a brave face and accept the goodbye. She had not wanted to go. "*Ashlyn needs you, and you must trust that the lightkeeper has told it to you true,*" she reminded herself, as the men beckoned them forward for the shove off.

"At least this time we will not have to do this alone," Ashlyn said to Roshin with a smile, before stepping up into Brian's hands to be lifted over the side.

"That is truly a relief," Roshin said with a nod before drawing in a deep breath and stepping up herself into his hands to be hoisted onto the boat. Her mind, however, was a churning whirlpool of emotions and uncertainties.

The men pushed the boat out into the water and then pulled themselves up over the side before grabbing an oar to row away from the shore. Roshin sat down beside Ashlyn near the bow of the boat, trying her best not to look back and cry.

When she glanced over to Ashlyn, the girl was gazing out into the bay with a near giddy expression *"She's finally going home,"* Roshin thought, *"This is not about you."* She took Ashlyn's hand and gave it a squeeze.

The last few days for the girl had no doubt been a whirlwind. After their breakfast that first morning Roshin had returned to the cottage. The girl had been feeling better and was preparing to come back out.

Roshin had stopped her to talk about what Deirdre had observed. "How long has it been since you have bled?" she asked.

The girl stood, looking at her puzzled for what felt like a long while. "I believe it was right before we were taken," she said, "but not since." She looked curiously at Roshin, as if seeking an explanation.

Roshin did not know how else to say it but to say it: "Deirdre suggested that your sickness may have nothing to do with the boat or the waves." There was an uncomfortable silence before Roshin finally finished,

"She says it is common to have such feelings when one is with child."

The statement hung in the air, unmet by anything apart from more silence. Roshin wished desperately she could hear the girl's thoughts, "*Or maybe I don't,*" she considered.

Finally, the girl broke the uncomfortable quiet, and her response surprised Roshin, "That does make a lot of sense." Her words were calm and measured, she did not seem angry or afraid as Roshin had expected.

"What will you do?" Roshin asked.

Ashlyn looked up at her, "I guess I am to be a mother."

The response again surprised Roshin, "I guess you are," she replied, not sure what else to say. The girl did not appear to be upset. If anything, she seemed to embody a new sense of joy over the following days.

Roshin found the experience a bit confusing and hard to understand until she finally managed the nerve to ask the girl about it three days later. They were alone in their cottage and Roshin had turned to Ashlyn to ask, "How can you not be angry or afraid to now carry a baby from such an awful experience? Does it not remind you of what happened?"

Ashlyn, a girl of seventeen, who set out with Roshin and Granya to experience the world beyond her village turned to Roshin and with the wisdom of someone much older, and much more worldly replied, "This child is mine, not his. I have made a choice to see it as a gift, a way to have meaning pulled from something that otherwise felt meaningless and empty."

Roshin nodded and then responded, "You will be a good mother."

The girl laughed and replied, "So long as I can get home, so my own mother can help." It was a harmless statement from a young girl seeking to get home, but it reminded Roshin that soon, she would again be alone.

The next day Roshin had moved through the settlement feeling clouded and uncertain. She attended the prayers, helped with the meals and the children, and found herself wondering if this might be a place she could stay.

She would need to see Ashlyn home, but was there not some way for her to return? Could she not get back to this island and make it to her home, so she was not stuck wandering without a sense of place or meaning?

She was not sure how it would work. She wondered if maybe the men could take Ashlyn not just across the sea, but also to her home. Maybe they could wait for her, or return a week later to retrieve her?

She decided to speak to the light keeper about it, "*He will know what to do.*" She wanted to stay, not go. She had no home in Perinthia, and she would very much like to make one here. She resolved to request an audience after the evening meal.

That time seemed to come quickly, and as the women were preparing to remove the food and bowls from the tables, so they too could be returned to their homes, she had rushed over and tapped on the shoulder of the light keeper.

"Might I have a word with you on a matter of some urgency?" she asked him eagerly. The men had already begun to repair the boat and she knew it would only be a few more days before they would be off.

The light keeper nodded his head. "Let us walk then down by the sea, so we might have some privacy," he smiled and gestured to the small children that had begun to run and play around their feet.

Roshin followed the light keeper down the trail, away from the settlement, and then down the hill toward the harbor light. As they reached it, he stopped and looked over to her, "I can tell you have an unsettled mind, how might I help to unburden it?"

With that Roshin took a breath to try and release the nervous knot that had settled around her stomach. She began in earnest, "Ashlyn will be going home, and when she does, I will have to say goodbye to my companion, and again face the world alone." She paused to carefully gather her thoughts.

"I have been alone for so much of my life, but I don't wish that to be the case, I want to serve and find meaning." She made a gesture back up the trail as the light keeper continued to carefully listen, "This place feels like the closest thing to a home I have ever known."

"And you wish to stay," The light keeper finished for her.

"I wish to stay," Roshin confirmed with a nod.

The light keeper made a move and began to walk down the beach, "Follow me child." They walked a time in silence, and the knot only tied itself tighter in her stomach "*He is going to tell me no,*" she thought bitterly.

"I had a feeling you may be about to ask this," he finally observed. "I could tell you have been seeking a place of belonging, and it is clear you like it here." He gave a little chuckle, "How could I blame you, I have strived to make this a community with just that purpose you are seeking." He paused.

"...But?" Roshin asked with some hesitation.

The old man again laughed, "You have a good intuition." He stopped and looked out at the sea before continuing, "Up until last night I likely would have said yes, but..." he drew out the word, "I had a dream."

"A dream?" Roshin asked, confused as to how the dream would have changed his mind.

"Aye, it was about you, my child. I no longer believe that your destiny is here. You need to continue on. It came to me that you will find your true direction when you reach the hometown of your friend.

Roshin jumped in to object, "But I have been to that village before, it is plenty nice, but I have no family there, no ties. I don't understand how that would be my destiny."

"You are tying yourself too much to places. It is not the place itself that is the answer, but it holds the answer," he explained.

Roshin found her frustration rising. The light keeper seemed to be keeping something from her about his dream, and yet he expected her to just accept it. "Can you not tell me more about what this path is? How will I know what the answer is when I get there?"

The old man put a hand on her shoulder, "Dreams are strange messengers, they are symbols, and do not always give clear instructions." He smiled back at her, "I believe however that this dream was an important message. I cannot tell you everything, and it likely would not even make sense to you. I just ask that you trust in me to not steer you away, down the wrong path."

Roshin looked out over the water. Her shoulders slumped, "Then I guess I am to go."

The old man just nodded and turned back toward the trail.

Roshin spent the few remaining days at The Light trying to stuff down growing pangs of uncertainty. Part of her would wish to defy the light keeper and stay, but she knew she really had no choice. He told her she must go, so now it was up to her to go on her own.

She had done her best to enjoy her time and take joy in seeing the excitement welling up in her friend as the boat was nearing completion. Now she was on the bow, heading out again into the sea. "*A few more days to my destiny,*" she thought with a bitter laugh.

21

Last Leg

The men had pulled the boat up onto the shore and helped the women down. They had been at sea for two days, and had finally reached the end of their voyage. Ashlyn jumped down and then laid her body on the sand as if hugging the land. "Oh, how I missed you!" she said with glee.

The men had sailed all through the day and night, choosing to take four-hour shifts to man the rudder and sail while still getting some sleep. They wanted to waste no time so that they might themselves make it safely back to the Gateway Island and their families.

Ashlyn had not enjoyed this extra time out on the water. She spent most of it queasy and unable to stomach anything. Roshin was a bit worried she was not eating but was hopeful that it would all be over now. Overall, the journey was quicker sailing, day and night. They were finally done with the sea.

"We will help you set up camp and see to it you have what you need for a few more days in the wild, but we cannot stay with you any longer than that. The Empire's eyes are everywhere," Brian explained as he pulled out a few bags from over the side of the boat.

They all set off to gather dry tinder from the shrubs at the edge of the beach. The landscape here was so different from what they had seen on the island. There were no trees here, only bushes, most of which were covered in thorns.

"*How will we get through this country?*" Roshin asked herself as she looked out over the thorny and weedy landscape.

As if reading her mind, Lochlan piped in, "There will likely be a trail toward your town. It may or may not be better than walking straight through this country, but I suggest walking a few miles up the beach to try to find it before pushing through."

Ashlyn agreed, "The townsfolk often made trips down to the sea, there should be a path." Roshin appreciated their confidence as she was not sharing in it.

Brian handed a pack to Roshin. "You have dried meats in your bag that should see you fed for a couple of days. You also have a bowl and a pot. Look out for the knife when digging around in there; it's sheathed, but it could come loose and cut you if you are not careful."

"Thank you," she responded, feeling grateful for all the supplies.

Lochlan passed a second pack to Ashlyn. "Yours has a couple of bedrolls and some extra linen. It is bulkier but a bit lighter to carry."

Ashlyn nodded and gave him thanks. "You both be careful out there, may Hulen Ahir see you safely home."

"And you too my lady," Lochlan said with a smile before turning back to Brian, "Are you ready to set back out to sea?"

"I am ready, Eadin's arms have been empty too long," Brian said with a sly grin. With that the men turned to the boat and prepared to shove off.

Minutes later, the women stood on the shore and watched them sail off back westward. Roshin said a prayer for their safe travels and then turned back to tend the small fire. They had no need to cook anything, for the dried strips of meat were ready to consume. Still, the light warmth made the beachside camp feel more comfortable.

Ashlyn poked a stick at the fire, scattering small sparks up into the sky around it, before turning to Roshin and asking, "What will you do when I am finally home with my mother?"

Roshin shrugged. "I had thought maybe to return to the island myself."

"Really?" Ashlyn asked with peaked curiosity.

"Aye, but the light keeper has told me that is not to be," she said, sadness still followed her words at her memory of the rejection.

Ashlyn looked at her surprised, "Wait? He would not let you stay?"

Roshin shifted a bit nervously in recounting his reason, "He told me he had a dream. No, more a premonition. He said my destiny was not there but that it would become clear once I see you home."

Ashlyn still seemed stunned, "Surely he told you more than that?"

Roshin shook her head and stared into the flames, "No, he was cryptic. Told me that if he explained his dream in more detail that I would not understand."

"Do you have any idea what he might mean by it?" Ashlyn asked curiosity flowing from her.

Roshin shrugged, "He did say it was not about the place itself, so maybe he's suggesting I will meet someone?"

Ashlyn nodded, "Maybe that is so." The conversation settled there with the girls chewing on jerky, before finally falling asleep. When they awoke the next morning, they gathered up the packs and set off down the beach to the east.

They walked near on to midday before finally coming across what looked to be an old trail to the north. "This looks like it!" Ashlyn announced triumphantly, and so they turned to follow it to the north.

The trail made Roshin feel claustrophobic, as the branches of the thorn bushes around them began to squeeze in on them. Several caught her sleeve and several more caught her flesh, biting into her and causing her to jump away and into another bush on the other side of the trail.

"I am not sure this trail is much better than just weaving through the bushes." She scoffed under her breath.

"A forest or field is kinder for traveling for sure," Ashlyn said as she too picked a branch of pickers from off her skirt. The travel went like that for much of the day. As the shadows got long, and they knew they would need to soon find a camp, the situation became even more concerning.

"There is nowhere clear enough to stop." Roshin observed bitterly. Her legs were tired, she was thirsty, and most of all she was sick of being jabbed. They continued on well past sunset, and into the twilight. There was still no place to camp off the narrow trail.

In frustration and desperation since the darkness settled all around them, they just gave up and laid their bodies along the trail, head to head.

Roshin awoke with her face in a bramble "Ow!" she howled before rolling over and sitting up to get a face full of a spider's web that had been built above her sometime during the night. She squealed and swatted at her face before resigning with a sigh, "The sea made travel much easier."

Ashlyn too had sat up and at that moment was rolling up her bedroll to pack it all away, "Maybe for you," she shot back in a playful manner in an attempt to lighten the mood. "We should not be long out now. Maybe one more full day of travel before we should make it to the river.

"I hope that is true," Roshin mumbled as she too turned to pack up her bedding.

The pair again walked well into the dark, but this time they did manage to find a clear space free of the blackberry canes and rose bushes that had plagued their time on the trail. They walked around it to flatten down some of the weeds and grasses before laying out their bedrolls.

"This should be our last night out on this path," Ashlyn whispered, her excitement was palpable, "Tomorrow I will get to see my mother! And you get to find your destiny," she added mischievously.

Roshin smiled. It was good to see the girl so bright, "I am going to miss her for sure," she thought as she settled down to fall asleep. It came easily that night. Her mind spun off into a strange dream, She was standing beside the Wynmridge Mountains.

Before her landed a massive turquoise dragon with glowing sapphire eyes. Its wings were spread wide. She stood in awe at its beauty. The dragon then folded its wings and bowed down before her.

She found herself feeling confused, but then the silhouette of a man appeared, and he stepped down off the dragon's back and onto the ground. She strained her eyes to try and see his features. "Who was he?" She wondered, "Was this real?"

He started to walk toward her, but then Ashlyn appeared off to her side, and he turned to walk toward her. Roshin could still not make out his features, and she thought to run toward him, but as she did, they all disappeared, and she found herself staring at the black of the night.

22

An Empty Cottage

The women stood on the shores of a wide river. "So how do we get across?" Roshin asked Ashlyn. "Is there a ferry or a bridge?"

Ashlyn shook her head, "I fear there is not. We will have to wade across."

"How deep is it?" Roshin asked with some concern.

"It's summer now, so likely up to our armpits. We should be able to touch the bottom all the way across."

Roshin took in a breath, "Is there a way we might be able to float these bags or our clothes across? If we don't make it to your home by nightfall, I don't want everything wet."

The girls began to look around on the banks of the river. They walked up and down it for over an hour before coming upon the remains of an old dock. "We might be able to pry a board or two off of that and set our things on top of it," Ashlyn observed.

"Good idea," Roshin responded making her way over to it. They had to get down into the river to access the boards. The girls took off their shoes and tucked their skirts into their collars. They both laughed at the sight of each other before wading out into the water beside the dock.

It had been a good idea, but prying free the boards proved more challenging than either girl had anticipated. In the end, it was actually easier to free a full section of the dock from the sides. The section was way bigger than what they needed, and it felt ridiculous to carry it together over to where they had set down their bags.

"This feels so heavy, I hope it will float," Ashlyn remarked.

"Boats are much heavier!" Roshin observed with a laugh.

The girl blushed and they continued shuffling down the bank. After a few more paces they set the section down and then they both slipped out of their dresses, and piled everything on top of the dock section. They then picked it up and carried it together out into the water.

The river was cold like the sea had been, but it felt good after having walked so far to have the dirt and sweat washed from their bodies and carried away in the current. The river got deeper, and soon they were no longer carrying the dock section, they were instead guiding it along.

Ashlyn had been right. The water had risen up until around their armpits as they hit the middle of the river. As they began to climb out on the other side a sense of finality came over Roshin. "We are almost there."

She was not just thinking about the river, but the reality that they had nearly made it back to Ashlyn's home. "I bet you are excited to see your mother again," Roshin commented, as the pair again shuffled the dock section up out of the water and onto the bank.

They gathered their things in their arms and, for a while, walked alongside the river back toward the east. They came to a pretty, open space, beside the river that it appeared had been trafficked fairly recently. The weeds and grasses had been pressed down flat into the earth. They settled there for a little while, getting themselves dressed and ready to walk on.

"Do you know what your will say to her when you get there?" Roshin asked Ashlyn.

She shook her head, "No, I have so much to say, I don't even know where I will start." The girl then let a large smile spread across her face, "I could start with how much I missed her."

The women walked along an old trail, which slowly started to pull away from the river and toward an open field. In the distance they could see what looked to be a cottage. Ashlyn's pace quickened, and she exclaimed, "That's it!"

Before Roshin knew it, they were both running down the narrow trail. Roshin thought to herself that the path seemed not very worn, and the field looked far wilder than she remembered from the last time she was there. "An old woman alone may not be much of a farmer," she assured herself.

Ashlyn had rushed ahead of her, but suddenly came to an abrupt stop. Roshin jogged up behind her and matched her gaze. Before them was the cottage, but it looked like a shadow of itself. The shutters were cocked, hanging from worn hinges, the weeds had grown up close around the building and vines had cracked the clay siding revealing the stones underneath.

The door stood open in a foreboding manner. The thatched roof looked to be rotting away. Ashlyn began to walk very timidly toward the structure. Roshin felt her mouth go dry, and her pulse quicken. She cast up a desperate prayer, "Please don't let her mother be dead."

Roshin's toe struck a small hand tool that had been obscured by the grass; much was left lying around as if whoever lived here had not planned to depart. Roshin repeated the prayer, "Let her mother not be dead."

At this point Ashlyn had gone inside. Roshin did not follow, instead she milled about outside looking at the artifacts of the family that were left behind. She saw the burial mound just off the path ahead of her and she walked over to look at it.

"There is still only one," she said to herself as she looked down at the pile of stones. Unlike the rest of the cottage, this place had seen some attention. The weeds were pulled back from around the mound and the space around it looked cleared. An idea struck her then, "Perhaps her mother has moved into the town?"

She looked up and toward the door of the cottage, she watched it a long while from beside the grave, Ashlyn finally emerged, tears streaming down her face. "She's gone! She's not here!" the girl wailed. "And it looks... It looks... It looks like it has been for a long while," she finally managed to squeak out through her sobs.

Roshin rushed over to the girl's side and wrapped her arms around her. "She might be in the town," Roshin exclaimed, pulling back a bit and pointing over to the mound. Someone appears to have been visiting your father recently. It's possible this farm was just too much for her after you left."

Ashlyn sniffed and then walked over to the mound. She stooped and put her hands on the marker stone, before turning to Roshin, "Do you think you could help me carve out his name on this stone before you go?"

"I can certainly do that," she said, doing her best to fight back her own tears. This was not how this day was supposed to go. "Shall we head into town?"

Ashlyn nodded before wiping her tears and rising up off the ground. Together they walked forward down the trail. At one point Roshin stopped to point out scratch marks on the ground. The weeds had been torn up in a few spots, "That seems odd," she noted in passing.

Ashlyn seemed too distracted to pay her any mind. The girl walked briskly down the trail as if in a rush to get into the town. They walked in silence, moving quicky down the trail. Soon the trail merged with several others and they were now on a road that was snaking back toward the river.

The town was ahead of them, "Taughmon," Ashlyn said in an excited whisper, before breaking out again into a jog to make it to the streets.

"Taughmon," Roshin repeated, "...*and my destiny?*" she added in her mind before jogging after her companion who was already nearing the main street of the town.

She caught up to Ashlyn beside the livery. There were clearly no horses there, "*Just and old saddle,*" she thought. She reached for Ashlyn's hand. And the two moved forward together.

"The town does not look the same," the girl noted, her words heavy with fear. Roshin agreed, she looked around and could see that it seemed to have been a while since anyone had made any investments into the town.

The buildings looked to be in far worse repair than they had been even a year prior. There was a boat sunk down into the river beside a rotting dock, the blacksmith's forge was cold, and the storage structure beside it looked to be losing its roof.

More striking than any of that, however, was the silence on the streets. They had yet to see a single person, no children, no dogs, no livestock, nothing. A dread settled in around Roshin and she looked over to see that same feeling reflected back on Ashlyn's face.

The pair reached the town square, and finally they saw some people milling about. Two old men were leaning up against an abandoned store stall. There was a woman winding up the rope on the well, and there was another woman who was about to walk past them without even paying them any notice.

"Do you recognize any of these people?" Roshin whispered to Ashlyn, who shook her head and then jogged over toward the woman who had passed them.

"Excuse me! Excuse me!" she shouted after the woman, reaching out to catch her arm. "I am sorry to bother you, but I need help," Ashlyn's voice was heavy with grief and desperation.

"No bother at all," the girl responded. She was a young girl like them, wearing a similar dress and veil, though her feet were bare.

Ashlyn wasted no time in peppering the girl with questions, "This is my hometown, I have been gone and just came home to find my mother gone. I am trying to find out what happened to her."

Roshin watched the girl's face grow pale and her expression darken, "I am sorry, I cannot help you."

Ashlyn grew more frantic, "Her name is Leesha. She lived in the cottage just up the road. You haven't seen her in town at all?"

The girl began to step back away from Ashlyn, her face mixed with sadness and fear, "I am sorry, the village was empty when we came. I do not know what happened to them."

Ashlyn froze with shock and for a moment silence hung over the group. Roshin stepped forward and tried to calm the situation, "Is there no one in town that was here a year ago?"

The girl's eyes became wild with fright. "There was one, and you are not the first to ask after him."

"What do you mean?" Ashlyn asked her, barely able to contain her tears.

The girl pointed out toward the windmill but said nothing further.

Ashlyn looked and turned back to the girl, "Awin?"

The girl nodded somberly, "He was burned."

Roshin became confused, "Burned? Like his cottage caught fire?"

The girl slowly shook her head, again terror filled her eyes, "No, he was burned by a dragon." Her voice went quiet as she said the words, an uneasy quaver in them as she looked around nervously. "There was a man who came through town, he too was asking after the people that were here before."

"I met him here, just a few days past. I told him of Awin and sent him up the road..." The girl trailed off as tears filled her eyes.

"What happened?" Roshin asked.

She looked back toward the windmill, "He left. He went up the road to speak with the man I assumed, but then..." again she trailed off.

"But then?" Roshin pressed her.

The girl swallowed and took a deep breath in. "It came out of the sky- it landed beside the cottage. We heard it roar and it set the place ablaze, and then it took off up into the sky. I think the man was on its back," she said with an uncertain confidence.

Roshin and Ashlyn just looked at each other, "He was on its back," Roshin said in a whisper.

23

Dragon Fire

The stones still felt hot, and the smell of wood smoke and brimstone hung in the air. The cottage was a ruin. The western wall had been smashed in, the field stones that had made up the side were dispersed all over the cottage floor.

The only thing that remained of the beams and the roof was a dusting of ashes all around them. The weeds around the cottage were also black and scorched. If there had been any furniture in the house, Roshin could not tell. All that remained was an empty shell.

Ashlyn stood still as stone, her mouth agape, with an expression of horror on her face as she took in the scene before her. "I don't understand. Awin was a gruff man, not exactly warm, but he was not bad," Ashlyn said, confusion spinning in her words. "How could a dragon rider do something like this? He was just an old man!"

Roshin took a few tentative steps forward toward the fallen wall of the structure. "Something must have happened here that merited the dragon's wrath," she asserted as she touched a stone on what remained of the wall. "There is something here we don't understand."

"What if it is just as it appears? What if this dragon rider is not a prophet, but is instead evil and cruel?" Ashlyn demanded.

Roshin looked back at Ashlyn. "You must have more faith than that," she said, her tone a gentle scold. "We were meant to be here. To see this! This was the light keeper's dream," she exclaimed. *"...And mine,"* she added to herself. "There is a new dragon rider, the darkness is at its end!"

Ashlyn looked down, the expression on her face was a mix of fear and doubt, but Roshin moved forward into the cottage. She kicked around at the ashes on the ground looking for answers. She found a pile of charred bones in one corner of the room.

She stooped down to get a closer look at them, whispering, "Awin..." As she cleared away more ashes, she caught a glint of steel in amongst the bones. Reaching for it, she pulled it free and then turned to face Ashlyn. "He was armed!" she exclaimed.

The long sword had been warped by the heat of the flames, but it was still recognizable as such. If Awin had been armed, then maybe this attack was really a defense. "Was Awin one to carry around a sword with him?" Roshin asked Ashlyn.

She didn't even have to think about it before she responded, "No, I never saw him with a sword, though I know he had one."

Roshin dropped the sword and then turned to her, "We should return to the village and see if we can't get more information from the woman that spoke with him. Maybe we can get an idea as to where he might be going."

Ashlyn agreed and together they returned to the town square. The girl was still there, leaning up against a door on one of the buildings and talking to another woman. Roshin locked onto her eyes and made her way over.

The girl saw them coming and began to flap her arms in a gesture to wave them away. "I don't know anything more about it," she called out, seeming to want to deter them.

"You said he spoke with you," Roshin dodged her dissuasion, "What did he look like, and what did he ask you?" Roshin asked her.

The girl went to turn away and open the door, but Roshin caught her shoulder and stopped her. She felt the girl's body tense. "*She seems scared,*" Roshin thought to herself. Changing her tone, she tried again, "I understand what happened here must have been terrifying, but we believe this may be of important significance. Please help us."

She felt the girl relax slightly, and then sigh, "He said he was a soldier, and he had been attacked. He looked it; he had the armor of a common soldier, and his face was covered in bruises. He had dirty and wild-looking dark hair," the girl said tentatively.

Ashlyn piped in, "You said he asked about the town?"

The girl responded, "Yes. He asked what town this was. He said he was lost and wanted to get his bearings. He was curious about what happened to the farmers outside of town."

"*So are we,*" Roshin thought, but she said nothing of it, "Was he an older man, or young?"

"He was young, but honestly the thing I remember most was how badly he looked hurt," the girl touched her face to indicate where he had bruises.

"Did he give you his name?" Ashlyn asked her.

The girl nodded, "He said it was Conan."

They managed a bit more information from the girl, but it was clear the man had other things on his mind beyond his conversation with her. She had told him they settled there recently and when he asked after the townspeople from before, she referred him to Awin. After that he apparently had left.

Not long after, the townsfolk had seen the dragon fly in in a wild hurry. It matched the description of the one that had appeared to her in her dream, a large turquoise beast with glowing sapphire eyes. They heard a commotion, and the beast roared before black smoke rose up into the air.

They saw the dragon fly off, heading east toward Lake Enda. "So we know he is out there, but what do we do about that? He could be across the entire country by now!" Ashlyn observed as they left the village square and headed back down the trail to her family home.

"He could be, but maybe finding him is less important than spreading the word that he has come," Roshin concluded. She watched the ground deep in thought about what this revelation meant. As they neared the cottage, she again noticed the scratches in sand, "*This must have been where he stayed,*" she thought.

Such a thing might explain the recent tending of the grave, but why he would have been interested in doing that, she was not sure. She was shaken from her thoughts when her mind registered the sound of sobbing.

She looked around her to find Ashlyn kneeling down beside the grave. Tears were pouring from her eyes. The excitement of the dragon rider had made her forget the fact that Ashlyn had come home to an empty house, and the fate of her mother was unknown.

Her spirit immediately sank. One thing she did know was how it felt to lose a mother. She knelt down beside the girl. "We could try and find her," she suggested.

"I don't even know where to look," Ashlyn squeaked out.

She was right, nobody knew where they were, the only one who might have had any answers was now a pile of burned bones. She said nothing more and just wrapped her arms around her friend, who in return leaned in against her and cried.

Section 3
Discipleship

24

Repairs

It had taken three weeks for Roshin to finally settle on a path forward beyond Taughmon. At first Ashlyn seemed determined to stay in her family home even without her mother there. The place was familiar, and if her mother was to return, she wanted to be there for her.

Roshin had agreed to stay and provide help to ensure that Ashlyn's family cottage was reclaimed and made suitable for this purpose. The agreement was struck in the musty home the first night they were there. Ashlyn had started a fire in the hearth and was pacing around looking at artifacts from her family.

Roshin had told her, "I would be happy to continue traveling with you should you not wish to stay here alone."

"I think I will stay. I cannot leave this house the way it is, and I want to be here should she return." The she, was of course Ashlyn's mother, and Roshin understood. The girl felt powerless to go out and try and find her, so the best she could do was wait and hope.

Roshin had nodded, "Then let me help you. We can work on the house together and see it done sooner. I can't just be off without a plan anyways. I will need some time to consider my path now that he has come."

The work to be done, at first, seemed overwhelming, the cottage was in such disrepair. The girls started with the greatest task, patching the thatched roof. Roshin did not know where to start with such an undertaking, but Ashlyn did.

The loss of her brothers at a young age had led her father to transition many of the chores that they would have been responsible for over to her. "First we need to go down along the river and look for willow stumps." She had instructed Roshin.

Willow trees would keep growing long after having been cut down. They sent up dozens of straight suckers off the main trunk, and these were perfect to use as spars to hold down the new thatching. They would need hundreds if not thousands of these things to make all the repairs required, but finding such quantities seem daunting.

They set off one morning with a hatchet and a barrow and walked up and down the river chopping off the suckers from every willow stump they found. They still came up short. "We can use bushes," Ashlyn offered. "They are not as good, but they will work in a pinch."

They took their borrow out in the scrub land and cut off v-shaped branches from different bushes using the hatchet. Later on, they worked to knock off the thorns and tighten up the cut so there was little left beyond the crotch of the branch. They returned home that evening exhausted, but with several hundred branches in total.

They spent the night beside the hearth, using knives to whittle points and trim the spars by the light of the fire, which they kept fed with their offcuts and mistakes. The work had only just begun and the next morning they had a new task.

They needed material for the roof. Typically, this would have been straw, but there were no crops that had been grown, so they had no straw to use, this meant they would need to use field grasses or reeds. The reeds were preferred as they were more course, so they again set off with the barrow but this time they went to a nearby marsh with a scythe to look for reed grasses. There were plenty available, but getting them was in itself an ordeal. They had to wade in the brackish water to cut and pass out the reeds. They sunk down into the muck and struggled to keep their footing.

They left the marsh with their barrow full of reeds, but their feet covered in leeches. "If we need more, we are going to get it from the grasses behind the cottage!" Roshin exclaimed as she used her nail to dislodge the tiny black blood suckers off her ankles.

They bundled and hung the reeds up to dry for a couple of days. They spent that time casting a net out into the river to try and build up a food supply, as what they had been given from the Gateway Island had all been consumed.

Aside from fishing, they cut back and trimmed the weeds from around the cottage and cleared the items that had been left out to rot. The place was again starting to have a lived in appearance, and Roshin was feeling better about having Ashlyn stay.

They got to work on the roof the next day. They took turns, with one up on the ladder using a stobstick to make a hole in the existing thatch where it seemed thin or soft. The other girl would grab a bundle of reeds, knock out any short bits and then twist the end to make a knot.

These knotted bundles were then passed up to the girl on the ladder to stuff in the hole with the little forked hand tool, while the girl on the ground bent and twisted a spar to pass up. These were then driven into the new thatching with a mallet to help keep the repair in place.

This was repeated over and over again until the girls ran out of reeds. The next day they were out in the field scything grasses and then back to the roof. Their arms ached but the roof looked so much better, "No more leaking in a storm!" Roshin announced triumphantly.

She had never thought she would be up thatching a roof, and she was grateful that Ashlyn had helped her father before with the repairs, so she knew what to do. The sense of accomplishment she got when they finally finished could hardly be matched. "Thank you," Ashlyn had said.

They were ready to move on to some smaller repairs, but for these they needed supplies. They traveled into town in hopes to get some nails and pegs from one of the abandoned shops. It had been a week since they were there.

The town looked much as it had on the first day of their arrival. Most of the people were held up inside some crumbling structure, trying to stave off starvation through an act of will alone. Nobody had stepped forth to take on the roles and responsibilities of operating the town as such.

Roshin reflected on what they had learned that first day from the girl in the square. "These people traveled here from somewhere in the north and stayed out of desperation when the cold hit. They were lucky the prior residents had thought to prepare for winter and left it all behind."

Now it was summer, and nobody seemed willing to work to prepare for the next winter. "They will either leave, or stay here and starve," she thought to herself.

Roshin and Ashlyn made their way to the blacksmith's now cold forge. Items were all about, including goods he had produced and left behind. They needed nails and hinges. They dug through the boxes and collected some items into a pile to take back with them to the cottage. As they did this, the girl from the square wandered over.

"You are still here?" she asked curiously.

It was Ashlyn that answered, "Aye, we are."

The girl leaned over to see what they were doing, "Why are you collecting nails?"

Again, Ashlyn gave her the answer, "We have been working to repair my family's home. We have patched the roof and now need to fix the door and shutters. We need nails and hinges."

The girl seemed surprised to learn about their efforts. "You patched the roof?" It almost seemed as if the thought of such a thing had never crossed her mind. "So, you plan to stay then?" she asked.

Ashlyn nodded, "That's my intention, but I couldn't the way it was, so, we are fixing it." Ashlyn beamed proudly for her efforts.

The girl turned and looked at Roshin, "Are you staying as well?"

Roshin shook her head, "No, this is not my home, and I have something important I must do."

The girl looked at her puzzled, "What is that?"

Roshin answered briskly, "I must spread the word that the dragon rider has come." Just saying the words kindled a warmth inside her.

The girl, however, clearly did not share her sentiments. Her face darkened and fear spread across her eyes. In a hushed tone she responded, "Ah yes the people should be warned."

It was all Roshin could do not to laugh. "No, this is not my intention; it is not a warning," she corrected the girl.

A look of disbelief struck her, "But what he did to Awin!" she exclaimed, "He is clearly a monster."

Roshin reached out to take the girl's hands and then leaned in really close, speaking in little more than a whisper, "Have you heard the name Hulen Ahir?"

The girl did not pull away, rather she seemed to lean in as if desiring to learn this secret. "No," she whispered back.

Still keeping close, Roshin's tone hushed, "We are his followers. He is the one true creator of this world." She paused to let the weight of that statement fall on the girl, "It has been lost with time, but this has not been the first time our world has fallen into darkness," she explained.

As if realizing the danger of the information being shared, the girl pulled back sharply and hissed, "You should be careful what you say, Life is hard, but the empire is good."

Roshin just shook her head, "Goodness cannot be created by words alone, it is reflected in the world around us," She gestured out to the decaying village, "look around you, this place is no longer a community working toward an end. It is hopelessness that leaves us unwilling to invest in it, or to care."

The girl said nothing, so Roshin continued, "If you had hope, you would have planted, you would have fixed, you would have built. The fact that you have not has told me that hopelessness and pessimism coat your existence. That is not goodness."

The girl looked around, her face grim and uncomfortable. Roshin kept going, "You came here, used what you needed to keep yourselves alive, and now you linger with no real plan for the future."

The girl responded defensively, "We are just not sure if we are going to stay or travel south."

Roshin responded sharply, "Then you need to decide, stay or go, but if you choose to go it will be no different there. The south is a slave market full of misery, there is no salvation closer to the heart of a dark thing."

The girl just stared at her, her mouth agape. Roshin had one last lesson she wished to convey. "The dragon riders gave hope and kept order, and now one has risen up as prophesied by the teachings of our faith. He will bring forth an end to the darkness."

The girl left the interaction unsettled, and wandered off back toward the village square, but the conversation had opened a door. Over the next couple weeks as the pair frequented the town for small items to make their repairs, they noticed a change.

The people started to come to them asking questions about the prophecy, the dragon riders, and the light of

Hulen Ahir. They also started working to improve the town. Ashlyn instructed several women on how they had patched the roof.

Others had started to clear away weeds and fix the docks. Nets were cast into the river and smokers came to life as the people prepared to dry and cure the fish they caught for long storage. "They have discovered hope," Roshin whispered to Ashlyn one morning as they passed through the square.

The change was rapid and as the third week came to a close it became clear that the town was becoming a town again. Roshin believed the change was inspired by her message about the prophet, and she felt assured that she needed to continue on from here to spread the word.

Ashlyn's home had been repaired as much as one could expect, it would be plenty solid for her to spend the winter and welcome a baby into it. The girls stood together and marveled at the fruit of their efforts.

Ashlyn, however, seemed a bit distant. Roshin turned and asked her what was on her mind. The girl looked over to her and what she said surprised Roshin. "I want to go with you. I want to go and spread the word. I want to seed hope in other places. I can't stay here."

Roshin nodded. It was a change of direction, but she felt better to know she was not about to embark on a journey alone. Ashlyn looked to her and smiled broadly, "And I know we will find him along the way."

25

Setting Off

The girls had gathered what they saw as essential supplies into packs that they would wear as they set forth. Fortunately, time on the road with Granya had given them a good idea as to what they were likely to need.

"Fishing supplies, a good knife, a pot, a bowl, water skins, salt, extra linen, some sisal cord for tying, and an assortment of small jars to store dried herbs," Ashlyn said, giving an inventory of all the supplies they had gathered. In addition, they also carried a bedroll to sleep in and a couple wooden spoons.

They would take it all in the wooden cart that they had used to collect the reeds and spars. They hoped the cart would ease the journey and allow them to collect more along the way. "If it becomes too burdensome, we can always leave it behind, or maybe even use it in trade," Roshin told herself.

She recounted the plan for their departure: "We will leave in the morning and follow the river to the east. It will connect to Lake Enda, which we will follow until it turns south. We can fish along the river to feed ourselves and gather wild plants and herbs as we come across them."

Ashlyn listened and nodded in agreement as she continued, "We will be seeking the south trade road which we shall take north toward Brenna. We will stop at every hole or hovel we find along the way should it host any people."

They decided to use their skills as healers to gain entry into the villages and homes. They would offer medicines, and services to anyone in need, and once they had an audience, they would seek to pass on the hope of the dragon rider and the prophesied end to the darkness.

It was risky. Speaking openly on matters of any kind of worship outside of one's dedication to the empire and the emperor was seen as treasonous. So many truth sayers of their faith had been put to death or enslaved for refusing to renounce their beliefs, deny the truth, or otherwise vow to put the empire above their god.

Those that carried on, like Granya, had mostly kept their devotions a private matter for their inner circle, doing good works out in the world in a centered way, but only exposing the truth of their beliefs to those they apprenticed directly.

Sacred texts and temples alike had both been burned and destroyed. They were playing with fire, but if the dragon rider had come, the people needed to know not to fear him, and instead see him for what he was, a symbol of hope, and the brightest of light to drive off the night.

Ashlyn and Roshin joined hands and offered up a prayer asking for courage from Hulen Ahir. They would need it on the road, of that there was no doubt. Once that was done, they settled in for one last night in Ashlyn's family home.

The girl's melancholy was palpable on this cusp of leaving, and for the first time Roshin could recall, Ashlyn began to speak of her family beyond just her parents. "When I was little, I thought we had it all. My brothers were so good to me, they would carry me around and include me in their adventures even though they were both older than me."

She looked over to the fire and laughed, "I think they scared my mother when they would do things like build me a raft to float across the river or help me climb trees that I probably should not have been climbing, but I never saw the harm. If anything, they made me feel stronger."

Her tone shifted, and her grief rose, "I was just seven when they were taken away. I had been so scared when the conscriptors came, and my parents ordered me to stay inside these walls. The soldiers looked so big, and they dragged my brothers out. They were crying and trying to fight."

Tears welled up in her eyes, "My parents went after them, but they could not stop the soldiers from taking them. I think my parents died a bit that day when they lost them. They were never quite the same."

"The hardest thing about it is that I am not sure I would even know them today if I were to see them." Ashlyn paused and looked over to Roshin, "I have no idea if they are still alive, if they are well? All the family I had was taken from me, and aside from my father who is buried outside, I have no idea where they are."

Roshin leaned in and embraced the girl. "I don't know if I have any brothers or sisters, but I understand what is to wonder after someone you don't even know if you would know." She was thinking of her father and wondering what had become of him after he sailed away from her mother.

The evening ended with these reflections on loss and family, and the pair settled and fell asleep. Roshin had another dream. In this one, she was walking, and a turquoise dragon flew over her head, she could see the outline of the rider on its back as it flew away. Ashlyn turned to her and said, "I know him!" and then ran down the trail ahead of her only to disappear in the darkness.

The dream was unsettling, and Roshin woke with a start. "Too much talk of loss," she thought as she lay awake in the dark, fretting over what her dream might mean. She struggled to get back to sleep so instead, she rose and went outside to look up at the stars.

She started to talk to herself, "What you are about to embark on is dangerous. Many have lost their lives to share such messages, but it must be shared. You have seen the hope these truths can bring."

She looked back to the cottage door. "But you need to be wise because you are not doing this alone, and it is two extra lives that you are responsible for here, not just one." Part of her wished that Ashlyn would again change her mind and decide to stay.

The anxiety that had jolted her awake after the dream would not seem to leave. Roshin tried to soothe herself. "She has chosen to do this on her own; you have done everything so that she might be able to stay. This is her baby and her fate; she has decided this for herself."

The words were of little comfort. She still felt the responsibility for the life of the girl, and the baby. Fortunately, the next morning came soon enough. It was the day they would leave. They gathered their things to go. "There is one more thing I must do," Ashlyn declared before trotting down the path toward the town.

She was back an hour or so later, dragging behind her the girl from the square. Ashlyn had stopped outside and was talking to her, Roshin went out to join them and caught the conversation, "All I ask is if my mother returns you bid her a welcome and let her know where we have gone."

Roshin looked over to Ashlyn with a puzzled expression. "Now remember to take care of it, and it will take care of you," she finished with a smile. The girl seemed surprised, but Ashlyn left it and turned to Roshin, "Let us be off!"

And with that the girls gathered their bags and packed them into the little wooden hand cart. Once they were confident, they had it all they turned, and down the trail they went, leaving the cottage, and its new owner, to fade into the landscape behind them.

"You gave her your home?" Roshin finally asked once they were some distance down the trail.

Ashlyn smiled, "I could not do all that work and then leave it empty. She will take care of it, of that I am certain."

Roshin just nodded in response as the pair arrived in Taughmon for what felt like the last time. They walked through the town pushing their little cart down the road, and the people waved to them and smiled. They waved back. A nervous pit filled Roshin's gut as the weight of their leaving settled upon her shoulders.

It was no time, however, before the windmill and the burned-out cottage loomed before her, and she reminded herself, "This is why you are going. You are a messenger, and your message will change lives." And with that the pair walked out of Taughmon and down the trail beside the river.

26

The Hermit

The women had been walking on the little trails for a week when the weather began to turn foul. The sky around them darkened. "This may be a wet few days if we don't find some shelter somewhere," Roshin asserted.

They had walked east from Lake Enda and were now walking along the shores of Lake Grom. The lake had turned toward the south and Roshin recalled there was a small settlement beside the river outlet that led to Lake Bahle.

It was the first place she knew of along the way, and she felt like they could not come upon it soon enough. Ominous thunder rumbled off in the distance, motivating her to pick up her pace as she dragged the cart down the trail behind her.

Ashlyn was holding steady, ready to offer a hand should they need to lift the little cart over an obstacle or carry it past a patch of sand. They had had to carry more than they would have liked to since reaching the western shores of the massive lake, and they were starting to feel fatigued.

The storm coming in from the west, however, was plenty motivating to push on past their discomfort. Roshin recalled to Ashlyn, "There should be a little fishing village. Last time we were there, only a dozen or so people remained." They had passed through it with Granya the last spring, shortly after having Ashlyn join them.

"I think I remember it. I was so excited to see my first little town that was not Taughmon!" Ashlyn observed with a cheery laugh, "It was not exactly what I was expecting!" she added before asking "Do you think they might remember us?"

"That would be good. I'm not sure they get that many passersby, and if they do remember us, that will be better for us in securing some shelter," Roshin asserted as they walked on.

Unfortunately, they did not make it to the town before the sky opened up. The rain started, slow at first, but it began to pick up shortly thereafter. The women soon found themselves soaked and navigating a now muddy path in the face of the harsh crosswind off the lake.

They had nowhere to go but forward. The lakeshore where they were traveling was open and bare, without any tree cover or bushes to serve as shelter for them. They were feeling right chilled after walking in the storm for the better part of an hour.

They kept having to stop and dump water from the cart; the herbs they were drying over the side had become soft and squishy. Their shoes sloshed as if they had been wading with them in the lake.

What a relief it was when they saw a small hovel appear out of the gloom just ahead. "Oh, I pray it has a roof!" Ashlyn pleaded to the raindrops.

It had a roof. The structure was not impressive, it was a small stone cottage clad with red clay, water dripped down from the thatched roof and created a trench in the sand beside the walls. The door was solid, and it had windows, through which they could see the warm glow of what appeared to be a lantern.

It was occupied, by who, they were not sure, but they were plenty eager to find out. It was likely a fisherman given the location, but maybe not as they did not see any signs of a boat on the shore.

Part of Roshin was nervous to encounter a stranger, but she had set out to meet with as many people as she could to share the tidings of the prophet, so she shoved her fear aside and reached out to knock on the door.

They stood before the door for an uncomfortably long time as the runoff from the roof dripped upon their heads. Ashlyn turned to Roshin and began to ask, "Should we knock again? Or just try to ope-"

The door cracked and cut her off as a dark brown eye ringed by patchy, pale, and furrowed skin peered out at them. "Who's there?" the words came out in a raspy croak, as if the man had not spoken a word in weeks.

"We are healers traveling from Taughmon seeking respite from the storm," Roshin announced to the crack in the door.

The door opened a bit wider, and out popped the head of an old man. He craned his neck around the door to get a better look at them. His hair was white, and he had a long unkempt beard that had a yellow tinge to it around his mouth and nose.

He looked tired with darkness under his eyes that contrasted with his splotchy linen white complexion. Had it not been for the deep furrows and ridgelines all over it, his skin would seem as fine as parchment.

He started to reply but found himself to be racked with a fit of coughing, "Hrrgh-hrrgh," he brought his hand up to his mouth and then cleared his throat, "Ahem, I suppose you want in."

Roshin looked at him alarmed, "Your cough, it sounds like you might be in need of some of our services," and she reached her hand up to her throat to bring attention to her observation of his aliments.

The old man grunted and again cleared his throat, trying to stave off another fit of coughing, "Ack, No I don't need anything," he objected as he pulled his head back in and moved to close the door.

Roshin reached out and used her hand to stop him. "Surely you would not shut your door and leave us out in the storm? Let us help you; we have medicine in our bag that can soothe that cough," she chided firmly.

The old man huffed but relented. "Curse you for thinking to bother me," he croaked. "But if you insist, I am not strong enough to stop you." He stepped aside and let her push open the door. Ashlyn grabbed their bags from the cart and followed Roshin inside.

The hovel was neither warm nor inviting. It was damp and musty, it reminded Roshin of Ashlyn's cottage before they put any work into it. The roof was leaking, and there were bowls and pots placed around to catch the water.

There was a fire in the hearth, which provided something by way of drying things out. A small pile of driftwood was set beside it. The floor was muddy, and a small cot was set in the corner with some old wool blankets. "No wonder he is so ill," Roshin thought as she looked around.

It did appear as though maybe once he had been a fisherman. There were old nets and traps strung up on the wall. Ashlyn asked after a kettle, but the old man seemed not to hear her, so instead, she pulled a waterskin and the pot from her bag and set them down on a small wooden table.

She fished around and pulled out the jars which had been filled with what they had collected on the road. "We collected lungmoss," she said as she turned each jar over and took a closer look.

The old man had sat down on his cot. He was still coughing, and seemed to be making a point to ignore them. Roshin used an iron poker to push around the coals to make a bed for the pot. Ashlyn brought it over to the fire to heat the water as she prepared a mixture of the medicinal plants to treat his cough.

Half an hour later she started searching for a mug, before giving up and pouring the tea into one of their bowls. The young girl walked over and stooped beside the old man. "I know you don't want us here to fuss over you, but we are grateful. Take this and drink it, it will help settle your chest."

The man grumbled, "Or it will simply just poison me and then you will be off with my things."

Ashlyn did not let that dissuade her, she set a soft hand on his, and simply turned to him with a chuckle stated, "You have nothing we want."

The comment broke the old man, who himself could not help but laugh. His laugh turned to a cough, and he finally took the bowl from her and drank. *"She has a way about her,"* Roshin thought with admiration.

The coughing ceased a few minutes later and the man's demeaner changed. He became curious, "Rough roads for women like yous to be traveling alone." He noted.

"Aye, they can be, but we have seen far worse than this storm in our travels," Ashlyn assured him.

"Like you have!" he said with some vigor in his words. "Still why bother doing such work?"

"Because we seek to be bringers of light, not followers of darkness." Roshin explained as she walked over.

This also got a rise out of the man, "Not much light in this world," he grumbled dryly.

A smile spread across Roshin's lips as she saw the opening she had been hoping for, "You might think that, but we know that things will soon change," she ensured her tone was infused with intrigue.

The old man was not buying it, "The only change will be for thing to get worse," he muttered harshly, "I like hope to be gone from this world before it does.

"Maybe you should not be in such a hurry" Roshin said as she knelt down beside him, "You have been around a long time have you not heard the tales about the dark times past?"

The old man gave her a suspicious look, as if testing to see how serious she was in her pursuit of such a topic. He had grown up in a time when such histories were not so forbidden, and as it happened he was familiar with the tales.

Roshin probed carefully to draw out what he knew, keeping in mind that she could be seen as a blasphemer against the emperor for saying too much. The old man for his part did not take things too seriously. He was a worldly man, and the world had destroyed his faith.

The stories to him were not histories, but rather just old superstitions and stories told to children, or those seeking false hope. Roshin saw her opportunity, "But what if the hope was not false?"

"Bah, people have been searching for some savior to see them from their misery for ages at this point. I will believe it when I see it," the old man said with a grunt.

Roshin's mouth drew up into a sly smile, "You might only need to watch the sky my friend. We have passed through villages that have seen it, a man on the back of a dragon like in the times of old."

This seemed to strike him as too much, he chided them both, "You are foolish women to think to walk around and weave such tales. You will likely find yourself strung up or in the stocks if you are not more careful."

Roshin crossed her arms defiantly, "That may be so, but it will not change the truth."

27

Drochit

The break in the storm turned out to be brief. For the second time in one day, the women found themselves struggling with their burden as they ran down a muddy trail in the rain. They were hoping desperately for another shelter.

The women had bid Branoc, the old hermit, farewell as soon as the weather had showed signs of breaking. Roshin would have liked to have stayed to help him fix his roof and clean up his home, but the old man had made it clear that he had no intention of hosting any overnight guests, so when the rain stopped, they left.

Ashlyn had been able to insist that he keep the jar of tea to treat his cough, "At least that is something," Roshin thought. When they set out, they were still wet, left to drag their barrow down the now muddy trail. "I hope the town is not too far off."

It was not far off, but it was not exactly close either. They were still walking well after the rain had started to pour down again as another savage summer storm cloud blew overhead. They were cold and miserable, and Roshin found herself thinking back to the storm on the boat out in Loch Da Crun.

When the shadows of some buildings came into view, the women nearly cheered with joy. They rushed ahead toward them, the cart bumping and splashing behind them. When they arrived, they felt a great sense of relief.

"Now if only I can remember where Granya went to secure accommodations last time," Roshin whispered as she scanned the different structures.

Their eyes settled on what looked to be an old tavern and inn, "We could start there for now," Ashlyn suggested. She had with her a few coppers she had found in a secret spot within her family home.

It would be more than enough to see them accommodated at least until the next morning when they could find the head of the town. They grabbed their bags and left the barrow beside the door and then pushed it open.

The door swung wide, but the inside was dark. Not a soul was there manning the counter. They walked around and called out "Hello?" hoping to find someone inside that could help them. It was not yet night, so it was not likely that the innkeep was asleep.

The building, for its part, seemed little used; the benches were pushed in underneath the tables, and cobwebs slung between them, indicating that it had been a while since there had been any human presence seated at them.

The environment made it an easy choice to give up on trying to find someone and they took it upon themselves to move over to the cold hearth and set a fire. There was a collection of sticks and driftwood piled in a cubby beside the stone fireplace.

Roshin used the edge of a knife to peel small shavings of bark from the sticks to make some fine tinder which she then piled atop the larger sticks. She leaned in and struck her flint to the blade to cast sparks upon it.

"Well, we might find ourselves extending a welcome that they do not feel we are owed, but the door was open, and we need to at least see ourselves dry," she justified nervously more to herself than anyone else.

Once the fire was going, the girls dusted off and dragged over a bench from under the nearest table. They then set down upon it in an attempt to warm their bones. Thunder rumbled loudly overhead. "I doubt we will have any other company tonight," Ashlyn squeaked after an especially loud crack.

She had been correct. Once they felt a bit warmer, the girls pulled over another couple benches and then removed their bedrolls from their soaked bag which they draped over benches beside the fire. "Maybe they will be dry by night?" Ashlyn shrugged optimistically.

Being in a common space, they did not feel comfortable removing anything else to lay out to dry, so they just stood by the fire, slowly turning to keep the chill at bay.

This time the storm was unceasing, and rain fell well into the night. They finally fell asleep on the hard wood planked floor beside the fire, only a bit damp. When they woke, they were both stiff and cold but mostly dry.

Roshin got up and peered out one of the windows onto the streets. They looked empty and it was still raining. "Maybe we should just rekindle the fire and wait a bit longer before going out to look for anyone?" she asked Ashlyn.

She was not exactly eager to see herself wet again, so this is what they did. An hour or so later the door opened and in stepped a man in a hooded cloak. "Hello?" he enquired into the open space of the tavern.

The women had their backs to the door, so when he spoke, they startled, jumping to their feet and turning to face him. "Oh I'm sorry!" Roshin exclaimed, "We did not see you come in."

"No, I see you did not." The man was shrouded by his hood so his expressions were unclear, his tone however, was firm and skeptical. "And so, I will ask just who you might be?"

"I am Roshin, this is my companion, Ashlyn." She stammered quickly, offering a quick curtsy to the shadowy man.

"Mhmmm, and why are you in THIS place?" he asked, his words slow and deliberate.

"We came in yesterday soaked from the storm and were seeking shelter," Roshin answered nervously, "This place looked to be an inn so we thought we might get a bed for the night and see ourselves dry."

The shadowy figure did not respond, he just stood there looming over the space, Roshin continued more nervous now, "But the building was empty, so we decided to stay, as we were loath to go back out in the weather searching for someone who could offer us some space."

"So, you just made yourself at home?" The man finally observed.

Ashlyn broke in, "We had expected to pay, and we have coin for the owner of the building. It was not our wish to just squat here, only the weather was just so bad."

"Indeed, it was. Mayhaps you can give me a copper apiece and I will forget the transgression." The man said simply, crossing his arms.

Ashlyn turned on her heel and quickly moved over to her bag. She fished out a couple coppers and then scurried over to the man to place them in his palm. With that he pulled off the hood of his woolen cloak and smiled broadly, "Well with that out of the way, welcome to Drochit, I am Fingal the mayor of the town."

The man had a commanding presence. His eyes were sharp and grey, with pronounced crow's feet that spoke to his years. He had a weathered but cleanly shaven face. His hair was also grey like his eyes and closely cropped like that of a military commander. Even his eyebrows looked to be trimmed.

Roshin thought that even despite his clear age, he looked quite intimidating. "Stay far from his bad side," she thought. The man stood tall and straight-backed before them. His arms and chest looked strong and tight. He studied them as they studied him.

"So, what brings you to our town, aside from the storms?" He asked them.

Ashlyn was first to respond, "We are healers that are passing through to offer our services to those in need."

"Healers you say?" he inquired scratching his chin. As it happens, I have a use for just such a trade." He stepped back and moved toward the door, "I suppose then you are thinking to stay some time here to offer your services?"

"That would be our plan, yes," Rosin answered.

"Good, we can use your skills." He paused as if combing his memory for a nugget from the past. "I think it has been a year since we last saw a healer here."

Roshin eagerly piped in, "It was last spring! And that was us! Well, we had another in our party who we have since parted ways with, but it was still us."

"So it was! Well in any case I can see you better accommodated than the floor of this old place," He opened the door and waved for them to follow him.

"Collect your things. I will take you to accommodations where you can stay, and then see about getting you work."

"That would be most agreeable, thank you," Ashlyn chirped. And with that the women hastily packed their bag to follow Fingal out into the rain. He took them to a small furnished cottage near the edge of the town.

It was not much to look at, as far as spaces go. It was small and the wood that made up it was grey and weathered. All the same the dirt floor was only damp, and it had a hearth, a table, and some blankets in the corner.

Fingal bid them a farewell for a time letting them know he would be back. The girls went in and latched the door from inside, remembering their intrusion in Veyah.

Once they felt secure, they worked to build a fire in the hearth again. "We have a kettle!" Ashlyn announced joyfully, and so they heated up some water and made a warming tea. It continued to rain so the girls decided to hold up inside and await a knock on the door before venturing out again.

The knock came somewhere around an hour later. It was Fingal, but he had brought another with him. Under a wool blanket hunched a shriveled old woman with a large lump on her neck, "Oh my" Roshin exclaimed.

"This is my mother, Nuala," Fingal explained. "She developed this mass, and it has only gotten larger. As it grows, she seems to be getting more tired and weak."

"I see," Roshin said, a look of concern on her face, "Come on in," she invited, stepping aside to let the pair enter. She closed the door to keep out the rain and then turned to get a better look at the old woman. She was a small woman, quite thin, and she stood hunched over. Her skin was pale and splotchy like the hermit's had been.

Roshin reached out a hand toward the mass, "May I?"

Fingal nodded. The old woman stood still as stone. Roshin reached out and palpated the mass, it felt cool and spongey. The old woman burbled and squinted her eyes. Roshin closed her own in thought. Ashlyn came over with a cup of tea and offered it to the woman as Roshin stepped back.

Roshin looked back to Fingal, "Do you have much salt here in town?" she inquired.

Fingal scratched his chin. "Not much," he said in a huff.

"Hmm." Roshin said in consideration, "She has a large goiter. To see this resolve, she will need her foods well salted, ideally with a salt from the brine mines in the south. It should have a rich golden color, as the gold is what will treat this condition."

Fingal looked up for a minute as if searching his mind for a cache of salt. He scowled in concern so Roshin continued, "We do have some, but she will likely need to take it for a few weeks to see this reduced in size. We won't have enough. I might suggest you seek a trader or send someone south to get a sack for your village, it's likely the others here don't have enough as well."

The man drew in a deep breath, "Well then, a task you have given me. If you can spare some for now, I can see what I can do in the meantime to try and get more. Not many traders pass this way anymore," Fingal's tone seemed to indicate some degree of defeat.

"If you get me a little pouch or something I can pour into, I will give you some salt." She will feel better after a few days regardless." Roshin stated.

The old woman let out a huff and a gurgle, and Fingal told them he would be back. He escorted his mother out the door and into the rain. "No salt in a village of fishermen. That does not bode well for their winter," Roshin said quietly.

"If he takes your advice and sends someone out, we may have saved them much misery," Ashlyn noted trying to stay positive.

"Assuming they can get it," Roshin finished for her a bit darkly.

28

Apostates

The women had been in the town for nearly two weeks. The work had been draining. The villagers all seemed to be suffering from some degree of malnutrition, of one type or another. Fingal had nobody to send to the south for salt, and aside from fish, there was not much available to eat.

The people in the town, however, seemed to be in denial. They would come to the girls and insist on whatever remedy they could offer, be it herb or tincture, but they refused to acknowledge or even face that the root of their problems was simply not having enough to eat. The girls themselves were starting to feel it, though they did go out to forage to supplement their paltry ration of fish.

The farms around them had collapsed, and no one was growing grains or raising any livestock anymore. The people had been pushed to source their food only from the lake, and as good as the fish might be, they were just not enough to balance out the needs of the people.

In response to this, Ashlyn and Roshin had tried to take a less direct approach. They had gotten a few women interested in the idea of being able to source their own remedies, so they made a plan to take them out into the fields and scrublands to source edible plants and berries.

While the girls' goal was to broaden the villagers' diets, and to improve their nutritional options, they sold the excursion as a chance to learn some preventive medicines. Roshin did not quite understand why she had to play this strange game to get them to go along with it, but she decided that, if nothing else, it was an opportunity to have more private time with some of the women.

"Maybe away from the village they will be able to handle more honesty," she hoped as she prepared herself to head out for the day.

Ashlyn turned to her before they went to out the door, "We have been here so long it feels, but I am not confident we are any closer to telling them about that with which we have come to share."

Roshin nodded, "I am feeling that as well. We need to be careful, but I am willing to try and open a door or two today and see where it gets us."

"Let's hope it doesn't get those doors slammed in our face," Ashlyn grumbled under her breath.

The girls met the women from the village outside, near to their cottage. Three women were joining them. There was Isa, the wife of one of the old fisherman, Bree, who was her daughter, and Mayve who lived alone on the other side of the village.

The women were all much older than them, and they looked it. Their puffy dresses and covered heads made their pale and gaunt faces stand out. "Let's hope this can help them," Roshin said as a prayer.

"Alright, let us be off," Ashlyn announced in a sing song voice before heading out into the field away from the town. They did not walk too far before stopping. "Ooh! Here we have some plantain. This one can fight off fatigue if you cook it up with your fish. It is also good in stews as well. And here we have some purslane..."

They picked the weeds and then sent the women off to find some of their own. When they returned with fists full of plants Roshin was quick to praise them, "Wonderful! Let's take a look and see what we have." She sorted plants and removed a few that were not edible.

Bree spoke up, "This is fine but what about a plant to treat my headache? And my mother's stiffness?"

Roshin's face dropped. This was, for sure, not going to be easy. She attempted to explain to them that the plants they were picking when incorporated into their diet would help with those things, but the women were having none of it.

"I thought we were here to source medicines, not greens for a salad!" Mayve barked with some force.

Roshin jumped back in to try and explain, "These plants can be medicines, your problems are just that you need to eat more than just fish."

She would have kept talking but Bree cut her off, "We have survived on fish in our village for as long as I can remember, we don't need this," she said tossing her fist full of the greens onto the ground.

Roshin tried desperately to save the outing, "Fish are wonderful, but we are designed by our creator to eat a variety of things-"

"Creator? What creator?" Mayve scoffed.

It was an opportunity, even if not ideal, and Ashlyn was eager to take it. She jumped in with youthful naivety, "Hulen Ahir teaches us that we are to eat of the land, forests, and seas."

She got no further as Isa, the matriarch of the group, swiftly jumped in, "We will not hear of your heresy here. You best mind your mouth. The empire itself is what we must elevate, fantasies of gods only steal devotion from the cause that is right in front of us."

Ashlyn seemed surprised at the pushback and before Roshin could stop her, she blurted out, "But it is not a fantasy, there is today a prophet of Hulen Ahir in the land, here to restore the light!" As if realizing her folly, she quickly clamped her mouth and diverted her eyes.

Roshin took in a breath and searched the faces of the women around her. Isa looked as though steam would soon come out her ears, "You are behaving as apostates, and you need to shut your mouth!" she excoriated.

Ashlyn seemed to shrink down low into herself. She had made an error of pride and did not attend well to her audience. "We are done here," the old woman's words were sharp, and she turned and walked back to the village.

The other two followed her sending a few glowering looks back there way before stomping off after the old woman. Roshin went over to her friend and wrapped her arms around her in a comforting hug. It was a mistake, but we can move forward," she said. She gave the girl's shoulders a squeeze before bending down to retrieve the plants that had been cast aside.

They then walked slowly back to the village, "We will get back, and never mind them, they are just a few women, and they are not the whole town," she said in an attempt to bolster Ashlyn's confidence.

When they got back, however, they realized that the situation might have been worse than what they had thought. Isa, Bree, and Mayve, had gone around and gathered some other elders, and they were all waiting for them beside their cottage, including Fingal.

Their faces looked grim as they stood with arms crossed before them. "We understand that you have spoken out against the Empire," Fingal stated in a mater-of-fact way.

"Against the Empire? We simply meant-" Ashlyn began to talk, trying to muster a defense, but Roshin firmly bumped her arm and stopped her before she could say anymore.

"I am sorry, we are just unclear about the accusation," Roshin finished for her calmly.

"It has come to our attention that you have been passing false teachings and myths," Fingal explained, "I would be loath to believe it, but I have passed by and heard what sounded like payers and chants from inside your cottage when I have dropped off your meals."

The mayor looked hard at them as if awaiting an explanation, when one was not forthcoming, he continued, "I fear you might be spreading false teachings that go against the Empire and its order."

The girls just stood there, as if frozen into a block of ice, *"They heard our prayers?"* Roshin's thoughts were incredulous.

"It's true," Mayve began, "They were talking of a prophet who has come against the Empire."

"We did not say that! We never said anything against the empire!" Ashlyn objected in frustration, as she shook her fists out in front of her.

Isa broke in chastising the girls, "You have been trying to sow seeds of doubt in this village for the entire two weeks you have been here. You have not acted as proper healers; you are just trying to convince us that we are wanting."

The accusation hit Roshin like a falling boulder, and she could bite her tongue no more, "But you are wanting!" she shouted in disbelief, "You are all suffering from ailments of malnutrition, you have no salt, no grains, or beans, or milk. All you have is fish and not even much of that!"

With that Fingal drew his sword and Roshin felt herself go cold. "Get your things and get out, or we will see to it that you are seized and taken to the road to be handed off as prisoners to the next group of soldiers that passes through." His words were as sharp as his blade which he pointed straight at the girl's chest.

She gasped and then scrambled back with Ashlyn through the door of the cottage. In a haphazard rush they stuffed their bags with whatever they could easily grab. They knew they had left things behind, including the barrow, but when they emerged there were more swords draw, and it was all Roshin could do to keep her heart from leaping out of her chest.

The girls ran out of the town away from the men and along the river. They ran as long as they could manage before finally, they could no longer run. They both found themselves doubled over with what felt like a dagger in their sides, gasping for breath.

"*How did that just happen?*" Roshin's head whirled around trying to figure out how things had gone so wrong, so fast. She thought back to Awin's burned out cabin, "*Was this the kind of trouble you found?*" she cast her question up to the sky. And then turned back to Ashlyn, "It looks like we are on to the next place then?" and she tried to crack her fear with a weak smile.

29

The Story of Soldiers

For five days, the women had been traveling on foot along the banks of various bodies of water. They were currently following Lake Bahle, which had turned south the evening before. They were now on the lookout for the road.

The South Trade Road ran alongside the lake for a bit before cutting back out into the country. They were hoping to find it and then head north toward the town of Brenna. They had chosen to continue to follow the lake in the wrong direction for the practicality of needing food and water.

It seemed easier to walk a bit out of the way, rather than having to push through the barren fields of the countries interior any longer than necessary. Fortunately, they found the road soon enough and turned toward the north.

As they were walking, they could see up ahead the shape of what looked to be mounted men and wagons. These were either soldiers or slavers; either way, the women opted to find a place to hunker down off the road. They settled behind some gnarly looking bushes with mean thorns and waited as the wagons went by.

They were soldiers, and Roshin felt her body relax a bit. It surprised her because she had not realized she had been so tense. The horses seemed nervous, and the men were also chattering, "Why won't it just leave us be?" Roshin heard one man ask.

"I think it's doing... it's doing it to get inside our heads. Maybe it prefers its meals tainted with fear," another man replied.

The horse snorted, and Roshin looked at Ashlyn with a curious expression. The soldiers seemed as though they had seen something, and Roshin's interest was piqued. They waited awhile longer until the wagons were well out of the way to get up.

"Did you hear that?" Roshin asked Ashlyn, her excitement bubbling over.

Ashlyn met her eyes, "I did, it sounds as though they saw something that has them on edge."

"We should follow them!" Roshin proposed excitedly and she started to move in the direction of the men.

Ashlyn hung back, her voice uncertain, "But they are heading south?"

"Yes, but I want to know what they saw," Roshin said. She did not seem to notice Ashlyn's reticence at the idea and left the bushes behind, making her way back onto the road. Ashlyn finally found her feet free and trotted after her.

The two broke out into a jog heading back south down the road. They trotted after the cart Roshin leading the way. It was still in their view and soon they started to close the distance. By the time they caught it they were well winded and panting.

One of the men noticed the women coming up behind them and announced to his companions, "Followers."

Both horses and carts ceased moving. There were six men mounted, and two ox carts with drivers, making eight men in all. The cargo appeared to be nothing but sacks and barrels. The men seemed to range in age, from older boys close in age to Ashlyn, all the way to seasoned men in their thirties

The mounted men all turned their horses to see who was coming to meet them. Roshin felt their stares as she timidly made her approach. "They look right young and pretty too," a plain-faced man with golden hair announced with a smile.

Roshin drew her own smile across her face, "Excuse me sirs, we came off the trail from Lake Bahle and caught sight of your carts. We wondered if we might be of any service to you?"

A dark-haired man with a large nose broke out in a laugh, "I can think of some services that would suit." The men around him began to laugh as well.

Roshin ignored the comment and offered a clarification, "We are trained in the healing arts. We can address any injury or ailment if you might be willing to exchange such a thing for a bite of bread?" She knew asking after food would seem normal to them and would not raise any hackles.

One of the wagon drivers shouted out, "I got a blister on me ass, you want to look at that?" again the men laughed.

"Cut it out," the stern reply came from one of the mounted men, who Roshin took to be the captain. He was a tall man with a helmet in his hand who looked to be in his thirties, he had crisp blue eyes, wavy chestnut hair, and a lean yet muscular body.

"I don't know that we need a healer's hand, but if you care to follow and cook for us tonight, we can spot you a bowl of something," he said, offering her a sly smile.

Roshin eagerly agreed, "Aye, we can do that!"

"Perfect," he said to Roshin before barking at his men, "Now all you lollygaggers get going, we still have miles to cover today." With that the men turned and continued down the trail with Roshin and Ashlyn following at a brisk pace.

They walked in near silence for what felt like hours before the company of men finally stopped. "Camp here tonight," the captain announced, and the men quickly moved off the road and went about their chores tending to their horses.

Roshin felt a nervous tension in her gut as she caught sight of the men shooting her glances, "It feels like I have just stepped into a pit of poisonous snakes," she thought to herself.

The captain came over and pointed to one of the carts, "Supplies are in there. You build us a fire and cook; there should be a sack of beans open."

Roshin nodded and she grabbed Ashlyn's hand and drug her over to the cart. The girl had not said a word since they had joined up with the company. She handed her the flint and steel from around her neck, "Can you start a fire, I will fill the pot."

Ashlyn nodded without a word, took the necklace, and went about setting up the cookfire. Roshin scooped beans into a large pot and covered them with water from one of the barrels before meeting back up with Ashlyn by the fire.

They worked together to prepare the meal, pulling out salt and herbs from their bags to improve the fare. Once they were done, they ladled the beans into bowls, which they handed out to the men. Roshin found herself holding her breath.

The first man took a bite and whooped, "Well I'll be! Lasses can cook! Turned stale beans into a feast fit for an officer."

"Grab yourselves a bowl and come sit with us." The captain said with a grin. Again, Roshin felt her nerves prick. She knew the role that most camp followers played. She glanced over to Ashlyn who looked as though she had just seen a ghost.

"*She is so uncomfortable,*" Roshin thought with a feeling of dismay. She took the girl's hand and gave it a squeeze, "I am with you," she whispered before walking over to the fire. They both sat down amongst the men.

"Have you seen any trouble on the road?" she asked, trying to keep her tone inquisitive and a bit flirty. The men responded to this immediately.

"Just a big blue monster hunting us from above!" the golden-haired soldier announced.

"Monster?" Roshin probed curiously.

"Aye, every day for the last month it seems we have seen a dragon fly overhead. We had just seen it again shortly before you showed up." One of the older cart drivers explained.

"Really? A dragon? I thought those were just stories told to scare children." Roshin asked feigning disbelief.

"A dragon, and a big one at that." The golden-haired man introjected, "It just flies over our heads does a circle like it is checking us out and then flies off again. Been that way every day since we left the camp."

Roshin brought her hands to her cheeks as if shocked by their story, "You must be so brave to keep a level head on you after that."

"Brave or plain stupid," laughed the man with the large nose.

The men chattered more about the dragon and Roshin did her best to demonstrate an interest in their ideas on how they might take down the beast. The sun had set and the golden-haired man called over to Roshin, "Why not come over here and have a sit down on my lap?" He patted his thighs with a dumb grin on his face.

She felt her face flush before Ashlyn came up behind her and ducked down to whisper in her ear, "Might we step away for a minute?" Roshin turned her face to meet Ashlyn's eyes and offer a nod. The girl looked white as snow. her mouth drawn tight in a nervous line.

Roshin stood and followed her a few paces back away from the fire, Ashlyn turned to her, taking her hands and leaning over to whisper again in her ear, "We should get out of here, there is nothing good that will come from our staying."

Roshin pulled back and shook her head, "But the dragon! If we follow them tomorrow, we are likely to see it too!" Roshin's words were quiet but excited.

"We might see it tomorrow, but at what cost tonight? These men... If we stay... I fear what we will be pushed into." Ashlyn's voice had a quiver and Roshin saw tears pooling in the corner of her eyes as her body shook like a leaf.

Roshin looked at her a long while, she studied her face drawn with fear and shame. She was scared, and Roshin had chosen not to see it earlier. She looked down in her own shame, "I am sorry, I was only thinking of the dragon."

She looked back over to the fire, a man waved to beckon them back, a wide smile across his face. She felt herself shudder, "*Ashlyn's right, this is too risky. It is not worth it, and we might still be able to follow them even if we don't go back,*" she thought.

"I will fix this," Roshin said, before turning and walking back to the fire. She found the captain and made her approach directly to him. She caught his eyes, gave him a coy smile, and with the softest tone she could manage she explained to him, "My friend is feeling ill, it seems the food has not settled well, we would wish to follow you again tomorrow, but we wish a pardon so that we might take our leave tonight."

The captain seemed adequately charmed, He nodded and said back to her "Some things are worth a wait," and he then took her hand and kissed it gently before she shyly pulled it back and walked off.

The men made their disappointment known, "Always getting cold feet when it counts!" one man shouted out.

The large nosed man shot back, "Naw, they Just couldn't decide which buck to pick,"

"Or they were too scared or your ugly mug!" the golden-haired man shot back with a roar of laughter.

"It was the threat of your lap that chased her off!" the large nosed man retorted.

The captain barked out sharply, "Shut your mouths and get yourselves in order!" The men fell silent after that, and Roshin shuddered as she met up with Ashlyn. Together they walked some way away from the soldiers' camp. The girl was still shaking.

They stopped and laid out their bedrolls beside each other near the edge of the road. Roshin turned to Ashlyn, "Again I am sorry."

Ashlyn managed a small smile, "Maybe tomorrow we will see the dragon, but can you promise me we will be away from them afterwards?"

Roshin bobbed her head in agreement, "We will leave right after." With that the women settled down next to each other, looking up at the light of the nearly full moon.

30

The Dragon

The next morning came without incident. Roshin woke early before dawn, her nervousness at the possibility of being left behind by the soldiers prevented her from settling and sleeping any longer. The sky was just starting to lighten, but it was not yet dawn.

She climbed out of her bedroll and walked toward the men's camp. It was still there, they were all still sleeping, save for the man pulling the guard shift. He did not see her, and she slinked back to her place beside Ashlyn to wait for the sunrise.

"We may see him today," was about the only thought that seemed to fill her head. She wondered if she would be able to make out the rider, or just the dragon. Either way, she could barely contain her excitement.

The dawn light finally broke, and the men in the soldiers' camp started to stir. They went about packing their bags and saddling their horses. The cart drivers yoked their oxen and prepared to go.

Roshin shook Ashlyn gently by the shoulder. "They are getting ready to go," she whispered. Ashlyn too stirred. Climbing out from under her cover, she moved to squat beside her bedroll and then rolled it up and packed it away.

"I am ready," she said in a whisper. Roshin smiled wide at her.

Before they rejoined the men, they went about fixing their veils and adjusting their skirts. They wanted to ensure they were ready for a long day of walking. Fortunately, it did not take them long to get ready and they were packed up and down the road well before the men were set to leave.

As they arrived at what remained of the camp, the men took notice, "Well, well, well, I wasn't sure they would be back," the big nosed man commented.

His golden-haired friend patted him on the back, "Looks like they didn't run off in fear after all."

One of the younger boys walked by and dryly observed, "They may later, once the dragon flies over."

Roshin found her heart rate quicken at the mention of the dragon. Ashlyn still stayed quiet as a mouse. The captain wandered over. He was buckling on his sword belt, and he regarded Roshin with a heated glance that made her palms sweat and her stomach flutter.

To her, he was an enigma. He had the formal mannerisms that told her he was likely a man who came from nobility, and he was impossibly handsome. At the same time, he scared her. His face was hard to read, as were his intentions.

It was clear he found her of interest, but she feared he might be the kind of man to take what he likes. She took a deep breath. "*We are only here to see the dragon,*" she reminded herself, as she smiled back and offered a slight curtsy.

The men scrambled around for a little while longer before they all mounted up and started off down the road. The captain rode over, "If you would like my lady, you could ride behind me, you would just need to hold on tight," his words were slow and inviting.

Roshin swallowed and then looked over to Ashlyn, who wore an expression like that of a frightened deer. "I would rather walk beside my friend," she croaked in barely more than a whisper.

"As you wish, my offer will stand should your feet grow weary." He gave her another sly smile, "I have no doubt that there will be a man here happy to ride with your friend as well."

Roshin sent back a nervous smile and gave him a nod.
When he turned back, she took Ashlyn's hand and gave
it a squeeze, "Hopefully it will not be too long on this
trail."

The walk was long, and they had to do it under a blazing
hot sun. The land along the road here was open, bare,
and dry, with only a few hardy weeds making a go at
surviving. Lake Bahle with its cool breeze was far off in
the distance.

She felt herself growing parched and tired; she looked
longingly at the men and their mounts, or even the cart.
"*I could ride,*" she thought, tempted by the captain's
offer. She shook off the thought after one look at Ashlyn,
and instead kept putting one foot in front of the
other. "For the dragon," she repeated to herself.

It was past midday and there was still no sign of any
dragon. Roshin was starting to feel a bit discouraged,
but more so thirsty. Her waterskin was now dry, and
her thoughts turned to the barrel in the cart filled with
water. "*Might they stop soon to drink?*" she wondered,
but they did not stop.

The men had more than one skin strapped on their
saddle, so to them the walk was not so grueling. She
again looked at the back of the captain's horse. "No,
keep walking," she encouraged herself.

She looked over at Ashlyn, who, like her, seemed hot
and parched. The girl's feet were marching forward as
her head hung low. It was well into the afternoon, and

they were still walking. There was no dragon. The men would be setting camp soon, and she had no idea how they might slip away at this point.

The men had also noticed the dragon's absence. "Where do you think it is?" the golden-haired man asked as he nervously scanned the sky.

"I don't know, it's never come this late," replied one of the ox cart drivers.

They moved on down the road as the sun began to sink. Roshin felt her heart drop, "*It's not coming,*" she thought in dismay. The carts bumped along as the air finally began to cool. Ahead of them was a small inland lake that butted up against the road.

"Camp here tonight," The captain shouted. Roshin turned to Ashlyn to see that her face too was drawn in disappointment, but also fear.

"*We need to find a way to duck out of here before they get settled,*" she thought as she scanned the landscape. There was much more greenery along the lake. She noticed a dense stand of bullrushes just off the road beside the water.

She turned to Ashlyn, "We could say we want to go off to harvest some roots to add to the pot, it might allow us enough cover to slip away."

Ashlyn looked over to the cattails and then back over to the men who were now working to setup their camp on the gravely beach between the water and the road. She nodded her approval at the plan. Roshin gathered her nerve and began to move over to the captain, when suddenly one of the men let out a whoop of surprise.

All around her, the heads of the men shot up. Several horses snorted and kicked at their riders, who had been trying to fasten their hobbles, before shooting off half-bound away from their handlers. Roshin turned and looked up.

"Ashlyn!" she cried out pointing up to the sky. It was flying in from the north, the sunlight streaming in from the west struck it and its scales, which shined like jewels. As it flew overhead, she could see better that the beast was much like her dream, turquoise in color, though in the yellow light of the fading day it almost looked green.

It was not colossal in size but still terrifying as it swooped low toward them. Its wings were fixed, and it soared around in a circle like a hawk. "Just like the men said," she whispered. Roshin thought it seemed to be trying purposely to intimidate the men. "*Whoever the rider it is, I wager to bet he does not much like the soldiers,*" she thought, as she stared at it in rapture.

The camp had spun off into chaos as men ran about trying to catch the spooked animals, Roshin snapped back to reality and looked around for Ashlyn. She grabbed her hand, "Lets run, now!" she called, and together they ran up the road to the north, as the men scampered to catch horses that had run off to the south away from the dragon.

Again, the pair ran until they could not anymore. When they looked behind them, the camp was off in the distance. This had not exactly turned out well as they still had no water. "We should keep going, it will be a full moon tonight, and if we keep walking, we might make it back near Lake Bahle sometime tomorrow.

This is exactly what they did. They walked long into the night. The moon was so bright the path ahead was easy to follow. They had no idea how long they were walking, but it became clear that soon they would need to stop.

A sound from above caught their attention. It was a rumbling wail. There was a trill of sadness in it. It was loud and almost other worldly. They looked back to see what it might be. A faint silhouette caught their eye in the night sky.

It looked like shining silver in the moonlight. "The dragon," Ashlyn whispered. Roshin had no words and again watched it. This time it was flying away, fast, to the north. It had a wave in its flight and seemed to be swinging a bit shoulder to shoulder.

It let out another mournful cry. "Something seems wrong with it," Ashlyn observed.

"It does seem somewhat distressed," Roshin found her pulse quickening. In her mind she worked to reassure herself, "Surely it is fine. He is fine."

31

A Smugglers Town

It had been five days since the women had seen the dragon. They continued moving north along the South Trade Road. They had made it past Lake Bahle and into the open landscape before having to ford across a river, reminiscent of their crossing of the Trout Run. Thankfully this river was shallower than that.

There was a new vigor in their mission. It was real, they had seen it, and while they had not seen the rider, it was not much more to believe that he too was real. They had spent much of their journey chattering about it.

It had been the nature of its sorrowful lamentations that night in the moonlit sky that had been of their primary interest. It had been tough to sleep with the excitement of it all. They walked instead, longer than they would have imagined they could.

Dawn had broken on this day, and the women joined hands facing the eastern sky and sang out a prayer:

> "The sun rises. May it bathe the land with its warmth and hope
> Hulen Ahir, we thank you for your gift sent on dragon's wings.
> For the one foretold has come to end the shroud of darkness.
> Guide us through the shadows and into your righteousness.
> Let your fire burn bright within us as we spread your message of hope."

And with that they set out again down the road toward the town of Brenna. They had reached another river crossing. This one had an old bridge. They lingered near it awhile watching the large river flow underneath it.

"This might be a good spot to fish," Roshin observed as she leaned out over the stone sides and peered down into the flowing water below.

Ashlyn tentatively stepped out onto the deck of the bridge. Her foot seemed to sink into the soft wood, and she leapt forward and jogged over the rest of the way. "I rather not stand on that any longer than I need to," she said gesturing back to the bridge. "How do they get Oxen and carts across that."

Roshin laughed. "The carts likely run over the stone arches, but you're right that this bridge could use some attention," she said as she picked at a flaked piece of stone under her arm.

"Do you know what river this is?" Ashlyn asked.

"I do not," she replied.

"Hopefully it is near Brenna, I would like to be done walking for a time." The girl had been holding up well, considering her situation. Her sickness had passed, and her energy and mood had been good for a while.

Roshin had noticed when they went to wash up that her stomach had, in fact, begun to swell. *The baby is growing well it seems,*" she thought to herself. They continued down the road.

At one point Ashlyn paused and with an "Oh!" she stopped and waited with her hand on her stomach. She turned and looked over to Roshin, her eyes wide and excited, "I think I felt it move."

Roshin beamed back at her, "Really?"

Ashlyn bobbed her head, "Yes, it's like a flutter, not much, but it feels distinctly unusual."

"Then it's getting right big! Soon it will be kicking you all day and you'll wonder when it will stop." She gave Ashlyn a gentle shove and they both laughed a minute, enjoying the moment.

As they continued on their way, talk turned to Brenna. "I hope they offer a place to sleep with a mattress," Ashlyn's tone betrayed her longing, "and I hope the people are not as tight lipped as at Drochit," she continued

"It will be nothing like Drochit; Brenna is a smuggler's town. We just need to be mindful of that and watch our backs, lest we get grabbed and taken south again." Roshin shuddered at the thought. "Either way we will not have to be as careful with our message. These people are no empire loyalists."

This seemed to please Ashlyn, "And we have seen it now with our own eyes, so that has to add power to our words."

"Indeed, we are no longer speaking of secondhand accounts," Roshin said with a nod.

They had spent these days on the road cultivating their message. This morning was no different. They had no sacred texts to reference, so they simply recounted the stories they had committed to memory. Roshin started:

"And so, he came down from on high, on the back of the dragon. The whispers of Hulen Ahir in his ears. He had come down to guide and direct those that would boldly follow. Set to vanquish the enemies that were turned toward the darkness."

With Ashlyn taking the next verse:

"As the rider landed among the people, he spoke unto them, saying 'I have been sent as was prophesied, to restore the light and stand against the shadows.' Then all who heard him knew hope again, for the promised one had arrived."

They went on like this for a few hours, deep in their memories of the sacred lore. They found such comfort in it, which was good for the world around them bled from the darkness. Soon the rutty road grew sandy. They could see tracks cut into the loose ground where carts had passed.

Hills rose and fell before them, and as they reached the top of one such rise, the town came into view. It was not yet midday. "Brenna?" Ashlyn asked Roshin, excitement in her words.

"Brenna," Roshin confirmed. It was all they could do not to trot off toward it, but they did not wish to expend such energy, as it would not shorten the trip by much, all things considered. So, they picked up their pace and walked briskly on toward the town set up beside Lake Bron.

The women entered it from the eastern roadside. They looked around. The edge of Brenna was ringed with shabby wooden huts, their windows missing panes. The street was dusty and covered with the manure of oxen and horses. They passed an old livery in which they saw at least half a dozen skinny rouncies. It was an unusual sight as they had not seen a town with a functional stable since Vargah.

The air between the buildings stank of dead fish. "It's like I am home," Roshin thought to herself with a chuckle. As they made their way toward the large stone inn near the center of the town the smell shifted, "and now is smells like a drunkards piss." Roshin crinkled her nose in disgust.

They looked around. The inn itself seemed solid as the stone walls were good for weathering the years, but the door was grey, and its shutters were not all straight. It seemed quiet this morning, but Roshin could imagine by evening this part of the town was likely to be lively.

Beside the inn was an old market square. The square had a public well and there were a few worn-looking stalls. In one of them she caught sight of an elderly bald man leaning over the counter, "*Well they have SOME kind of commerce here,*" she thought to herself.

She tugged on Ashlyn's sleeve and pointed over to the man, "He might know who to talk to about accommodations and work."

Ashlyn nodded and the pair walked over to the old man. He looked to be dozing, "Excuse us sir," Roshin asked in a bright and cheery tone, the man did not stir, she looked nervously over to Ashlyn as the thought of him actually being dead passed through her mind.

Ashlyn reached out a hand and shook his boney shoulder repeating "Excuse us, Sir? Sir?" She got louder with each repetition of the word. Finally with a snort the man stood up and blinked at them.

"Gah, yes, yes, sorry how can I help you?" The old man grumbled.

"Do you know if this town has a lord, or mayor, or leader of some kind we might speak with?"

"Ah, Ah... well," The man stuttered and considered. "Best to go in and speak with the inn keep, He's like to be the closest thing to something like that here." And with that the women smiled at him gave a slight curtsy and turned to make their way to the door of the inn.

As they reached the entrance, Roshin rolled back her shoulders and took a deep breath before pulling it open.

The room on the other side was a dimly lit tavern. There were wood tables and benches all around. Two men leaned against a wall in one corner each holding a mug, and they leered at the girls as they walked by.

Near the far side of the room was a long stone counter, beside it a dark stairwell. The place smelt of cider with an undertone of vomit, and Roshin could not help but think how unappealing it seemed to her. "*May Hulen Ahir consider the souls of the poor drinker.*" She prayed silently.

Ashlyn tucked in close to her and they walked in sync toward the counter. They stood before it for what felt like a long time, just looking around. They observed a large stone hearth in the center of the room, they observed the cobwebs hanging from the ceiling.

Everything was stone or wood, or both. There was a lingering scent of pipe smoke near the counter. Finally, after what seemed like an eternity a broad chested fat man came down the stairs and spotted them.

He looked to be a stern man with pitch-black hair. He had hard dark eyes and a wild looking black beard, "Something tells me you're not here to drink," he grumbled as he crossed his arms against his chest.

Roshin felt nervous and spent a second searching for her words, "Aye, sir. The merchant outside told us we might speak to the inn keep," she fumbled a bit as his stare bore down into her. "You see we are traveling healers, and we typically stay in towns and offer services to the residence in exchange for food and lodging," she finished in a rush.

The inn keep jumped in, "So why are you speaking to me?" His tone felt cold as ice.

"Well…. we had asked after a lord or mayor, and the old man outside said you might be the closest thing to that," Roshin wished she might shrink down into the floor. Ashlyn was holding her arm and standing behind her clearly also nervous.

The inn keep erupted into a roar of laughter, "And how about that, boys!?" he thundered out to the men in the corner, "I'm now the mayor of Brenna! I think I might order you all to get another round!" He slapped his stomach as he laughed.

Once he calmed a bit he turned back to Roshin, "Look, girly, there is no mayor here, and there would be no one to make such an arrangement with." He pointed to a pouch on his waist belt, "My inn costs coin if you have it, I don't need no healer."

A smile broke out across his face, "I am likely to find you a few patients come nightfall; just get these men enough drink and they are bound to break a nose or poke a hole into someone. Maybe they would pay you for your work and you can buy a room."

"I see," Roshin gave the man a thin smile.

"Sorry, lass, there is a place for women across the lane. Maybe you might have better luck there trading work for board," he said, pointing out toward the door. "Just look for the red sign."

And with that the women scurried out of the inn. As they hit the light of the street, they began to look around, Roshin saw the red sign, but her chest sank at the shape. It was a place for women alright, "It's a brothel," she stated grimly.

"Well, we might still be able to get a room," Ashlyn tried to be optimistic, but her face looked concerned.

"I am not sure this is what we want, but I suppose these women need hope just as much as any," and so together they walked over to the door and knocked.

32

The Faith of Women

Roshin ran a thick wooden comb through the ends of her long auburn hair. She teased out the tangles, starting near the bottom and then working her way up toward her scalp until she could run her fingers through it all.

From there, she collected it up to the side and began to fold it into a long and thick braid, which she tied off with a fat section of yarn. Once her hair had been bound, she pulled on her snood, attached her veil, and then looked around her room.

It was a small space with threadbare curtains and a broken window. A rag had been stuffed into the missing pane to keep the evening chill at bay. Roshin went ahead and pulled it out to let in the breeze from the street.

She looked at Ashlyn, who was still lying asleep on her small cot, wrapped in a moth-eaten wool blanket. She did not wish to begrudge her friend more time to sleep. They had had a long and late night, and she no doubt deserved the rest.

Roshin squeezed past her and slipped out the door, cringing as it squeaked on its hinges when she pulled it closed. She crept down the hall toward the stairs and peered into the open doors of a few of the other rooms to find them empty save for the blankets and cots.

Down the narrow staircase she went, until she reached the ground floor by the front entryway. She looked out the window at the bottom of the stairs and saw the sign hanging. The painted red shape of a woman's body.

They had knocked on the brothel door ten days earlier, uncertain as to what they were walking into. They were greeted by a number of bubbly young women eager to learn more about them.

At first Roshin had been afraid to walk through the door, but now part of her feared leaving more. She entered the common area, an open room with a hearth and a couple wooden tables with long wooden benches.

"Good morning!" came the bright chirp of Clohda, a slightly built blonde haired girl with a wide mouth and bright smile.

Roshin smiled back. "Blessings on this bright morning."

"I've got a kettle hanging with tea," Clohda announced, "Can I pour you some? I even added the sweet leaf you gave me."

Roshin smiled back gently, "That would be lovely." Clohda had been the first girl they had met, she was young, close in age to Ashlyn and nearly as gentle.

"So, broken nose, rib, or black eye last night?" another voice inquired.

Roshin turned to see Orla standing behind her with a covered basket in her hand, "None! But we did have to stitch up a gash from a sword," Roshin said with a giggle.

Orla waddled over, her belly bulging out before her. She awkwardly tried to slip past Roshin to set down her bundle but ended up knocking her stomach into the table and grunting. "You would think those men would put more value on their flesh than they do," she said, rubbing the spot she had knocked.

A third woman laughed, "You don't understand the value of a fine scar!" It was Fiah, a dark-haired woman in her mid-twenties.

Orla laughed and she attempted to sit down, legs wide apart on the bench. "From beating back the guard sure, but a crooked nose from a tavern brawl is not exactly what I call appealing," she objected.

Fiah smiled, "That's why they will never tell you the truth of it!" Fiah looked over to Roshin. "What do you say? Ever ask a man about his scars and have him tell it true?" She did not wait for an answer, "There is always more valor recounted than likely earned."

Clohda hummed and turned to Roshin, "I bet your rider has some scars!" Her voice was eager and excited.

"Yeah, but they are probably just from getting poked with those spines on the back of the beast," Fiah countered as she crinkled her nose and bit her tongue.

"No I like to think it would be a real righteous cause," Clohda shot back.

"That's how you will know him Roshin, righteous scars," Orla said with a smile.

At that moment Ashlyn walked into the room, and the women turned and offered her greetings. "Oh we have bread!" Orla announced, "It was a real surprise, but a cart came through with flour the other day and the tavern was able to make bread!"

She pulled back the cover on her basket, "Ashlyn dear come get yourself a first helping. You have another mouth to feed with as well," she said as she patted her stomach. The women all sat down to sip the tea and eat the bread.

After eating, the women went about their chores to clean up the building and prepare for the evening. Orla did not move, "Are you alright?" Roshin asked.

"My low back, it just hurts, and I feel like the baby is just in a bad position."

"Try this," Roshin said getting down on her knees before the bench, The woman got down with her and Roshin nodded, "Yes, now sway a bit and see if we can't get the baby repositioned." She then stood and put some pressure down on the back of the woman who sighed in relief.

As the day wore on the women again settled in the common area, "So if the darkness is near an end, does that mean the empire will fall? What about the smugglers and the slave markets?" Clohda asked her eyes bright with curiosity.

Roshin caught her hands, "That is all darkness. It had no place in the world of light."

"So what will life look like?" Clohda asked as if perplexed by the idea of what goodness was.

Roshin understood. The girl's life had not been easy. Like Roshin, she had been orphaned. She was from Brenna, and her parents had starved one winter, doing their best to keep her fed so she might survive. The women in the brothel had taken her in out of pity when she was wandering the streets, a girl of ten. She had spent seven years living here.

The other women had similarly difficult stories, Fiah had managed to escape from a village on which the Empire had taken out its wrath. They had come through with a company of soldiers and murdered the unarmed peasants before burning the town to the ground.

She hated the soldiers for the destruction they caused, and she came to Brenna when she learned that it operated mostly outside of the Empire's control. The brothel had been her lifeline, allowing her to support herself and stay.

Orla had been the first in this home, having found her way here when looking for an opportunity to make something of herself. She had thought to be a performer in the taverns, but she found more coin available to her through the sale of her body.

"We will be able to have families again, and farms for food. Our towns will function, people will have true trades." Roshin recounted a story of the good times before, the bounty and peace. The women sat and listened, with a look of longing on their faces.

The recounting was interrupted by a knock on the door. Fiah stood and excused herself. Roshin heard her conversing with a man on the other side of the door, negotiating a fee. She cringed and closed her eyes as she heard the man come in. Fiah made her way up the stairs, making small talk and giggling at the lewd comments of the man.

This was the part of their day she hated so much. She looked over to Ashlyn to get her attention so that they might head out the door, but before that happened the door swung open, and a drunk man stumbled in, Clohda and Orla both stood and moved over to intercept him before he made it too far. Roshin stood, "Let us go quick," and they rushed out the door and into the street. The square had come to life, and several men flowed in and out of the tavern.

They mostly still had their wits about them, but Roshin knew that was soon to change, so they prepared again for another night tending to the men on the streets.

33

The Doubt of Men

The light from a dozen lanterns bounced off the stone walls only to be swallowed up by the shroud of swirling pipe smoke that had dispersed into the air above the tables. The tavern was not yet full and only two tables had occupants beside the one where Roshin and Ashlyn sat.

The women had settled themselves back in a corner facing the counter. Though they did not order any drinks, the innkeeper let them sit there. As he discovered, their presence seemed to interest the men and drive them to stay and spend more of their coppers.

They had selected their location as it allowed them to see what was happening, while staying out of the thick of things. As the inn keep had suggested, the tavern was good for providing them with work to do. Each night there was at least one fight, and most nights a few.

Occasionally a man would hurt himself as he fumbled with a blade while attempting some feat, despite being thoroughly inebriated. The women had needed to invest in line and needles and had become quite adept at stitching up gaping and bleeding wounds.

The innkeeper, for his part, liked this all the more, as stitching wounds required even more alcohol, both in and on the man being stitched." For the most part they sat quietly, not demanding much attention, but they still received it.

Each night men would come over and sit down before them. They often tried to engage the men, but usually by the time they had gotten the nerve to come over, their minds were already cloudy. This night however a group of three men entered the tavern, spotted them, and came right over.

The first man to approach was a broad-chested fellow with a mop of light brown hair. He had hazel eyes and was clean-shaven. Roshin guessed he was in his late twenties. He looked to be a guard from a wagon train.

He had a sword strapped to his side, a dagger, and a pouch full of coins. He had a long linen tunic and leather vest with leather vambraces, which he was working to untie as he walked over. He gave them a flirtatious look before stepping one leg over the bench and setting down straddled over it, "My eyes may be playing tricks on me, but I believe you two came out of a brothel."

Roshin gave him a polite smile as acknowledgement. "No tricks, we are staying in a room over there," she was quick to add, "but we are not working there."

The man pushed back against the table and shot over a look of disappointment, "Too bad, I would have liked some company tonight." He then shot glances over to his two companions and made to leave.

Roshin for her part could have let them go, but she found she was actually eager for an opportunity to speak to some men who were not yet drunk. "No need to run off. You're welcome to sit here, so long as you don't interfere with our work." She shot him a shy smile.

The man settled back down and waved to his friends to join him. One went off to secure some mugs and the other sat down. The new man was rail thin with a long face. He was also dressed as a guard and she thought him to be younger. The first man returned his eyes to Roshin, "Work eh? What work would that be?"

It was Ashlyn that answered, seeming to want to be involved in the conversation, "We are trained healers, and we are here to tend to any injuries that happen to befall the patrons of this establishment."

The man just roared with laughter. "So formal!" He again leaned back and looked around before turning to face to the women, "No doubt this place keeps you plenty busy," his tone seemed a taunt toward the Inn Keep, whose eyes had been firmly set on him while he wiped out a mug from behind the counter.

His companion returned and slid a mug in front of him. He took it, and after a long draw set it down and leaned in, "It's a hopeless endeavor really, patching these men back together, they are all on borrowed time, eventually we will all lose our heads for being traitors to the Empire," he hissed before turning back to his companions, "Right boys?"

Roshin countered his assertion, "But that assumes the Empire will endure."

The long-faced man took this one with a chuckle, "Why wouldn't it? Desertion has only gotten harder, and the military just grows."

Roshin did not disagree, but she pictured the dragon, "The Empire is a blight, but we believe it's days to be numbered," she had a calm confidence and authority in her tone. The first man took notice and looked at her a bit taken aback.

"Why believe such a thing?" the broad chested man asked, then poking a finger at her chest he continued, "Are you planning to slip a poison into the stew of the emperor?"

His companion who brought over the mugs scoffed, "Like his son would be any better anyways."

The first man nodded in agreement, "We are ruled by men and therefore we will suffer under them."

Ashlyn shot back, sounding a bit defensive, "Then we should seek to be ruled by a god and not by man."

This got another hardy laugh to rumble from the broad chested man, "All the gods were burned away with their temples when Belenos took power." His tone was full of contempt, but in relation to what, Roshin was not sure.

Ashlyn again broke in defensively, "That is not true!"

Roshin put a hand on her arm to quiet the girl before calmly finishing for her, "We are followers of Hulen Ahir. There are many like us who have been practicing the faith in secret, but no more."

This piqued the men's curiosity, and they learned in. The first man poked at her to try and get a rise, "No more? So you wish to see yourself extinct?"

Roshin crossed her arms and sat up tall. "No, our prophet has come."

This again set the men roaring with laughter, "Prophet, eh? I bet he's just another man seeking power over others," he sneered.

Roshin shook her head "No, the prophet is a dragon rider, and he has come to deliver us from the darkness," her words carried with them her own iron clad confidence.

The men were not buying it. The long face man shot back a sarcastic, "And did he tell you that?"

Roshin was growing frustrated, and she found it hard not to just shout back at them. She looked at Ashlyn who was also showing signs for frustration, then she took a slow breath, and responded as calmly as possible, "No it is written in our sacred texts and recorded in our histories."

She was not ready to let this go, "This world had peace when the dragon riders last flew." Ashlyn nodded in approval at the statement, but it was just met with the cold skepticism of the men.

"No doubt they wrote those histories," the first man said, his voice full of scorn. He leaned in toward the women and in a low voice explained, "Look, I like you both, you seem innocent enough, but if you think some man will come here and save us all from our misery then you have truly much to learn."

He was not done, this time he made his voice loud, "Men are petty, and men want power." He seemed to be seeking the ear of the entire room at this point, "Sure a man on the back of a fire breathing monster could gather much power, but what makes him good? And who is to say a man who rules on dragon back would rule any better than a man who rules from a gilded throne?

His companions agreed. "Exactly!" trumpeted the man with the long face.

Roshin truly was upset now, and she felt herself having to fight back tears. She was not sure what to say, but she felt herself losing the argument. Ashlyn tried to bolster her, "But he had the wisdom of Hulen Ahir, he can hear his words."

The first man just shook his head and derided her as if she were a small child, "Says who, the man?" he laughed, "You can't hear it. Who's to say, even if these dragon riders did exist, that they did not just make up such things?"

He turned and spat on the floor, "Bah! Your prophet may be a better ruler than our dear Lord Belenos, but I will not follow him. I am done following anyone but myself, and so are most the men here."

For the first time Roshin felt doubt start to creep in around the edges of her beliefs. The man had made good points that she did not have an answer for. "*He didn't have to be so mean about it though,*" she lamented to herself, thinking back to his scornful tone.

The men eventually left, and the women remained in an uncomfortable silence in the corner of the Inn. Clearly the words of the men had dug into Ashlyn too. "How do we know he can hear the voice of our god, and how do we know he is good?" The answer came back to her in one word, faith.

It was at that moment that a fight broke out. Two men exchanged blows before drawing swords and stumbling back out the door. "*Well, there is one thing I know for sure,*" she thought, "*and that is how to stich up a stab wound.*" She rose with Ashlyn and made for the door.

34

The Raid

Despite their injuries, the blood of each man was still running hot. Roshin assumed that had they not been drunk and clumsy they truly would have cut each other into pieces. "*Or maybe they could have avoided this altogether,*" she thought. She didn't even know what the dispute was about.

Usually it was thievery, an insult, or some question of honor that would trigger the altercations. It hardly mattered, but the man she was trying to look at would not settle while his foe was nearby. Roshin bid Ashlyn to direct his opponent to the other side of the building and treat him over there.

It took some negotiation to get the other man to move, but Ashlyn had a calming presence. It was a few gentle touches, and an effort made to keep his eyes upon her, that eventually resulted in his compliance. Roshin was left to evaluate her patient undistracted.

He was holding on to his forearm and sitting down in the dirt. He looked to be bleeding on his leg as well as his arm under his hand. She pulled up the leg on his breeches and he cursed at her. "Now hold still. I am trying to help here. No sense in making it harder for me," she scolded, before quickly pulling up the cloth.

The sword had bitten into his leg just below his knee. It did not, by any measure, look good. "I need to get some ale for you, and to clean out this wound before I can stich it up. Give me one of your coppers and I will be right back," she asked in a gentle voice.

The man cursed and with a drunken slur refused, "No! You use your own coppers, these are mine, and I earned them."

Roshin began to lose her patience, "You also earned yourself a gaping wound," she barked, "I can stich you right here like this, I will ask some of these men to come hold you down," she gestured out to the square where some men were milling about. "But you are not going to like it, and it would be easier if you just give me a coin so we can make this less painful."

The man finally relented, and Roshin took the coin and ran into the inn. The man was still on the ground when she came back out. "Now you drink this," she ordered as she shoved a mug into his hands. "Drink it fast for maximum effect, you have no doubt had a lot already, but I need you right loose."

The man drunk from the mug and Roshin saw Ashlyn creep by and into the Inn as well. "It looks like you put a hole in your friend as well. I thought you might like to know that." Ashlyn left a minute later with her own two mugs. Roshin splashed the wound on the man's leg with the drink.

"Hey, I bought that!" he called out, reaching for the mug.

She swung it away from him. "You did, to soften your mind and to clean this," she said, gesturing to the slice on his leg. "Now let me see your arm."

His arm was not so bad so she nodded, "We can pack and wrap that one, only your leg needs a stitch." She let him finish the rest of the second mug, and by that time he was starting to look quite wobbly and slow.

"*Good,*" she thought as she reached for her bag and pulled out the needle and horsehair thread. She moved over to the lantern next to the door of the Inn, opened the glass and stuck the needle in the flame. She then threaded it with the hair, and wiped the whole thing off with an ale-soaked rag.

She sat down beside the man and began stitching. "*No doubt Ashlyn is stitching up the other one,*" she thought as she worked. The man before her looked about ready to pass out, which she thought was good as it made her work easier. She made another careful stitch.

His inebriation became a problem, however, as suddenly a bell tolled, and two men ran through the streets in a panic. "Raid! Raid!" they called out. One man went to the brothel, another to the Inn, and soon there were at least a dozen men out on the streets.

A sudden realization hit her as she watched them all run off toward the edge of town. "Soldiers," she whispered.

She tried to stir the man before her. She looked at her work and realized she was only half done, she stooped and made a few more passes to try and close it up quick. "*If I can finish, I might be able to drag him off with a little help,*" she thought."

Her hands moved faster at her task than she ever thought would be wise. She almost had it, and was about to tie it off when she saw four mounted men arrive in the square. "Get up, Get up!" she shouted and she stood and tugged on his arm, and the man slowly moved but did not get to his feet.

"Get to your senses! You have to move!" she demanded as she tugged desperately on his arm, but his body was like an anchor stuck on a rock. Her eyes darted around for anyone that might help her, but the only men she saw were soldiers in polished helms.

A man jumped off a horse beside her. "Well look here, is he alive?" The soldier grabbed the injured man's arm and pressed his thumb into the wound, the man burbled and moaned. "He is! Well at least for now," he sneered, and he pulled the man toward him.

Roshin had not let go of his other arm and so she came too, "Let him go girl," he hissed, and when she did not, he kicked her hard in the stomach. Her breath went out of her, and she lost hold of his arm. She found herself falling backwards and gasping for air.

The dirt met her shoulder with a jar, and she tried to sit up quickly to look and see what had happened to her patient. She heard steel crashing from behind her and turned to see a stumbling drunk man trying fight off two soldiers.

He swung wildly but was no match for the men before him. They laughed and jeered, running him back hard until he stumbled and fell. He dropped his sword and then one of the solders put steel to his throat.

She watched as they seized him and dragged him away. Then she realized she had forgotten her patient, and she whirled her head around to look. He was gone, but to where she did not know. She rose and began to walk off in the direction she had seen the soldier drag the other man.

She heard a woman scream, and then spun and looked around, "Ashlyn?" she called out. Ashlyn appeared behind her, her movement timid and careful as if she was sneaking away from something.

"They took him," she stammered out. "They pulled from me, and drug him away!" her words came out in barely more than a whisper.

"They did the same to me as well," Roshin said. "Did you see where they took him?"

"I think back out toward the road," she squeaked.

Behind them a door slammed, there was some cursing from an old man and then a woman yelled. *"They are going in the homes and looking for men,"* she thought as she watched a soldier, sword in hand burst out of one building before moving over to the next and kicking in the door.

He emerged from the building some moments later pulling out a boy who looked no more than 12. He dragged the boy off, kicking and squirming, back toward the road. A pit formed in Roshin's stomach, "I must see where they are taking them," she announced in a hushed tone.

Ashlyn nodded and took her hand. Together they crept along the buildings and down the lane toward the edge of town where they had come in. Roshin was not exactly sure why she wanted to follow them but something in her told her she needed to know, to see, and so they made their way to the edge of town and ducked behind an old cart that was parked just past the last building. The light was quickly fading as the sun had set.

The solders had gathered along the road. They had two carts and looked to be maybe a dozen strong. Roshin through of the men she had seen run out of Brenna, "There were at least that many if not more." Most had scattered to the wind however as soon as the bell had tolled, and the criers ran through the town.

Lying bound on the ground, before the assembled soldiers were several prisoners. Roshin saw the men they had been treating, lying in a heap off to the side. There were three other men that had been caught, and then three boys who were in the process for being bound and tossed in the back of one of the carts.

The sight of the boys being hauled off for conscription made her feel sick, "*They are just children,*" she screamed in her mind. She had seen the conscriptors as a child, it was the one time she was not afraid to be seen as the girl she was.

At one point a soldier had grabbed her thinking she might be a boy, but she screamed and kicked and told him she was a girl. He did not believe her until one of the fishermen ran over and confirmed it by pulling down her trousers in a panic. It had been shameful, and embarrassing, but even still as the soldier dropped her and she ran back to the docks, it was a relief.

The boys looked afraid. The bound men looked defeated. The solders, however, they looked as though they had just taken a prize in a hunt and were jovially bumping arms and laughing.

Three more men joined their ranks empty-handed, and one of the soldiers said, "Looks like the haul tonight, boys! Five! Not bad."

Roshin could not help but think that if all the men in town had joined forces, instead of drinking themselves stupid and then running away, they could have easily bested the soldiers, but they didn't, they ran or let themselves be taken.

"If only the rider could give them all a spine," she thought bitterly. What followed was a horror unlike any she had seen. A hulking man stepped forward, in the dim twilight she though he looked like Toran. "Another monster," she whispered.

Two soldiers would grab the shoulders of one of the prisoners and heave them forward. One of the soldiers would announce the sentence, "You are charged guilty for the crime of desertion from your service from the Empire, your sentence is death which shall be carried out henceforth."

The headsman stepped forward, hefted his sword and brought it down with a thundering force that bit through flesh and bone alike. The prisoner's head came free from his body and the man was no more.

This was repeated five times. The boys were sobbing in the cart, a few men laughed and joked about the crumpled bodies. Roshin watched as the man she had stitched up was hefted and held so the headsman could end his life with a single swing.

Roshin heard Ashlyn retch, and then she turned to her, and in a mousy voice pleaded, "Can we please go?"

"Aye," she said in a whisper and the women slinked back toward the now dark and quiet town, and the door of the brothel.

35

Unwelcome Reunion

Roshin laid awake on her cot for a long while that night, replaying the executions in her head. *"The man in the tavern was right; the men truly are living on borrowed time,"* she started to understand their behavior more.

"They are drinking because they are running away. They are trying to forget what their lives are and how tenuous it all is." She looked over to see Ashlyn lying on her side facing the door. Eventually sleep took her and when she awoke the light was streaming into the window of her room.

Ashlyn was gone, which struck her as unusual, since typically she was the first one to wake. Roshin sat up and began the ritual of readying herself for the day, but somehow, she found it a struggle. She stopped, and sat, and stared at her hands.

"Will you be able to end this? Do you have this power?" she closed her eyes and asked up to the sky. She wished she could speak to him. Seeing the dragon was a gift, but to speak to the man? She needed to know that her belief was not misplaced. Her hope felt as though it was faltering.

The sun rose higher, it was above the window now, Afternoon was not too far away. "I need to get up. I need to get out of this room," she mumbled. She finally found the energy to braid her hair, slip on her veil, and stand. She looked out the windows. There were soldiers wandering around the streets.

The pit in her stomach returned. *This will not be a regular day she thought."* She emerged into the hall and began to walk toward the stairs. Suddenly, she heard the front door burst open. She heard Clohda rush over to attend to the visitor.

"Welcome! We don't typically see guests so early," she said in a rush.

"So you don't," the voice responded. She recognized the voice. "I am lookin' for someone. Move!" he barked, and then she heard Clohda grunt and bump into a wall.

"You!" was what she heard next, and her heart began to pound.

She heard Ashlyn squeal. "Excuse me, let her go," Clohda pleaded. Roshin began to rush down the stairs, but she was caught by Fiah who wrapped her arms around her tight. Roshin turned her head to look back at the woman who stared at her white faced and scared,

She put her fingers to her lips to hush Roshin, and then slowly pointed out the window. Roshin timidly looked out. That's when she saw him, standing cross-armed outside the door. It was Toran. He was standing sentinel outside.

Roshin could hear Ashlyn struggling, Fiah began to slowly draw her back up the stairs. "I thought I saw you last night. Ya made me feel right guilty, and here I find you in a brothel. Imagine my surprise."

"She's not working here!" Clohda called out, "She's helping the town."

"You shut your mouth," Delvin said to the girl. "You have no idea the trouble you caused me," Again Ashlyn squealed and Clohda burst out, "Watch out! She's with child!"

"Is that so?" his voice rang out. "From who, some deserter in this brothel?"

"YOU!" Ashlyn barked out in a tearful cry. Roshin strained against Fiah, wanting to run down the stairs, but the woman held her tight and set back on her heels. Roshin found tears were rolling down her cheeks. It was like that night when she could not get to Ashlyn. She found herself resigned to the hold.

"ME?" Delvin barked out as if in disbelief and then he laughed his voice sounding bright, "How about that?" His voice then darkened, "And is she here with you?"

"No." Ashlyn said solemnly, "She stayed at a village beside the sea. I went on to my home but found it empty, and so I came here to not be alone."

"I see." There was a pause, "Is she alone?" Delvin asked.

Clohda replied, "Yes, she came a couple weeks ago, we took her in."

Delvin huffed. "That's not what I want, but either way, this is a plenty fortunate surprise." There was another pause and then a scraping sound. "Come on." His voice grew closer as he neared the door.

"Where are you taking her?" Clohda begged as Ashlyn cried.

"Where she belongs – which ain't in this filthy brothel." Roshin heard him spit. "She's my woman, carrying my child. This place is no place for her, she belongs with me." His words rang with passionate intensity before the door opened and slammed closed."

Roshin strained to get loose. "Stop!" Fiah scolded her. "She protected you. Don't let that be in vain." It didn't matter, Roshin wrenched herself free and ran over to the window to look out. She could hear Clohda crying,

Ashlyn was being pulled away by Delvin, and Toran was following behind him.

She fell to her knees and began to weep bitter tears. She wanted to go after them, she had to rescue her friend, but how could she? "That monster, that beast of a man!" she wailed.

Fiah knelt beside her and wrapped her arms around her. "It should have been me he took. I'm the one he wants," she cried into her hands.

Fiah stroked her back, "I am not sure that is true. He might want you to repay what he is like now to owe, but if that is the child's father, then I would guess he wants her more." Roshin looked up and sniffed, her tears would not cease.

"What do I do now?" she wept.

"You have to keep going," Fiah said sharply, "Those bastards just take everything, so don't give them yourself. Go east."

Roshin looked up at her, "East? What is East?"

Fiah sat back and looked toward the window, "It's likely those soldiers are heading back south now. Stay low and once they go, you get on the road, and you take it east to Dunmaer."

She felt confused, "What's in Dunmaer?"

Fiah cracked into a slight chuckle, "Well no soldiers for one." She nodded, "It's a smugglers town. The empire leaves it alone."

This didn't make sense. It seemed the Empire left nothing alone. "Why?" she asked.

Fiah gave her a sly smile. "They have tried before to siege the city, but it is well fortified and protected by a thick wall. They were able to resist and stand." She moved to rise and offered a hand to Roshin to help her up, "If the empire wants to take it, they would need more forces then I think the Emperor is willing to send so far away."

Roshin stood but fixed her eyes out the window. "But how can I leave her?" she howled.

Fiah shook her head as Clohda joined them by the stairs, "She is gone now." The woman gave her shoulder a squeeze. "Look, whoever he is, he is a soldier. He does not look to be an officer so he can't marry, he's wandering around now, but at some point, he will need to return to his host and when he does she will be free, so take some comfort in that."

Roshin objected, "He could desert."

"I doubt his tall friend would permit that," Fiah noted, joining her gaze out the window.

Roshin knew she was right. "Go to your room and stay there today. I will come up and let you know when the company have all gone, and then you can be away." Roshin nodded with a sniffle and then allowed the woman to lead her up the stairs.

It was a cold feeling, sitting alone in her room, staring at Ashlyn's empty cot. She decided she could no longer look at it, so instead she laid down upon it. A new wave of grief washed over her and she held the blankets that smelled of her friend.

"I will find a way to get you. I will find some way to find you again and see you safe," she whispered as tears soaked the blanket. "If I have to climb a mountain to drag the rider himself to your cause, then I will do that, but I will not forget you."

36

Eastern Road

Orla removed another bowl of uneaten stew from Roshin's room and replaced it with a crust of bread. She touched the girl's shoulder and peered over her as if to ensure she was still breathing, before stepping back and slipping out of the room.

Roshin did not move. Fiah had come the day prior to tell her that the town was now clear and that she could go, but she did not. She did not even rise. It had been two days since Ashlyn was taken, and aside from the use of a chamber pot, Roshin had not left Ashlyn's cot.

The women in the brothel were worried, they checked on her regularly. They sat and talked to her, though she did not reply. They tried to recount the stories she had told them, they reminded her of the rider, but none of it was enough to fill the hole she felt.

She had lost everything she ever cared for. She lost her father before she knew him, her mother as a child. She left Granya behind on the road to Ancalah, and now Ashlyn was gone. They were all gone, and it felt so bitter to her.

She had thought to just sit there and waste away. She could die and find her way to the kingdom of Hulen Ahir. Maybe then she would not have to face a road alone. It was that road that scared her. She was not sure she could do it. Not on her own.

She had thought about it before, in Taughmon, but maybe part of her always knew Ashlyn would come, so she was not too afraid. But now, now she truly was alone. What kind of place was Dunmaer? Could she make it back to The Light? Was there somewhere else she could go to find a home?

Her mind seemed to be a swirling whirlpool dredging up the memories of the past and mixing them with her feelings of today. How could she do it alone? She closed her eyes and conjured up the memory of the dragon, flying in the moonlight. She remembered its sorrowful cries, "*What hurt you so?*" she asked silently.

It was hurt, but it was flying forward still. Maybe that was to be taken as some kind of sign. For the first time she rose off the cot. She ran her hands along the blankets and closed her eyes as a new wave of grief hit her.

She took a breath and then turned toward the window. Light was streaming in. It was morning, and there was plenty of time. She cast up a prayer: "Hulen Ahir, give me the strength I need to continue forward. Help me make it into the light of this new day."

She stretched her hand forward into the rays of sun that were dancing on her cot. They felt warm, and in that she found comfort. She removed her crooked veil, and then undid her braid, her auburn hair spilled all around her.

She looked to her lap and sighed before picking up her head. "Just a little strength is all I need. Enough to get started," she continued her prayer, but this time to herself and not a god. She re-braided her hair, and she fixed her veil upon her head.

It was one more breath and she made it to her feet. She took a bag, and filled it with her belongings. She stuffed in her bedroll and then placed it over her shoulder. She again placed her arms into the warmth of the sun.

A few more breaths and then she took the piece of bread. She looked at it, but she did not feel hungry, so she packed it away and then opened the door. She looked long down the hall before beginning to walk, and she again stopped at the top of the stairs.

"Just one step, just one step." She repeated, and soon she was moving down the stairs. When she reached the bottom, the women saw her, and they all jumped to their feet and ran over to her. "You are up!" Orla called.

Clodah ran over and gave her a hug. She melted a moment in her embrace, and had to again fight back the tears, "Thank you," She managed to whisper before looking up, "Thank you all."

Fiah came over, "Ready to go east then?" she asked with a crooked smile.

"No, but I guess I am going anyways," she said looking at the door.

"Hold on!" called Orla who shuffled back into the common area and returned with another bundle of bread. "For your trip," she said, and she too hugged Roshin, her bulging belly pushing her out and away.

"Please take care and be careful," she said in a tearful voice. Clodah started to cry and Fiah put an arm around her.

"Off you go," Fiah encouraged, and Roshin turned to face the door. Another breath and she opened it. Out into the streets she went, past the inn and then toward the road. She was moving now but it almost felt as though it was someone else driving her body.

She felt like she was still lying down on that cot. Who was making her go? She did not know, but she kept going. The road stretching out before her had looked so long and lonely. She had nobody to talk to, nothing to keep her mind off her loss.

She kept walking. Hours had passed. There was something off the road just ahead. She felt compelled to see what it was. It was the remains of a few wagons, they looked to have been sitting there for months as the weeds had grown up and around them.

One had been burned; two others had been scavenged until almost nothing remained. She looked around and saw what looked to be bones. "People died here." She reflected solemnly. "Was it by the Empire's hand, or some other misery?" she wondered darkly.

She turned and kept walking east. She had no idea how long it would take her to get to Dunmaer. It felt too long, too far, but she kept going all the same. The first night was lonely and cold. She found it hard to sleep as every sound jerked her awake in a panic.

The next day she started, already feeling exhausted. She was moving through the barren plains. The land was dry and cracked; only a few weeds showed signs of life. She passed the ruins of what was once a farm. "*The darkness,*" she thought looking at it.

She was parched, and as she walked on, she desperately looked for a stream or some place to get water, but it was not until late in the evening that she finally found one. She dipped her feet in it and sat a while as the water flowed past her.

She made her camp there and again she found she could barely sleep. Where was she going? A thought came into her head. She was going to find him. That seemed ridiculous and she pushed it out.

Day came once more, and she started walking again toward the east. "*How am I still going?*" She wondered. She had barely slept; she had not eaten in days. Again, a thought entered her mind, "*Find him.*" She started to feel like maybe she was going mad.

She could not push the thought away, however. She reached into her bag and pulled out the bread, now stale from the days it spent not being eaten. She chewed on it, and then she realized how hungry she was.

It was the night of the third day. She had walked until she felt she would collapse. This time she slept. Her mind settled deep into a much-needed rest, and the world disappeared around her. She saw something. It was mountains; they towered above her.

She found herself moving toward the mountains till she saw the turquoise shape ahead of her. She walked toward it. It was the dragon. It was perched at the base of a rocky cliff, it was huge, majestic.

It looked at her with sapphire eyes and then looked down. She saw him, he was standing at the dragon's feet, wrapped in a dark cloak and facing away from her. He had dark hair, and he was looking down. He looked overcome, he looked lost, he was moving away from her, his shoulders slumped in defeat.

"No!" she found herself saying, and she started to run toward him. "You are so dark; you are supposed to be the light!" she called out. For a moment he stopped, but then he kept going. "We need you to bring the light." She saw him shake his head, and she willed herself to run faster.

She ran toward him and reached out a hand to grab him by the shoulder and whirl him toward her, but then she woke up. She lay there blinking up at the sky, the sun was just beginning to lighten the sky. "*What did that mean?*" she wondered. The thought again entered her mind, "*Find him.*"

She sat up. It was just as good a time as any to start walking again, and so she packed away her bedroll, the mountains were ahead of her. "*Maybe I will make it to Dunmaer this very day,*" she thought. And again she started walking, but this time, she felt like it was her own feet driving her.

37

Dunmaer

The mountainside loomed large, and before Roshin were the walls of Dunmaer. "I have made it," she thought. She had no idea what she would find behind the walls, but she took a breath and walked forward.

The air had a bit of a chill, fall was near and Roshin reflected that she was going to need a plan to stay warm come winter. "Something tells me I am going to need coppers to survive here," she mumbled, thinking back to Brenna.

It was then a realization hit her, and she stopped and began to dig around in her bag. She found the little pouch that Ashlyn had taken from Taughmon and she peaked inside. It still had five coppers in it. It would be more than enough to get her a room until she could figure things out.

A feeling of relief fell over her, and then guilt at the idea that she was taking money from Ashlyn and her family, "She would want me to use it," she reassured herself squeezing the pouch in her fingers.

She was nearing the gate now, it was closed. A sleepy-looking guard was perched above it. She paused and looked up at him. He was young and his face was a patchwork of sparce whiskers. His armor was all leather, so he didn't look like a man with much authority, but still he looked to be the guard, as he was there at the gate holding a spear.

He did not notice her, so she called up to him. "Excuse me! Hello?"

The man jerked forward and peered down at her, then squinted his eyes as if confused by her presence. He looked around behind her as if expecting some trap and then returned his gaze to her, "Business?" he asked with a flavor of piqued curiosity.

"I have come here from Brenna seeking sanctuary from the Empire's soldiers. I was told Dunmaer would be such a haven."

The man laughed. "Haven of some kind, I s'pose," he said, then added, "Aite." A moment later, the gates of the town opened. She walked through, her heart pounding as she made it to the streets. They were bustling much like the streets of cities in the south, but there were so many young men.

She could not recall ever seeing so many men in one place, not even Brenna. "There has to be hundreds of men here," she whispered to herself as she began counting bodies. The town was alive, that was for sure, and her arrival had caught many of their eyes.

"I need to find an inn or boarding house, some place I can stay at," she told herself as she skirted past the men and scurried briskly down the road. The buildings were mostly made of limestone, with clean-looking thatched roofs. It looked as though they had been carved from the limestone peaks of the mountain behind them.

They all looked in good repair, clearly the town was not lacking for hands to work. The buildings were all stacked against each other in a row, most rising two or three stories. The streets were wide and full of carts. Many were empty as if awaiting cargo. Some were full of barrels and sacks. And to her dismay others had people with grim looking faces.

She squeezed the coin pouch harder as she thought back to the slave markets in Vargah, *"Perhaps this is where it all begins,"* she thought grimly. But then again, she had been taken by smugglers, much like these men, out of Veyah and sold off like nothing. "*Are any of these men actually free?*" she wondered sourly.

She continued down the street. She passed a blacksmith's forge, and three men were inside hammering hot steel. It was another surprising sight as a blacksmith still in operation was a rare thing indeed.

A few towns still had an old man making nails and spikes and other things, but these were young men, and they looked to be crafting swords and other more advanced metalworks. "*What the Empire is missing by sending them all into service,*" she thought

A fight broke out in front of her as a man punched another, who staggered back, nearly knocking her over. She gasped and then rushed past, "*I imagine this is a common occurrence here,*" she thought as she looked back

A whistle came next, and she turned to see several young men with drinks in their hands milling beside an alley way. One winked and blew her a kiss. She blushed and walked faster. "One of these must be an Inn," she muttered to herself looking at the buildings for any signs or symbols.

She finally found a building with a wooden sign on which was carved three circles and an arrow. This was a common sign for lodging amongst the common people in Perinthia, so she walked up the steps and slipped into the door.

The building was poorly lit, with only a few lanterns. Men were milling around beside a limestone fireplace set into the far wall. She saw what looked to be a counter and behind it was a thin man who she hoped to be the inn keeper.

"Excuse me sir, I need accommodations, is this an inn?" she asked, trying to be as polite as possible.

The man looked down at her and laughed, "Aye, it's an inn alright, but I don't serve no women here. Don't got no private rooms here, only shared space, and I don't want no trouble for trying to house no lady," he explained gesturing out to the men in the room.

Roshin looked around and felt discouraged, "So is there any place that will host women in this town?" she asked feeling a growing sense of unease. *"Or I might end up exposed, sleeping in some alley,"* she thought grimly.

The man seemed sympathetic, "Aye, if you wish to stay out of the brothel, there is a building set back beside the training yard that should be able to serve you. It's small, ain't much, but the old woman who keeps it will sell you a space if you can pay."

Roshin nodded her thanks and worked her way past the leering eyes of the men in the dark common area and back out to the light of the street. "The training yard," she repeated, and she looked around trying to determine where that might be.

Her ears gave her the first clue, as she could hear cracking, and grunting, and yells off toward the north.

She left the steps of the inn and ran down an ally that took her past the row of buildings that otherwise blocked her path. She broke out into a clear space that looked to be the training yard.

Before her sat several archery targets. She walked down the lane away from them to find an open area where men were gathered watching pairs fight with practice swords. She stood and watched them duel for a moment, taking in the brutality and strength on display, "This is practice," she mumbled to herself before pulling her eyes away and looking for the accommodations.

She saw what she guessed to be it ahead of her, an old woman with tanned leathery skin and steely grey hair sat on a stool watching the men fight as she smoked a pipe. Roshin thought it looked odd but shook it off and moved forward.

Like all the other buildings, this one was also made of stone. It was two stories, and quite narrow, sandwiched between two larger structures, she understood what the inn keeper meant. The building did not look like much, especially when compared with its neighbors, but it should serve.

She approached the old woman who saw her coming and regarded her. "I was told you may host accommodations for women?" she asked timidly.

The old woman had turned her eyes back to the combat and took another puff of the pipe. "Aye," was all that came out of her mouth.

Roshin again squeezed the pouch in her hand and continued to probe the old woman, "And you have space?"

The woman cringed and Roshin followed her eyes out to the yard where a man was now standing doubled over with pain, "Aye, it'll cost ya two coppers a night," she finally croaked but still she made no bother to look at Roshin.

It was an exorbitant price and Roshin knew it. After a pause she got up the nerve to ask, "Is that for a private room?"

This finally got her attention, and the old woman cackled with amusement. "No child, that gets you a space on the floor. Try and keep it right, covered in straw, refreshed weekly, sometimes every other week."

Roshin nodded grimly, "*How can anyone afford to pay that?*" She wondered, but she had little choice, "Well, I would take the space for at least two nights," she said, and she opened her hands to expose the pouch.

She fished out four of the coppers to hand the old woman and then looked in her bag at the one that remained. "*I will need to work out how to make more of these and hopefully find a different place to stay,*" she thought uncertainly.

"Good, I will show you the space." She rose off the stool and then smoothed her many layered skirts before adding, "I say not to leave your bag, things have a tendency of disappearing here." She gestured to Roshin's pack.

"Good to know," Roshin thanked her, and she followed the woman inside. The building was dark and cramped and the ceiling seemed too low leaving her to duck to get around. She followed the old woman up a narrow staircase.

Everything here felt cramped, and the space was no exception. It was hardly bigger than the room she shared with Ashlyn in the brothel, but she figured it would do. "How many other women are here?" she queried.

"Right now, you make four," her raspy voice returned, to which Roshin had to blink her eyes to make sure she could see it.

"Sounds as though I will be getting quite comfortable with my roommates," she commented, trying to keep her good humor about her, but at the moment she could feel little more than exploited.

The old woman just laughed and then wandered back down the stairs. "Two nights and then I will need more payment," the old woman reminded Roshin before returning to her pipe and stool.

I will need to figure this one out," she thought feeling a sickness enter her. She walked away from the building to now try and use her last copper for some food. At that moment a man howled in pain, and she look up.

It was another injury in the sparring yard. An idea struck her. She had been treating stab wounds and fighting injuries for nearly two weeks at Brenna. These were the same men, and she knew they had money, they also seemed prone to injury. She could charge for her services and use that money to keep herself fed and housed.

It was a good idea, but how to make her offering known? She decided to return to the match area and just wait, a man was bound to try and leave bloodied at some point. It might just work.

38

Ciran

Roshin stooped over a young man, checking his face carefully. "Well, you look to have chipped a tooth, possibly broken a nose, and you definitely split your lip," Roshin reported as she dabbed a rag over his mouth to sop up the blood.

"They're not supposed to swing for your face," the man grumbled with a curse before turning his head to spit.

Roshin gave him a gentle chiding. "And you are supposed to block the strikes."

The man growled in contempt. "Bah! It wasn't a fair strike."

"Either way, you would be dead," she noted dryly before offering him a tied bundle of leaves and stems. "I can't do anything for the bruising, and no need to stitch up your lip, but I can help with the pain, chew these leaves, 3 or 4 at a time until you can no longer stand it. Don't spit them out until you feel the pain begin to numb."

The man nodded and pulled off some of the leaves which he began to chew. His face twisted a bit as he swallowed down some of the bitterness from their juices, but after few minutes he spat them out, "Aye, it does feel better." Roshin reached out her hand in which he then set a copper into. "Thank you," he managed before turning and leaving.

Roshin had been in Dunmaer for over a week now and had amassed what felt to her, at least, to be an impressive purse. She was treating three or four men every day, and the men had now learned to seek her out. It was mostly pain relief, wrappings, or stitches, with an occasional splint.

She had found the forest nearby to host an impressive array of medicinal herbs and plants which she would bundle and carry about hanging off her person from cords of twine during the day, and then from the curtain rod of the shared room at night.

It was a lot, but so far at least, she had been able to source the two coppers she needed each day for her room. The space was cramped and full of fleas, but it suited her for now. She was hopeful that given some more time, she may even be able to collect enough coins to rent some smaller room in another building from which she could better treat the men.

The nights were growing colder, so she had invested in several more jars and spent more time in and around the forest collecting the plants that would soon die back and be blanketed in snow. "I will need enough to see me through the winter," she thought surveying the number of jars she had managed to fill.

Carrying everything with her had made her feel so weary, but she had headed the old woman's warning to not leave anything behind, as she could not risk losing any of her precious supplies to thievery. The women she was sleeping beside changed nearly every day, and she did not feel she had adequate time to get to know any of them. "*I miss having Ashlyn around,*" she thought as a desperate sadness and sense of worry settled over her.

She wondered where the others went, and she figured they had just run out of coins. "*Hard to make a go of it here without a good skill,*" she thought, as another man approached her cradling a gash on his arm. She looked at him, "We best head to the tavern my brother, you will need some drinks."

One thing she had yet to figure out was how to speak to the men about the rider, or any matters of faith. She had had a few chances, where a man expressed curiosity at her own story, and how she ended up here. She would tell them of Hulen Ahir, and the dragon rider, and how she had set out to spread the word, and they would mostly just laugh at her.

If there was a conversation, it reminded her of the men in the tavern at Brenna, she was less angry about it now and at least answered their questions with the truth. She had chosen to believe it because it gave her hope and purpose. She would then ask what their rejection was like to bring them when faced with a company of soldiers out on the road.

The men did not seem to like this, as it struck a nerve. She thought it was just as well, "*If I can show them their folly, it may save them their head someday.*" She remembered the executions in Brenna and shuttered.

Upon stitching up her latest charge, Roshin decided it was time to find something to eat. She had realized it was well into the afternoon, and she had had no food that day. The town seemed busier than normal. A large wagon train from Garvahal had come in to resupply before heading south through the forest. "*Vargah.*" She thought with bitter resentment.

She had not forgotten the nature of the industry that seemed to keep the coins flowing here. It was her own ability to source coins that likely kept her off of one of those carts, "*That is likely where those women went when they could no longer pay,*" she thought with a huff.

Injustice was all around her, and she did not know how she felt about being there. She squeezed Ashlyn's coin pouch, "The one saving grace is that money can buy men here." When she started to get paid for her work the realization had come to her that if she was to earn enough coins, she might be able to buy her own guards to go hunt for Toran and Delvin and find Ashlyn.

"*I am going to need a lot of coins,*" she thought recalling Toran's wild swings and brutality. Her mind again turned to Ashlyn being trapped with them. She wanted desperately to at least know that she was alright. "*I am never going to be able to settle here,*" she thought as her melancholy fell in around her.

She walked further down the street and found her way into a tavern that was known for its rich stews and fine ciders. A woman was working as a server and she flagged her down, slipping half a copper into her hand for a bowl of soup and crust of bread.

The woman nodded and disappeared behind a door. She returned a few minutes later with a bowl and some bread, and with it Roshin sat down, unburdening herself of her pack and dipping into the warm bowl.

She had not seen them come in behind her. She was too engrossed in her fears over her friend and thinking how long she might need to work before she would be able to hire a few swords. "*Maybe Fiah was right, and they will have to let her go when they get called back to the camp."*

"Delvin may not be able to return without a bride for his officer," she thought. It was the joyful laughing and greetings that broke her from her mind.

"We were certain you were dead!" a voice announced jubilantly followed by the sound of a slap.

It was the pained groan that followed that caused Roshin's head to snap around. She looked behind herself and saw a group of five men. Four seemed to be gathered around one in the middle, and he was the one wearing an uncomfortable grimace.

"Sorry brother, I forgot! I didn't mean to hurt ya," a tall blonde-haired man said, squeezing the shoulder of the man in the middle. "Let's get drinks around to celebrate the return of our long-lost friend Ciran! Afterall, he looks truly like he needs it."

"Aye," said Ciran with a wince as he looked around the room. He briefly caught Roshin's eyes but his attention was quickly diverted back to the men around him. Roshin could not help but study him, something about him looked familiar to her, but she could not quite place it.

He was young, a tall man, who seemed like he could have been quite strong, but he did not look well, his skin was ashen and pale, his cheeks sunk in, and he looked malnourished. His tunic was worn, torn, and stained in blood, as were his breeches. He had a belt with a knife and a dagger, but no sword, a bow was slung over his shoulder along with a quiver and a few arrows.

His hair was dark and wavy, like Ashlyn's had been, and his eyes were a deep blue, not light and icy. He had a short beard that looked as though it had just started growing in, and most of his wavy hair was long enough to be tied back with some around his face spilling free and framing his features.

Something about his presence seemed different. He lacked the bravado and carefree nature of most of the men around him. There seemed to be a concern or tension in him riding under the surface as if he was not sure he should even be there.

She found him interesting, but decided to move on, back to her meal, and her planning for the rescue of her friend. She left the tavern awhile later, and as she did, she could not help but to again glance over at the table of men who had come in to celebrate their friend's return.

The cider was flowing, and four of the men were starting to show it. Ciran however was mostly just observing. He had a mug, but she noticed it was mostly still full, and by his mannerisms, it was likely not his second or third, she wondered what he was thinking about, before slipping out the door.

Another night passed, this time only two other women shared her space. She got back late having been stopped to treat an injury from another tavern brawl.

Fortunately, this one was mostly mild and did not require much skill.

She was exhausted. She laid down and quickly fell asleep. She had another dream; this time she saw the man from the tavern in it. He was standing before Toran, with a sword in his hand. His face drawn with determination and rage. She startled awake before any swords flew to find light streaming into the window.

She gathered her bag, draped the bundles over her shoulders, and went out into the yard. It was only a few hours later before she was treating the first injury of the day. As she worked to wrap up the wound a familiar group walked by.

"We recently got our own healer to patch us all up right good. She'll cost ya, but it seems a worthwhile price to pay," the tall blonde man from the night before announced. She looked up and caught Ciran with him. "Say, she might even be able to look at that back of yours,"

"No it'll be fine," he deflected.

 "Yeah, but then you won't get to hear her spin tales of her god and the dragon riders that will save us all," the blonde man burst out laughing and slapped his leg. The man she was working on chuckled too.

Roshin looked up from her wrapping and felt herself blush. Again, she caught the eyes of Ciran. He was not laughing, instead his face was inquisitive. She felt her skin prickle a bit before the men began to move on. As they passed Ciran nodded to her and offered a thin half smile.

Later that afternoon she was walking to the tavern to get her meal, a hand caught her by the shoulder, and she whirled around, the bundles draped over her swung outwards and smacked into the man who was standing behind her.

It was Ciran. "I'm sorry," he said with a bit of a stammer," I didn't mean to startle you. I just had a question, and it may seem completely strange to you, but do you by chance know anything of the faith of Hulen Ahir?"

Roshin just stared at him for a long while, until his face began to drop, and he looked like he wanted to just run off. "I do," she said simply. She then looked inquisitively back to him, "and you know of it as well?"

Ciran tipped his head back and forth a bit as if considering how to best answer, "Well I know of it, but not much about what they actually believe. I was curious to know if you did?"

Roshin brightened considerably at the opportunity to share her knowledge. "Of course, I am going to eat. You are welcome to join me. I would be happy to tell you about my faith, though to understand it fully, we are likely to need more than one meal."

Ciran also brightened and straightened his body. "I understand. I would be happy to join you."

And with that they walked together toward the tavern. Once inside they each ordered some food and then settled down across from each other at a table near the back of the room and awaited its arrival. "I'm Ciran by the way," he introduced himself.

"Roshin," she responded with a smile.

Ciran gestured to her bags and bundles which she had yet to remove, "You are carrying much Roshin. Is there a reason?"

"I was told I was like to get robbed if I left my belongings where I am sleeping, so I carry it all on me," she explained with a shrug as she went about unburdening herself.

"I understand that," he said before tapping his own bag. The food came, and he was quick to start eating. The joy in his eyes was evident as he savored the taste of the stew. "This is so good," he exalted, before catching himself and explaining, "You would understand if you had any idea of what my last few months had been."

Roshin nodded. She had already thought he looked half-starved so his behavior did not come as a surprise. She offered him a smile and then started sipping her own soup. "So, you wish to know about Hulen Ahir?" she asked looking to redirect the conversation.

"Aye, I do," he affirmed between spoonfuls.

Roshin offered him a curious smile. "Might I start by asking how you learned the name?"

He winced a bit, "You might not believe me, but in my travels, I came across a temple and a man. I believe he called himself a 'Truth Sayer?' Anyway, I saw carvings in the temple of dragon riders. The man would not tell me the significance, so I have been left guessing for quite a while."

She considered him and then responded, "I see" She looked up and away a moment before continuing, "Well you likely saw carvings to recognize the prophets of old."

"Prophets?" Ciran asked curiously.

She began to wave her hands a bit as she explained, "Yes. To start simply, there are dragons and there are men. Hulen Ahir created both, but the dragons have a special gift that connects them to the spirit world."

Ciran did not make any comment, he just seemed to stare intently at her as if wanting to hear more. So, she continued, "The story goes that men drove off the dragons out of jealousy, and then we entered a period of darkness. It was a group of believers that climbed up the mountains and sought out the dragons."

This seemed to connect with him, and he observed, "That explains one of the carvings."

She nodded and then continued, "These men were each joined in mind and spirit with a dragon, and this connected them to Hulen Ahir, they were able to guide the people into a long period of light before they finally all died."

At this he scowled, "I see."

She was quick to observe, "I imagine given where you are now, you would likely agree we are again in a dark time."

Ciran snorted in derision, "That I agree with."

At this point Roshin grew quite bright, and her voice rose, "But no more! It is foretold that a new prophet will come, a new rider who will again speak to our god and guide us out of the darkness." She beamed with the joy of a child.

At this, Ciran could not help but laugh.

Her face darkened a bit, as once again she found her audience throwing up walls at the idea of a savior, "I get it, you don't believe me, none of the men seem to believe me, but I have seen it. I have seen the dragon with my own eyes, and I know it has a rider."

This seemed to especially interest Ciran, and he leaned in toward her, "And how do you know that?"

Roshin nodded and explained, "I passed through a town that saw him. I spoke to a girl that met the man. He said his name was Conan, the villagers saw him leave on dragon back."

At this Ciran seemed to grow even more pale, "Mhmm, well I thank you for this lesson. It has been truly most informative. I think I understand more now of what I saw, and I don't think I have any questions," He rose and began to gather his things, "Thank you, thank you again." And with that he backed away from the table and left the tavern.

Roshin watched him go, and she wondered what had just happened. It seemed strange indeed, and she decided then that she wanted to know more about this man, and the journey he had been on.

Epilogue:

Arrival at Dunmaer

There was a knot in Ciran's stomach as he stood before the gates of Dunmaer, but also a feeling of relief for having made it across the open space carrying his bag and the hide. "*I need to drop this off,*" he thought wearily.

He looked up at the gate guard. "I need entry!" he called up, and a man looked down nodded and then opened the gate. Ciran took a breath and then walked in. Before him the streets were crowded with carts, and it was all he could do to put down his anger.

"*Find the tanner, sell your hide, and then get your answers,*" he told himself as he forced his legs on past the carts. He could not help but look at them, women of all ages, old men, and children filled them. "Get to the tanner, sell the hide, get your answers," he repeated, this time out loud.

Still, he searched the faces for any sign of his mother or sister. "*I don't even know that I would recognize them if I saw them,*" he thought bitterly as he glanced upon each thin, sad, and bony face. They looked back at him and the ball in his gut grew. "Get to the tanner," he reminded himself one more time.

And so, he did. The head and hide had fetched him two and a half coppers. "*Imagine what I could earn if I brought in all of Lorcan's kills,*" he thought. It would be a helpful start anyways. "*I'll need silvers or maybe even gold for a sword,*" he thought, feeling like he was quite far off.

Now feeling less burdened, he walked off in search of accommodation. He found the inn he had stayed at the winter prior and walked in, half a copper a night would get him a space on the floor with some 15 or 20 other men depending on the season.

At least he was used to it, having just spent over a month sleeping on the ground in a military camp. The guard runs paid two coppers per night, so as long as the men didn't drink away all their coins most could manage it for a season.

"*The trains would be moving for at least another couple of months,*" he thought, so he had some time before things would get too crowded. He fished out four coppers and handed them to the man. "Eight nights," he said. A voice from behind him grabbed his attention.

"Ciran?" it enquired. He turned. "It is you! I thought I was seeing a ghost! We all thought you were long dead!" a tall and lanky blonde-haired man trumpeted. The man was named Edin, and he was a fellow guard Ciran had traveled with several times over the years.

"I honestly don't believe it myself," he said as Edin came right up next to him.

"Well Welcome back friend!" he celebrated. Ciran did not have a moment to wheel away before Edin took a swing and slapped him on the back hard. This brought Ciran to his knees and he howled out in pain.

Edin looked shocked and out of curiosity peeled back the collar of Ciran's tunic to look. His face grew grim, "How did you get away?" he asked in a croak as if knowing exactly what he saw.

"The fortunate arrival of a friend, lest I would have been dead," he explained before rolling up his sleeves to show the marks that remained from his wrist bindings.

"Well, you let me know who, because if we ever see 'em, we'll be buying him a drink as well," Edin said, reaching out an arm to help Ciran back up to his feet. "Come on then, I know there are others who will be pleased to see you are in fact not dead." And with that Ciran followed his old friend back out onto the streets.

Ciran was starting to feel as though he should have just sent Edin out alone to find the others, as he was growing tired and sore from all the walking around. Edin did eventually gather three more men who were just as happy to see Ciran was alive.

It was heartening to see the joy and surprise on their faces when they laid eyes on him, "You look absolutely terrible," they told him before laughing and offering his shoulder a squeeze.

"Time for drinks boys!" Edin announced and together they walked down another street to find their way to one of the many taverns in town. When they arrived Edin had announced their celebration and slapped his back again without thinking about it.

Ciran had again groaned, but this time he stayed on his feet. He had a mind to turn and take a swing at him, but he winced and let it go. The men ordered mugs of cider and passed one to Ciran and then they gathered around him.

He felt unprepared to tell his story, "*I still don't know what to say,*" he thought, and he looked around the room as if searching for an answer. He spotted another group of men well into their enjoyment of the evening, and a girl with a covered head sipping from a bowl. "*I could get some food,*" he thought, but his stomach felt too knotted with nerves.

Fortunately, the men did not dwell much on his story beyond him explaining the attack on the wagon train this spring. They started cursing the outlanders and lamenting how many had been lost this year in raids near Brenna.

He learned that the wagons had mostly diverted their course staying near to the forests, and that this had thus far worked to keep more men alive. It was Ciran's first opportunity to ask about the size of the trains.

Edin, well into his first mug, had no problem telling him how the people they were moving were mostly those fleeing some famine in the north, and they took them south in trade for grains, beans, and salt.

"They have farms in the south that need workers and so we take the people down to work which helps keep us all fed."

"Maybe my family was taken south too," he pondered. For the first time in months feeling like he was learning something useful. *"I may end up wintering in the south after all,"* he thought.

The cider was good, but he nursed it slowly, wanting to ensure that he kept his head about him. As his friends drank, their lips got looser, but the sense they made reduced. He did not get an impression that any of these men had actively worked to march anyone out of a town, they mostly just guided the people south from here.

It was late into the night when Edin walked him back to the inn. He thought to maybe leave and go find Lorcan but decided it could wait for the next day. When he woke the next morning with a new set of flea bites he had regretted that choice.

Edin had been waiting for him and insisted that Ciran join him to go find some food to break their fast. After which Edin thought to drag him around as if Ciran had never been to Dunmaer before.

Having nothing better to do at that moment he continued to follow him. They walked along around the edge of the sparring yard. Edin cracked jokes about the skills of the men, and the quality of the practice swords. Ciran laughed to himself, as everything he saw here was in much better condition than anything he had seen in the camp.

Edin pointed to a young woman who was stooped over a young man just outside the Archery range. She was wrapping up his bleeding arm with some linen. "We recently got our own healer to patch us all up right good. She'll cost ya, but it seems a worthwhile price to pay." She looked up and Ciran recognized her from the tavern the day before. "Say, she might even be able to look at that back of yours," Edin continued.

Ciran just shook his head. He did not want to show that to anyone else, "No it'll be fine," he said flatly. He noted the bundles of herbs hanging from her shoulders and thought back to Lidan's cottage.

 Edin broke the memory, "Yeah, but then you won't get to hear her spin tales of her god and the dragon riders that will save us all." He broke out into a hearty laugh, but the comment pricked Ciran's ears. "*God? Dragon riders?*" He was now curious. He ignored the laughing and studied her closer, hoping to be able to find her again before he was dragged off.

She was a young woman with striking green eyes and a smattering of freckles across her nose. Her head was covered in white linen, so he could not see her hair. She wore a simple brown linen dress with an apron, but it was the bundles of herbs that made her stand out.

It took several more hours for Ciran to finally get free from Edin, and he had hoped to use the opportunity to slip out and return to the mountainside to meet up with Lorcan. On his way, however, he saw the girl from the sparring yard, the one Edin had said spoke of dragons and gods.

She was hard to miss with the bulging pack and the bundles of herbs hanging from her shoulders. "*The alter,*" he thought, "*she might be able to give me some answers.*"

He broke into a jog to try to catch her but slowed to a brisk walk as the foot traffic intensified and he needed to weave past some men. Finally, he caught up to her and reached out to grab her shoulder.

The young woman whirled around; her herb bundles whipped out, away from her body, and smacked into his arm. "I'm sorry, I didn't mean to startle you," he stammered, feeling about as startled by her reaction as she had been by his touch.

He continued in a rush, feeling awkward for his query, "I just had a question, and it may seem completely strange to you, but do you by chance know anything of the faith of Hulen Ahir?"

The girl did not immediately respond; she looked at him with an expression that he could not read. He started to wonder if maybe he said something he should not have, *"Did I offend her somehow?"*

Finally, she opened her mouth and offered him a simple, "I do." His heart began beat with excitement before she continued, "and you know of it as well?"

He was not sure how to answer, He knew of the faith, the fact that Hulen Ahir was some kind of god, and that they seemed to believe something about dragons, but he really knew little else, he tried a response that reflected the most honesty, "Well I know of it, but not much about what they actually believe. I was curious to know if you did?"

He watched as a smile spread across her face, *"She must know something,"* he reassured himself.

The girl opened up, "Of course! I am going to eat, you are welcome to join me, I would be happy to tell you about my faith, though to understand it fully, we are likely to need more than one meal."

The invitation was welcome, and anticipation rose inside of him, *"I may be about to get an answer I have spent months wondering about."* He prepared himself to follow her and then graciously accepted the offer, "I understand, I would be happy to join you."

She nodded and he followed, thinking over the questions he had, *"What did the carvings mean? Where are there other dragon riders? What was the significance of being such? How big might Lorcan get? Would their connection change or grow?"*

He had no expectation that she would have all these answers, nor was he sure how to ask some of the questions without starting with something along the lines of *"Hello I'm Ciran, and I happen to be bonded to a huge turquoise dragon named Lorcan."* He scolded himself for his foolishness, *"Maybe I can at least get an understanding of the carvings."*

They made it to the tavern. It was the same one he had been to the day before. *"If I recall correctly, this place was also known for its food,"* he thought as he fished out half a copper from his pouch to hand to the attendant.

He let the girl led him to a table, and he sat down on the bench across from her, acutely aware of the way his tunic was rubbing against the scabs on his back. He shifted a bit and began to unburden himself of his bag. He then looked at her realizing she had no idea his name, "I'm Ciran by the way."

"Roshin," she responded with a smile.

Ciran noticed she had not bothered to try to remove the bundles or her bag, and he thought it seemed odd. He made a gesture to them, "You are carrying much Roshin. Is there a reason?" His inquiry was gentle.

Roshin looked a bit nervous, and he watched her grip the strap of her bag. She answered him, "I was told I was like to get robbed if I left my belongings where I am sleeping, so I carry it all on me," and then finally, as if realizing how strange it seemed herself, she began to remove the items from around her body.

She was not wrong, thieves were all around in Dunmaer. He tried to offer a half-smile. "I understand that," he said as he tapped his own bag which was pushed close to his body.

It was around that time when the food came. The smell hit Ciran's nose, and he found himself salivating. "*Oh, a good stew with meat, spices, and root vegetables. What a rich treat indeed.*" He had just nearly starved, not just on the wheel, but in the camp, so the idea of plentiful food still hit him in an especially strong way.

He put a spoonful in his mouth and soon found that he could hardly stop himself as the memory of such desperate hunger met with this taste of bounty. "This is so good," his words trimmed with his pleasure, but then he suddenly noticed she was staring at him strange, and he began to feel self-conscious, "You would understand if you had any idea of what my last few months had been," he explained in a rush.

This seemed to satisfy her, and he felt relieved as she went about calmly eating. His focus on the food in front of him was broken with a question "So, you wish to know about Hulen Ahir?"

He had nearly forgotten why he was there once the bowl came. He scooped another bite into his mouth before pausing to confirm for her, "Aye, I do," and then he kept on eating, hoping to see it all finished so his mind could move off from the food.

The girl seemed more interested in him then explaining the faith, "Might I start by asking how you learned the name?" she asked.

His first thought was of Lorcan, but he stuffed it away as really the answer was Terranwood, "You might not believe me, but in my travels, I came across a temple and a man. I believe he called himself a 'Truth Sayer?' Anyway, I saw carvings in the temple of dragon riders. The man would not tell me the significance, so I have been left guessing for quite a while."

She did not respond right away, and he prepared himself for some cryptic line. But instead, she gave an, "I see" before looking away. It was a great relief to him when she continued, "Well you likely saw carvings to recognize the prophets of old."

"Prophets?" Ciran asked curiously.

The young woman came to life, "Yes. To start simply there are dragons and there are men, Hulen Ahir created both, but the dragons have a special gift that connects them to the spirit world."

"*Spirit world?*" He sat on that a bit considering if it made any sense to him. "*I mean Lorcan is clearly some kind of magical creature, but spiritual?*" His mind began to spin. He now wanted more, and she continued.

"The story goes that men drove off the dragons out of jealousy, and then we entered a period of darkness. It was a group of believers that climbed up the mountains and sought out the dragons."

"*The robed men approaching the large dragon,*" he thought, "That explains one of the carvings," he informed her.

She nodded and then continued, "These men were each joined in mind and spirit with a dragon, and this connected them to Hulen Ahir, they were able to guide the people into a long period of light before they finally all died."

He pictured these regal men ruling from dragon back, "I see."

The woman broke in "I imagine given where you are now, you would likely agree we are again in a dark time."

Ciran snorted in derision, "That I agree with."

The girl grew excited, "But no more! It is foretold that a new prophet will come, a new rider who will again speak to our god and guide us out of the darkness." She beamed with the joy of a child.

Ciran burst out laughing. *"Speak to a god? Leading the people? She can't be serious,"* he roared in his mind, before noticing that her expression had fallen.

"I get it, you don't believe me, none of the men seem to believe me, but I have seen it. I have seen the dragon with my own eyes, and I know it has a rider," her tone seemed forceful and intense.

Ciran could not help but lean forward, "And how do you know that?"

Roshin nodded and explained, "I passed through a town that saw him. I spoke to a girl that met the man. He said his name was Conan, the villagers saw him leave on dragon back."

Ciran felt the blood leave his face, *"Taughmon."* he thought. He needed to go. He responded to her, "Mhmm, well I thank you for this lesson. It has been truly most informative. I think I understand more now of what I saw, and I don't think I have any questions," Jumped up and began to gather his bags.

"I need to get to Lorcan," told himself, and then added to her, "Thank you, thank you again," before slipping away out of the tavern and taking off down the streets and toward the gate.

Milton Keynes UK
Ingram Content Group UK Ltd.
UKHW031153061224
452240UK00001B/199

9 798227 236470